W9-BON-915

The Angels' Share

By Rayme Waters

Winter Goose Publishing

This publication is a work of fiction. Names, characters, places, and incidents either are products of the author's imagination or are used fictitiously. This work is protected in full by all applicable copyright laws, as well as by misappropriation, trade secret, unfair competition, and other applicable laws. No part of this book may be reproduced or transmitted in any manner without written permission from Winter Goose Publishing, except in the case of brief quotations embodied in critical articles or reviews. All rights reserved.

Winter Goose Publishing
2701 Del Paso Road, 130-92
Sacramento, CA 95835

www.wintergoosepublishing.com

Contact Information: info@wintergoosepublishing.com

The Angels' Share

COPYRIGHT © 2012 Rayme Waters

First Edition, August 2012

Cover Art by Winter Goose Publishing
Typeset by Victoriakumar Yallamelli

Published in the United States of America

For K, who makes everything possible

Chapter 1

At first I thought I was alone. I woke face down in the gravel to rivets of pain when I tried to blink or move or take more than a tiny sip of air. Willing myself forward, I crawled out of the harsh sunlight to the coiled hose by the side of the garage. Hot, plastic-tasting water turned sweet and cold giving my cells something to work with. I lay back down on the sharp muddy stones. What had happened? I felt my face with my fingertips. My left eye was swollen shut and there was a thick cake of blood on the side of my head. I couldn't open my mouth without wanting to scream. Yellow jackets buzzed near my face, drawn by the smell of my wounds. I tried to sit up, but it felt like someone had poured acid into my hip joints and ground the bones around like a pestle. Then I heard Kevin, scrubbing something in the trailer, not more than twenty feet away. He was awake which meant he was still high, and dangerous.

Could I escape? My car keys were on the dresser in the house, but I was scared to get them. I considered crawling into deeper shade and waiting until Kevin was sober enough to be devastated by what he'd done. He'd rush me to the doctor, guilty and full of apologies. But the doctor would see my infected arms, my bony body and this beating, and that would be trouble I couldn't explain away.

I got to my knees and tried to stand. The world spun and I stumbled. I rose again, this time leaning against the aluminum side of the garage while my pulse steadied. Beneath my feet were various shades of red gravel and mud where Kevin had poured the toxic leftovers from his lab. Nothing grew where I stood. Not even a thistle or dandelion, although they blanketed the fields twenty yards away.

I knew I would have to walk out of there. In the distance, I heard the whine of eighteen-wheelers braking on Highway 101, the tires rotating on pavement made the highway seem reachable. If I could make it there, I figured someone would stop and help me.

Slowly, I limped through a break in the split-rail fence into the old vineyard adjacent to Kevin's, hoping he wouldn't see me and come with his steel-toed boots to finish the job he'd started. Once I was hidden by the grapevines, I could move without being seen. I'd make it to the freeway faster that way and if Kevin came looking for me, he'd search the road.

Because of the crags of the land, the wire-trellised grapevines wove like a maze. The sun beat down. Each step required all my concentration, all my effort. When it felt like I'd been walking for hours, but hadn't gone more than a hundred yards, I fell, catching myself on a trellis post. Something popped in my ribcage and the pain made me wonder how many of my ribs were broken and what walking with smashed-up bones was doing to my insides. I considered turning around, crawling between Kevin's dirty sheets once again. I tried to determine the direction back, but the vines had closed around me. The sound of the road was louder than it was before. I kept moving forward.

In the late summer heat, stumbling going downhill, clawing on all fours going up, my mouth became desert-like, insistent. Thirst wound into my spinal cord then up into my brain searching for moisture. The sun's rays hit me like bullets. I tripped and fell into the dust as fine as talc.

Cursed are you . . . upon your belly shall you crawl and dirt shall you eat.

Was this the place beyond hope from which I'd be born again?

I tried to think of the next line from Genesis, something to hold onto, but my mind was muddled—a jukebox shuffling through my knowledge for something to keep me alive—it had stopped at the Bible, but the needle lifted again, looking for the right record to play.

I came to the top of a hill, my vision going black at the sides. I had hoped for the freeway. Instead, I saw a white farmhouse, with a wide

front porch. Was it real? How long would it take me to get there?

Then a new voice shuffled to the front of my brain.

And I sank down . . . the night-wind swept over the hill and died moaning in the distance . . . would I stiffen to the friendly numbness of death? A light in the distance was my forlorn hope: I must gain it.

I worked toward that farmhouse, falling, getting up and falling again. My mouth felt moist and I looked down to see myself exhale a fine mist of blood. I'm all ripped apart, I thought as I sank to the ground, this time into darkness, a comforting chill working its way from my fingers and toes toward my heart, the cold soothing my thirst, my broken face, the last bit of exhausted muscle the meth hadn't destroyed. Gravity welcomed me into the soil, and exhaustion tucked me in. Now my mind was quiet, but out of the silence there came one man's voice, then another; fingertips at my throat, my wrist. No use in getting up. I wanted them to leave, let me circle down into the cavern that was opening for me in the ground, where memory and mistakes and pain could drown in the darkness below.

Chapter 2

The best place for make-believe in Bolinas was the graveyard. On a foggy May morning when I was seven, I played house between wide rows of headstones, using abalone shells, some as big as dinner plates, to mark the boundaries of my rooms. To keep me company, I wished for, but could never quite conjure, imaginary friends. I wanted two: a girl, my age, like a sister, and a boy, a protective brother in our gravestone and abalone house. Whenever an unfamiliar car would slow on the road, its driver watching me play alone, I closed my eyes and wished for my friends to appear, but could never make them solid. Some days when I invoked them, when I tried to will playmates from rocks and stumps, I'd look into the mossy forest above the church and they'd be there, walking toward me between trees that looked like columns, but we never reached each other. When I blinked, they'd be gone.

I heard my father's motorcycle, the rhythm of popping misfires growing louder, and ran to the fence. Usually, he'd look for me, slow down and wave as he headed over the hill to town. This time he didn't. The back of his bike, where my mother or I sometimes perched—we could never travel all three of us together—held his canvas duffel, stuffed full.

"Dad!" I cried, loud enough so the whole town could hear, but he didn't turn his head. He ran the stop sign at Highway One and rode south toward San Francisco. For a few minutes the Indian Chief sputtered at full throttle along the cliffs of Muir Cove, then trailed off until I couldn't distinguish it from the cry of the birds or the pound of the ocean.

The firehouse sounded its noon siren and I walked back to the place I lived for real: a drafty one-room cottage with a wall of windows that rattled in the wind. This morning when I'd woken, my fingers had been stiff from the cold, but now the house was humid and rank. My mother was drying wool again.

My dad had bartered a five-gallon bucket filled with the green weeds he grew in the hills for two demon-eyed sheep.

"They'll feed us and clothe us, Stephen. I can sell the extra yarn," my mother had insisted.

The sheep ate our patch of grass down to dust and pooped on our front step. Despite the Mary-Had-a-Little-Lamb plans I'd hatched, these were not the friendly creatures of nursery rhymes and when they followed me, it only was to bite at my clothes or hair. I spent playtime well out of their radius. My mother managed to shear off some of their winter coat and spin it into a warbled thread, some parts thick as your thumb and others wispy as gossamer. Then she boiled the whole mess with herbs my dad foraged.

"This one's blue," she said, stringing up a dripping length between the icebox and the bed. Half a skein already hung like the work of a psychotic spider.

"It looks gray," I said. I knew it would annoy her, but I couldn't stop myself from saying what was true, correcting an error, attempting to set the world right.

"Well, you're wrong. It's blue," she answered, standing on a chair, a dozen clothespins clipped to her long red hair. "When it dries, you'll see."

My mother was twenty-six. Her outfit was another self-creation. She'd liberated a garbage bag of men's clothes from the Goodwill donation bin, cut them into odd-sized pieces, and then quilted herself a sack dress. She decided, back when she was trying to mount the Bolinas social strata, that we should only wear clothes that she could make. Even after she had abandoned her quest for acceptance, the homemade clothing philosophy stuck.

In addition to the sheep, my dad bartered more green weeds to an elderly Dutch lady in Stinson Beach for knitting lessons. My mother had learned how to cast on and purl before Mrs. Van Tassen found out

I didn't go to school.

"But every child must go to school."

"Cinnamon learns from the sky and the sea. School is poison to a child's imagination. She has no need for desks in rows."

Mrs. Van Tassen had delft-blue eyes behind her spectacles and white hair in a messy bun. Like so many other adults, Mrs. Van Tassen had disliked my mother instantly. But she'd leave me a plate of her fudge made with real chocolate in the kitchen. I'd sneak in there during my mother's lesson and cram the gooey delight into my mouth.

"How will she read, write, make friends? How will she live if something happens to you?"

My mother, Linda Pierpoint, former San Francisco debutante, had set her mouth and lifted her nose. I could hear her doing it from where I was standing in the kitchen eating fudge and drinking a cold glass of cow's milk.

"How I raise my daughter is none of your business. If you'd like to discuss personal matters do it with someone else on your own time."

When my mother talked like that, my dad got mad and called her a bitch. No one liked bitches as far as I could tell, so I choke-gulped the milk and the last piece of candy.

Mrs. Van Tassen had stuffed the pink (gray) yarn she'd been using to show my mother how to construct a sleeve into my mother's satchel.

"For the child's sake I should teach you this, but I've lived too long to put up with a beggar who thinks she's a princess."

We had walked home, my mother muttering about how no busybody was going to stop her from making sweaters.

There were two failed attempts and then one that looked enough like outerwear to try on. One arm was longer than the other; it looked small.

"It'll give, it'll give," she'd said as I tugged the sweater over my too-short corduroy jumper.

After a few minutes I'd lost feeling in my left hand. I pulled at the seam under my arm until a dropped stitch ran, making a hole that allowed sensation back into my limb. But that created a place for the sweater to unravel and I knew it was only a matter of time.

By now I'd outgrown that first sweater and dreamed of something pink, bubblegum pink, but blue (gray) would have to work. I scooted over to the wood stove, where the embers were low, and waited for my mother to finish her web.

When she was done, she cut a leaden piece of wheat bread and poured a glass of sheep's milk from the previous day's pitcher. I'd never taken more than two full sips of that rank fluid in my life, but my mother was always surprised when I didn't finish.

"Not thirsty?" I knew she'd ask me in about an hour, putting the jelly jar of milk into the icebox next to so many others, curdled and molding.

"Where's Daddy?"

She was quiet and I thought she hadn't heard me. When I started to ask again, she cut me off.

"Gone."

"Where?"

She began to clean the counter.

"Forever?"

She shrugged.

I was frightened of my father. Just as easily as he could come through the door, smiling, and swing me up onto his shoulders, he could come in angry and kick whatever I was playing with, sending it skidding while I ran for cover. I never knew what to expect. But I knew he was the one that kept our little raft afloat. Whenever we were out of food, he'd do an odd job or trade some of his green weeds for groceries. My father split and stacked wood for the stove. He paid rent. Without him, I didn't know how we'd get by.

"Why did he leave?" I asked.

My mother attacked the counter with vigor, wiping crumbs, which had been there for days, into the basin. I thought she might not have heard me again, but then she said:

"You are too young to understand irony, Cinnamon, but if you did, what I'm going to tell you is funny."

Irony? My father was a machinist; he worked with metal. I leaned forward.

"He's leaving because I don't cook and clean well enough. He said I'm not a good enough wife. I ran away with him because he begged me to leave all those phonies and conformists behind. Now he's deserted me because I can't make dinner the way he likes it. And when you get to be my age, you will see that your father is a very ironic man. Now, stop it with the questions and help me wind the yarn."

Chapter 3

After Sam Gladstone found me in his vineyard, my first memory of something more than a doctor's penlight or the bang of a nurse coming through the door was being transferred from the ICU to a regular hospital room. Most patients moved in a wheelchair, but so many of my ribs were broken that I was rolled on a gurney to avoid the agony of sitting up. The hospital ceiling flowed by, the distance between the ICU and the elevator marked by a repeating pattern of acoustic tiles and fluorescent lights. The interior walls of the elevator were burnished steel, giving me the first mirror I'd had in weeks. I turned my head so I could see. My fractured skull was wrapped in a foam helmet because I'd had seizures after they operated on me. One of the blows from Kevin's boots had ruptured my sinuses and the pooled blood had given me two long-lasting black eyes. My jaw, still swollen, was wired shut and throbbed even under the pain-blunting weight of a morphine drip.

The new room was smaller, but had fewer tubes and machines than the one I'd been in before. Unlike the ICU, I had it to myself.

I woke later and watched the slow, steady drip of the morphine from one bag and nutrition from another. The medicated saline and the thick yellow goop combined in an IV tube and disappeared underneath the edge of my blankets. Usually, I went back to sleep after just a few minutes of consciousness, but this time I stayed awake. There was a white plastic box taped to my bed with a red button. Eventually, I pressed it.

A nurse with crooked, yellowing teeth stood over my bed until a doctor arrived. I couldn't speak through my frozen jaw, so the doctor handed me paper and pen while the nurse freed my right hand from its soft tie. I grasped the pen but couldn't remember how to hold it. Did it thread through my middle or ring finger? Neither felt right. The yellow-toothed nurse with breath that smelled of eggs helped position the pen and held the pad while my shaky hand scrawled answers to the doctor's questions:

Cinnamon.

1995?

Clinton.

That afternoon there was another MRI and more blood draws from the catheter in my chest because my arms were septic. When I woke again there was a nicer nurse on duty and a fanned bouquet of pink roses on the windowsill.

"Who?" I wrote with an arrow toward the flowers. I remembered my grandmother, her rose garden. But she had disowned me years before. Who could have sent them? My mom? Kevin?

The generic florist's card said simply, "Get Well Soon."

"Mother?" I wrote.

The nurse swapped an empty bag of morphine-laced saline for a full one.

"Don't think so, m'dear. She got very angry when she couldn't see you in surgery. Refused to wait. Screamed and threw things until she was asked to leave. The doctors thought it best that her visits be suspended until you were . . . better."

"Dad?" I wrote.

"Haven't seen him," she said.

The police came next. I knew I should tell them how to find Kevin, but when they questioned me, I couldn't turn him in.

"The hospital filed a report that your mother arrived intoxicated and tried to fight her way into intensive care," said one of the officers. "Could she have done this to you?"

"No," I wrote. They asked about my father, about boyfriends. I shook my head.

Stupid and ridiculous girl, I told myself. I was the one who had always gotten into so much trouble telling the truth and now I was lying to protect someone who'd nearly killed me. But I'd tossed my moral compass away ten years before, and could no longer guess what direction was north. And, despite everything that had happened, Kevin had once been my white knight, the best protector I'd ever had. I wasn't ready to turn him in. After fifteen minutes of them asking me the same question in different permutations, I wrote "tired," pushed the nurse's call button, and closed my eyes.

New flowers came every few days: lilacs, peonies, blue delphinium. I knew how expensive flowers were, and bouquets that nice had to be from my grandmother. Maybe it was her way of apologizing for shutting me out. Maybe it was on behalf of my mother. The nurse with the yellow teeth told me I was too little of a girl to be getting so many pretty flowers.

"Lucky you're not allergic," she said, yanking my sheet tight. "We'd have to take them all away."

The police came again, told me they'd searched the property adjacent to where I'd been found, and discovered evidence of a lab.

"You had meth in your system on intake. What do you know about it?" the male cop asked.

"Don't remember," I lied out loud this time, my jaw now unwired.

I wanted to ask if they'd arrested anyone, get some dribble of information about Kevin, but that would be suspicious. If they'd found the lab, he'd be in enough trouble already.

The female officer sitting in the chair beside my bed looked me in the eye.

"What about the next girl who loves him?" she asked. "Can you remember something to keep her safe?"

Her brown eyes and her badge were insistent. She thought there was a chance I'd trust her, give her enough to get Kevin, Tony and everyone else I could identify thrown in jail. But that wasn't the way it really worked. Even the bad people got plea bargains. They'd come for me. And no matter how many times he'd beaten me, the real Kevin, the sober Kevin, didn't mean it. So, I turned my face to the wall, wanting to disentangle from the police, the druggies, the horrendous mess

I'd made of my life. "I'm sorry," I said, hating myself. "I really don't remember much before the accident."

After a month more in the hospital, a dozen CT scans, vancomycin drip for my infected arms, physical therapy, heparin flushes, tapering off of pain killers, and oral surgery for my shattered teeth, they pulled the catheter from its lair in my right ventricle, wrapped my healing ribs tight one last time, and discharged me to a rehabilitation center called Napa Meadows that was nicer than any house I'd ever lived in. The hospital's social worker told me I was lucky; Napa Meadows was expensive and my grandmother had agreed to pay. I wrote her a long letter, thanking her for her generosity, the flowers, asking if, when I was better, I might be able to tell her these things in person. I also wrote Sam Gladstone, the man who'd found me in his vineyard, called the ambulance and saved my life. I thought about asking him to come and visit, telling him I'd like to say thank you, but I didn't want him to feel obligated.

At Napa Meadows, I was protected. In the beginning there were no visitors, no TV, no tell-all group sessions. Between physical therapy and twice-daily appointments with my counselor, Dr. Falk, all I managed to do was sleep. I was treated like an infant, cocooned, watched over. I fainted in my shower the second day and after that, I wore a delicate monitoring device on my ankle. Instead of it being intrusive, I felt like someone was finally, finally looking out for me. I saw patients who'd been there longer helping cook meals, going out in the van for off-property hikes, but I was relieved that I wasn't allowed to do any of this. When I could go a few hours in the afternoon without napping, I sat on a chair in the courtyard and watched the bees dance between the lavender bushes while I waited for my next appointment.

Physically, I was a mess: a slip of bones and skin, my hair growing back in patches and a tangled, pink worm of scar above my left ear. The inside of my elbows burned and itched from nerve damage. On bad nights the burn would work in between my shoulder blades where it seared through my chest and left me feeling like I'd had a sledgehammer to the back. My visible bruises had faded to yellow, but my chest was still healing, causing me to swear whenever I sneezed or coughed. Getting the hiccups was a trip to hell. But each day my body felt a little stronger, more coordinated.

It was the condition of my mind that scared me. A month in, it was worse than when I'd arrived. Trying to follow a conversation, answer more than a yes or no question, my brain scrambled. I had bizarre reactions to everyday things—I sobbed inconsolably when I saw a bowl with bananas and oranges nestled together on the cafeteria counter. At Christmas, when the staff played the Overture to The Nutcracker in the rec room, I put my hands over my ears and howled to drown out the music—and I had no idea why.

In a counseling session with Dr. Falk, she asked me about the first time I'd ever gotten high. I wanted to answer but the weave of my thoughts unraveled faster than I could speak. I couldn't focus long enough to answer a question.

"In my mouth," I said. "He said if I didn't get it, my mouth, inside. Also, hurt."

Dr. Falk nodded, waited for me to continue. But the freight train of my story had passed by, leaving only a retreating rumble. I'd forgotten what I'd already said. I was exhausted.

"I'm not okay," I cried out. "I'm worse!"

Esther Falk's voice was quiet, clinical. "You have brain damage from the drugs and the beating you took. You'd been running on adrenaline for who knows how long and now you're not, so it seems worse. But you're young. Your brain is plastic. I've seen kids your age get a lot of it back. That you recognize there is damage is more important than you know."

Dr. Falk videotaped each session, and later, when I was better able to concentrate, she showed me some from my early days. It was a good tactic and harder to watch than The Texas Chainsaw Massacre:

"Tell me," Dr. Falk asks from off camera, "What do you want?"

I tilt to the right in my chair; my head shakes like I'm 82 instead of 22. My still-bandaged hand tries to brush something from my face—a strand of hair? A bug? If it exists, it can't be seen.

After forty minutes of my scattershot rambling and Dr. Falk taking different tacks to engage me, she asks a final time:

"What do you want?"

"I can't find them," I inch out.

"You can't find who?"

"I meant . . . I don't know."

"You said you couldn't find them. Who can't you find?"

I put my head in my hands and call my own name.

Dr. Falk repeats her question.

Then all the electrical impulses racing around the maze of my brain, hitting dead ends, connect, uniting into one emotional cable: anger.

"Friends!" I shout.

"Which friends?"

"The ones who never come!"

"Who doesn't come?"

I open my mouth to answer her, but I'm lost again. "I don't know what you're talking about." I say, near tears.

The tape goes to fuzz.

It took longer than my body, but Dr. Falk was right, my mind began to heal. Part of my daily routine was cognitive therapy, where they first had me summarize a children's book, then a newspaper article, then short stories. Re-teaching me to think linearly and logically was a process like anything else I did at Napa Meadows. The staff gave me small goals, applauded my minuscule improvements, and I began to gain confidence that I could heal and be as good as new. I could have another chance.

In our sessions, Dr. Falk kept circling back to me saying my friends didn't come, that I couldn't find them. At one of our meetings she encouraged me to draw the place where I'd find them, a place where I'd have the other things I told her I wanted: clean sheets, warm rooms, a place where my scars could fade away.

"There are three of you," Dr. Falk said when I handed her the barely preschool-worthy drawing of a cottage covered in roses with stick figures in a circle out front. "Who are they?"

I searched my healing memory, but it was blank. Only I was recognizable in the picture, the other two figures looked away, their faces hidden.

Chapter 4

After my father deserted us in Bolinas, I distracted my mother by begging her to tell me stories. Most had to do with The Pierpoint, the Nob Hill hotel my mother's family had owned before I was born. At its peak, The Pierpoint hosted heads of state, society balls, and celebrities like Rita Hayworth who got her ball gown stuck in the revolving door, ripped off the bottom half of her skirt, and went on to the party anyhow. Built by my great-grandparents, The Pierpoint had been a grand hotel, providing my mother with a royal childhood until my grandfather, Jasper, who favored high-stakes poker and Betty Page look-alikes, embezzled enough to bankrupt the business.

Although our family's hotel had survived the great earthquake and fire of 1906, the Depression, and two world wars, it couldn't survive my grandfather. By the mid-1960s, the hotel was borrowing money every month to make payroll and had past-due bills as thick as the phone book. The interest on my grandfather's gambling debt alone was more than The Pierpoint's monthly gross revenue. Within a year of declaring bankruptcy, Jasper died of a heart attack.

My grandmother, Elaine, remarried a man named Frank Ferguson, who owned a chain of by-the-hour motels in Northern California and Nevada. My uncle, Victor, was shipped off to a mediocre boarding school in Bakersfield, and my mother, humiliated when her socialite friends deserted her, became an easy conquest for my father, a blue-eyed bohemian she met at the Café Trieste.

But my mother didn't like to tell me stories about after our family had lost their fortune and social standing; instead she talked about galas, movie stars, and fun.

"A massage for each story," she said.

She'd take her shirt off, lay on her stomach with her arms tucked underneath, and I'd rub baby oil into her back while she told me more about who she'd been and all the great times she'd had before I arrived on the scene.

When she was happy with my father there was a coda to most stories, about how glad she was to be away from that old life: "This is much better than being stuck with all those Junior League jerks," she'd say. "You're having what I never did, Cinnamon: a real childhood around real people."

As I saw it, the hippies in Bolinas—especially the men who claimed they were inventing a new culture based on love and equality, but at the end of the day expected dinner served by pliant, sweet females—were no different than the legions of phonies and fair-weather friends my mother had left behind in the city. They'd just cultivated a grubbier façade.

But my mother still desired to be at the apex of whatever group would take her. She pretended it had been her idea to dump the heiress life and start sprouting whole grains, reading Carlos Castaneda, and raising her love child, me. There, then, in the counterculture, she hustled for inclusion in a different kind of in-crowd. But between her domestic incompetence, her congenital sense of entitlement, and lack of judgment before opening her mouth—a trait I so unfortunately inherited—she floundered. While the hippies accepted my artsy, rage-prone father, my mom was branded a snob, a mellow-harsher. She, and therefore I, became misfits on the fringe.

Within a week of my father's desertion, our money and food were gone.

"Call Grandma," I pleaded when we'd used the last bit of change from the Mason jar on the counter. I had never met my grandmother, but knew from my mother's stories that she and her new husband lived in a mansion with eight bedrooms.

"No way," my mother said through her teeth as she searched for her other brown thong sandal at the bottom of a pile of mildewed clothes. I ran to keep up with her as she marched down the hill toward the raised boardwalk that led to the Bolinas Post Office. She read notices posted on the bulletin board there. *Help wanted: Stinson fishing crew. Help wanted: oyster shucker. Help wanted: Bolinas Real Estate, ten hours a week typing, filing, apply in person.* My mother took that one and pulled me further along the boardwalk to the real estate office.

"Look hungry," she said.

I was hungry.

They agreed to try her and she lasted two hours. She'd lied about being able to type.

"I never learned anything like that in school," she told me when we were back in the cottage. Her voice was muffled because she lay face down on the bed. "Why would anyone put the Q and the W next to each other?"

"Call Grandma," I said.

She thrashed her head no.

"We need help, Mommy."

"I already asked," she cried into the pillow.

"When?"

"About twenty times. All the time. Your grandmother's mad at me for running off. She's doubly mad because I had you."

"When she knows he's gone, won't she feel sorry for us? Won't she change her mind?"

"She told me . . ." my mother said, choking on her words, "she told me, I'd made my bed and now I could lie in it."

The guy from Bolinas Real Estate found my mother a job cleaning the weekend home of a doctor and his wife from San Rafael. Getting ready to go, she smiled at me and pulled her hair back into a ponytail.

"Don't ever say you're too good for anything, Cinnamon. I never cleaned a toilet until I was nineteen years old. Never washed my own clothes, never cooked anything. Everyone told me I was better than all that. But," she said, pulling on her patchwork skirt and kneeling down so she could look me in the face, "your mother does what she has to. Gandhi scoured toilets and I can too."

She marched down the hill again, this time in the rain, to clean the house of the rich people while I stayed at the cottage and looked at my illustrated fairy tales. She came home a few hours later. Her long, red hair stuck to her face, her cheeks flushed.

"Get your jacket, Cinnamon."

"Why?"

"Just get it."

We walked to the bus stop in the rain and she pleaded with the driver to take us as far as San Rafael for free. We rode the bus an hour, stopping in Olema, Lauginitas, and Fairfax before we wound down Sir Francis Drake to San Rafael.

In San Rafael, another driver let us board the bus to San Francisco with a shrug; I crossed the Golden Gate Bridge for the first time and saw the mythical skyline that contained both my mother's childhood and the hotel I'd heard all the stories about.

"Will we pass by The Pierpoint?" I asked.

"Good God, no," my mother said. "I've heard it's a dump these days."

From the Transbay Terminal we walked, still in a downpour, the six blocks to Cal Train and jumped on without a ticket, keeping one car ahead of the conductor for the twenty-minute ride to Hillsborough. My mother hitched us a spot in a bakery van up Ralston Avenue to the black iron gates of my grandmother's house.

"Don't you dare tell her that I don't send you to school," my mother said. "She'd never understand."

Hungry, tired and needing a bathroom, I trudged behind my mother up the rain-slicked drive. At the top, under the shelter of the porte co-chère, a small group of women, all in stockings and heels, one with what looked like a dead fox wrapped around her shoulders, waited for their cars to be brought around.

"Linda?" one of the women said, half-stooped into her Jaguar.

I'd find out later these women were my grandmother's bridge part-ners. The last time they'd seen my mother was at her disaster of a debut, and however bad things had been then, they were worse now. She was bedraggled in soaking, mismatched clothes and held the hand of a raggedy child, only a rumor until now.

One of the women had gone inside to get my grandmother and now Elaine Pierpoint Ferguson, dressed in a beige wool skirt and matching cashmere sweater, stood in the doorway.

"Linda?" my grandmother called out. "Is that you?"

My mother's copper-colored hair was unmistakable and was now longer than ever, to the point she could sit on it if she wanted, because that's how my dad liked it. Long. So long it was impractical.

"Linda, come over here and get out of the rain." Although we'd just arrived, my grandmother sounded like we'd been pestering her for hours.

I pulled my mother's hand toward shelter, but she kept her feet where they were. Behind the trim figure of my grandmother, I could see inside the house: big bunches of flowers in vases along the hall and a tremendous fireplace aglow in the distance.

My floppy boots squelched with water every time I shifted from side to side, which was frequently because I really needed to use the toilet. I was thirsty, too, and I couldn't stop staring at the cluster of coiffured ladies, a species I'd been told about but never seen until now.

"Linda, for God's sake!" my grandmother called through the downpour. But my mother didn't budge.

Elaine Ferguson put the last of her friends in their cars and waved them away, although they all slowed their descent on the driveway and craned their necks so they could watch the scene unfolding back up the hill. A uniformed man hustled to us with a big black umbrella that he put over our heads.

"Miss Linda. Won't you come inside?" His accent was thick like the fish scalers' at Stinson pier.

My mother tilted her chin, and with a tone both cold and acquiescent, answered, "Yes, Jorge, we'd love to."

"Your timing is impeccable," my grandmother said when we were under the porte cochère. But when she knelt down near me, her knees never touching the stone porch, she asked, "Are you my granddaughter?"

I nodded.

She looked me up and down. Her green eyes like moss trapped in ice stared into mine.

"Well, you don't look like much. But let's get you cleaned up and see," she said.

I stepped over the threshold into a hall with harlequin tiles and pendant lamps that dripped a honey glow. The warmth and dryness of the house hit me. I thought for sure things would be all right now. Then, I peed on the floor.

Chapter 5

When I'd made enough progress at Napa Meadows to be allowed visits, I asked them to call Oh Holy Mountain, the commune where my mother lived. She came the next Tuesday at visiting hours, wearing a floor-length, tie-dyed muumuu. When she saw me she dropped the paper grocery bag she used as a purse to the floor and covered her mouth with her hands. My bruising was almost gone, but the hollows under my eyes were still purplish-yellow and my hair hadn't fully grown in. I'd tried to hide the scar by gelling some hair over the bald spot.

"Oh my darling!" she cried, enveloping me.

Under a thick coating of Jean Nate body splash, my mother reeked of not showering and grain alcohol. I had forgotten the power of that smell and couldn't help but hold my breath and pull away. She took a crumpled napkin from the paper-bag purse, dabbed her eyes and blew her nose.

"I'm not going to forgive you for refusing to see your own mother," she announced.

"That wasn't my choice, Mom. At the hospital . . ." but she'd already dismissed the topic and presented her hand to Dr. Falk.

"Pleasure to meet you," my mother said, her eyes lingering on Dr. Falk's cropped hair and plain, unmade-up features.

Dr. Falk only nodded.

With an exaggerated sigh, my mother collapsed into a chair like it was a fainting couch, pulled her Bible out of her bag and put it in her lap. She opened and shut it several times, then looked up at us.

"Okay, when do we start blaming everything on me?" she said, giggling.

Five minutes before, I'd felt fine, optimistic that my time at Napa Meadows had made me a strong enough person to handle this visit, but at those words the bottom dropped out of my energy. My head felt like it weighed a hundred pounds.

"I need to lie down," I said. "I can't do this today."

"What? You can't just walk out," my mother said. "I drove an hour."

"We need to take this process slowly," Dr. Falk said. "You and she have made great progress today, just sitting together in the same room."

My mother crossed her arms, pouted for a moment then asked Dr. Falk where she might find the ladies' room. She got up quickly, as if leaving before I did could make a point. Before she left I remembered something I wanted to tell her.

"Mom, thanks for the flowers. I know Grandmother couldn't have done it on her own."

She paused in the doorway. "What flowers?"

"The ones in the hospital," I said. "They were beautiful. They made a difference."

"I never sent you any flowers."

My mother returned the following Tuesday with Phil. I looked at Dr. Falk, who waited for me to tell her who the stranger was.

"This is . . ." I said, not knowing how to introduce him.

Phil was founder and guru of Oh Holy Mountain or OHM, pronounced like the yogic chant. His followers called themselves Pilgrims for Phil and put their faith in a version of the Bible he had edited, making himself a direct descendent of Jesus and a divine prophet. Access to Phil's spiritual guidance wasn't cheap: to live at OHM, Phil required power of attorney and the relinquishment of all personal assets to his control.

"Phil is my spiritual adviser," my mother said. "I was so distraught after our last visit; I brought him today as my support."

"Is this okay with you?" Dr. Falk asked me.

"Okay with her?" my mother shrieked. "She's got you; I need someone on my side!"

Phil touched her arm and she went quiet. "Let's get started with love in our hearts," he said, a saccharine-voiced, blue-eyed Buddha.

It was silent in the room for longer than what seemed right. Phil stared at me, I watched the floor.

"Are you better yet?" my mother blurted out.

Her question grated. After so many years of problems, she expected me to be better, voila.

"I'm no worse," I said, wanting to keep all my good news, how many days sober, how much better I was thinking, feeling, to myself.

"Jesus caught me when I was falling," she said.

"Praise be," said Phil, keeping his gaze on me.

My left temple began to pound, but I took a breath.

"This isn't about my religious salvation, but about my ability to stop injecting meth into my veins. It's about making better life decisions and—"

"To save yourself, Cinnamon, you've got to find God," my mother insisted.

"I don't think so," I said.

My mother recited: "I will see what their end will be; for they are a perverse generation, children in whom there is no faithfulness." She quoted chapter and verse.

I looked at Dr. Falk. She gave me a gentle nod and a smile. Go on if you're comfortable, her look said, I'm here.

"I'd love to have faith, Mom. It would make things easier. But for me, God and the Bible, like you use them, it doesn't work."

"Without God," my mother shook her head, "how will you avoid going to hell?"

"By taking better care of myself and never dying," I said, the words familiar although I could not remember where I'd heard them.

"She's a cold child," my mother said. Phil continued to stare at me. While my mother had so far done most of the talking, his presence was stronger. I felt him studying me like a chessboard, considering his strategy. Stupidly, I kept talking.

I could feel my still-healing brain starting to overheat. I was better, for certain, but the intensity in the room coupled with my nervousness was making it harder to think clearly. "This is me, this is who I am," I said as much to him as to her. At that, Phil nodded like he understood something important and rose to leave.

"But Phil," my mother whined, "we've barely started. This is my baby, my chance to save her soul . . ."

Phil, already at the door, motioned to my mother. She looked between him and me, her eyes uncertain. For a moment, I wished that she could be the one to live in the cocoon of Napa Meadows, that she could be protected and taken care of. But she followed Phil, walking out without saying goodbye.

Phil accompanied my mother again on her visit the following week.

"You don't have to do this," Dr. Falk said before we met them in the library.

"I've got to learn to deal with him, with all kinds of difficulties, when I'm out of here, right?" I said, not convinced at all, but hoping that this meeting would be better, that we could make some rules about what we could talk about, in the beginning at least.

"It is important to your mother that you understand the cost of your treatment," Phil opened.

"I understand," I said, though I didn't.

"Over twelve thousand dollars a month," he said.

I tried to stifle my gasp. I had assumed it wasn't cheap, but twelve thousand dollars a month?

"This meeting should not center on finances," Dr. Falk said.

My mother looked into the middle distance, her eyes unfocused. Phil continued. "Considering the pace of your progress, this facility is too expensive. You will have to move to something cheaper, or better yet to OHM, where our community will support you in your process."

"How I get better is none of your business, not your decision," I said. "You have no say."

"Now that your father has left again—" my mother started, but Phil raised his hand and she went silent.

"Besides, neither one of you is paying for it, Grandmother is."

"Your grandmother is no longer wealthy," said Phil.

"I think these meetings would be the most productive if we didn't focus on costs," Dr. Falk said again, a warning in her voice.

"I didn't want to have to tell you this, Cinnamon, but your grandmother has been selling her personal items to pay your bills," Phil said, sighing.

I could tell he thought that would be a gotcha, but I already knew how my grandmother financed family charity. "So she has to sell one of her hundred, ugly, jewel-encrusted brooches. What do I care?" He'd ambushed me and I wanted to find something that would wipe away his stupid, saintly grin. "That she subjected me to Frank Ferguson in any kind of capacity creates a debt that cannot be repaid, even with a lifetime in cushy rehab," I said, more clear and sharp than I had felt in years. Phil was used to dealing with followers, those who gravitated toward cults like his and belonged at all costs. I refused to belong at all costs and I was quivering with my ability to take him down.

"Her jewelry is one of the few things our family has left," my mother said.

"Our family?" I said. "You are actually trying to claim the hideous jewelry that Frank Ferguson paid her off with as some kind of heirloom? You just want to hock it yourselves so Phil can buy another Mercedes, take another trip to Hawaii with his new female converts. Am I better yet? Fuck you both. You're the ones who need to get better."

I sat back, trembling, but elated. My brain teetered, holding just to this edge of reason.

"Your mother has told me of your troubled heart," Phil said, his voice placid, but his mouth pulled tight. "Pray for forgiveness. To find a way to give instead of just taking."

I laughed. "This coming from two of the biggest freeloaders I've ever met."

My mother's look went from unfocused to shocked, hurt at what I'd said. It might have been true, but I'd gone too far.

"We're going to end the visit now," Dr. Falk said.

"I should have never been born."

"Why do you say that?" Dr. Falk asked.

"Phil's a hypocrite and a freeloader, but honestly, look at me. I am draining money from my grandmother. I'm a failure. I don't know how to be a good person.

"Think about that house you drew," Dr. Falk said. "Pretend those roses, with roots deep in the ground, belong to you. Think about that circle of friends in the front yard. Decide who you want to be, where you want to be, and then find them."

"Look for your higher power," she continued. "God doesn't work for you. That's fine. I've had lots of clients choose another way," Dr. Falk said.

She was right. Before I could graduate, start a real life, I needed to have a firm recovery plan, a set of behaviors to emulate.

Dr. Falk left me alone in the library. The sun was setting and I knew if I looked out the window, the meadow and gardens would stretch before me. There were some people who chose the beauty of nature to be their higher power; they hiked and found solace and direction in the rustle of the trees and the sway of the grass. While I loved the setting at Napa Meadows, I needed more substantial direction than that. I needed someone who would instruct me on right and wrong, show me how to be a grown up. The library chair was on casters and I began to push myself from one side of the narrow, book-lined room to the other with dramatic spins that reminded me of the gazebo scene in *The Sound of Music*.

"I need someone, older and wiser, telling me what to dooooh," I sang as I swiveled myself around. I pushed too hard the next time and the chair tipped, landing me on the gray wall-to-wall carpet shoulder first. It hurt, but not too much. Here, eye level to the floor, I surveyed books on the low shelf. *Jonathan Livingston Seagull*, *The Fountainhead*, and then, in a worn paperback, black text on a peach-colored spine: *Jane Eyre*. I pulled it from the shelf, remembering this book, the one I'd once stolen and read a hundred times.

It is a very strange sensation for inexperienced youth to feel itself quite alone in the world, cut adrift from every connection, uncertain whether the port

to which it is bound can be reached, and prevented by many impediments from returning to that it has quitted.

I lay on the floor of the library until the light was gone, absorbed in a tale I hadn't read since junior high. Scattered among the self-help books were some other favorite novels and I pulled them from the shelves. Dickens' *Bleak House*, Eliot's *Middlemarch*, Sewell's *Black Beauty*, and took them back to my room. Unable to sleep that night, my mind turned these rediscovered stories over and over, kneading them back into my circuitry.

These were books I'd once very much enjoyed, but as I turned their pages with the mind I possessed that day I realized they were more than that. Between their covers were step-by-step guides for leaving bad circumstances, for creating a life with dignity, for coping with abandonment, injustice, hypocrisy. Against the odds, the characters in these novels raised themselves to be good and strong. Virtue was rewarded and wrong doers punished. Lost family and friends were found. That these novels might be a part of my salvation was perhaps unrealistic, but was it any less probable than the Bible?

I requested a break from my mother's visits. And after I read Burnett's *A Secret Garden* I asked for my own row of herbs and flowers. Like Mary in that story, I anticipated watching new green shoot through my bit of earth. After my first afternoon working in the dirt, the muscles in my arms were sore, but there was a natural pink in my cheeks by dinner. I began to look forward to meals, to volunteer in the kitchen, to cry when I watched a sad movie, to laugh when someone told a joke.

When I had a bad day and my brain buzzed like angry ants and I couldn't think or talk straight, I thought of what the characters I admired would do. Would Jane Eyre throw her cafeteria tray to the floor when she couldn't get the ketchup dispenser to work? Would Esther Summerson sneak out with some newer patients and smoke smuggled-in pot in the woods? Although Sara Crewe had every reason in the world to be as messed up as I was, she picked her battles and otherwise restrained herself. I read for hours a day absorbing so much Victorian literature that my internal diction started shaping into something more formal, more old-fashioned. I'd catch myself thinking without contractions, pronouncing all my consonants and speaking, at least to myself, in a voice that was more nineteenth-century Britain than near twenty-first century California. I was going to pretend to be an independent, upstanding person, and these novels were going to help me until I became one for real and I didn't have to pretend anymore. My bad days came less frequently and I started taking on tasks at Napa Meadows that I'd been in awe of my first weeks there. I was proud to be handling them just fine.

I was getting better, better than I ever thought I might.

But a month later, without a visit or a phone call, I received a letter from my grandmother withdrawing her financial support. I walked to Dr. Falk's office, showed her the note, requested and received sleeping pills. While I was waiting for them to take effect, I thought about what I knew. My grandmother's decision was harsh, but in all honesty, as a member of the Pierpoint family, I should have expected it. Napa Meadows was expensive and I was lucky I'd gotten as much time there as I had. Her paying my way was nothing I'd deserved or earned.

Chapter 6

Socorro, Jorge's wife and the female half of my grandmother's live-in staff, cleaned up the mess I'd made on the hallway floor and drew me a bath. I couldn't stop crying because I was certain I'd ruined any chance of my grandmother loving me. Socorro spoke soothing and low, ladling warm, soapy water on my skin, massaging my scalp and promising that everyone would forget about it by dinner. My cheeks burned every time I remembered the sound of liquid hitting stone. As Socorro dried me with a thick, white towel, I buried my face in the support of her steady hands and believed her. She combed through my long, knotted hair with patience, humming a little, tying my black curls back with a ribbon. I looked in the mirror and saw my pink lips looking pretty against my fair skin, my brown eyes holding some of my grandmother's green.

Socorro held my hand down the curving staircase. At the bottom, in the center of the high-ceiling foyer on a marble-topped table was a bronze cherub. No more than a foot high, its arrow pointed in the direction we headed.

"What's this?" I asked, stopping.

"How we find your grandmother. She points it in the direction she's going. Now it points toward the living room, so she will be there. Or in the mornings it can point to the rose garden when she cuts flowers, or it can point to the morning room when Mr. Ferguson is at work. If it points to the garage, we know she's out."

The cherub and I were eye-to-eye, its chubby arm forever drawing back the bow.

Frank Ferguson, the only grandfather I'd ever know, grunted an acknowledgement at me over his newspaper. He sat, ankle over knee, reading the Wall Street Journal and drinking a whiskey sour. My grand-mother, in a fancier dress than she had worn that afternoon, sat in a matching chair beside him smoking a brown cigarette in a long black holder.

"Good evening, Cinnamon," she said. "Ready for dinner?"

There'd been nothing to eat or drink since morning. I was so thirsty I'd drank some of the bathwater when Socorro wasn't looking.

"I'm starving," I blurted out.

My grandmother's face tensed, her expression soured. Had what I said been too loud? Or was it the words that were wrong? I bit my lip looking back at her, but she'd replaced her irritation with the same placid look she'd had when I entered the room.

"Waiting on your mother," said Frank, not looking up.

The way his short, thick neck overlapped his collar reminded me of the snapping turtles in Bolinas Lagoon.

When my mother walked in, I was glad I hadn't been offered any-thing to drink; I would have dropped it. Her coppery hair was combed into a twist and pinned up. She must have borrowed the blue silk dress from my grandmother—it was a little short—but it still fit her better than anything else I'd seen her wear. Her lips were frosted, shimmery, and her eyes lined dark like Elizabeth Taylor. My mother now was as gorgeous as any of those ladies I'd seen this afternoon.

She smiled at me and I felt a charge of electricity, so certain my mother's beauty meant better things ahead for us.

"The look behooves you, Linda," my grandmother said.

My mother nodded, waiting for Frank to notice her appearance. He did not look up or say anything, but shook his paper straight, stood, and walked past her.

"You're like a movie star!" I said, taking her hand. "You are the most gorgeous mother ever!"

"That's enough enthusiasm," my grandmother said.

Like the rest of the house, ceilings in the dining room were high and the décor was formal: French, stuffed, and lacquered into some-thing austere. I measured each breath I took. Socorro stood ready and completely still next to the louvered doors that swung into the kitchen.

The mohair upholstery of the dining chairs scratched the backs of my legs. Frank fussed with laying his napkin on his lap; the rest of us were still, waiting for him.

"They want to raise the greens fees at the Club," Frank said, finally satisfied with the positioning of his napkin. My grandmother, like a statue awoken, motioned to Socorro who appeared with a platter of warm rolls and then with salad plates. I noticed there was a whole different set of rules for eating at a table like this. In Bolinas I foraged our countertops for food, eating with my fingers, leaning on my elbows. Here, I followed my grandmother's cues, breaking my roll into small pieces before buttering it with the little knife, laying my heavy silver fork down between bites, touching the corners of my mouth with my napkin every time she did. If I could mimic her behavior, perhaps she wouldn't notice how out of place I was and would want me to stay.

Frank said very little during dinner, grunting acknowledgement if prompted to my grandmother's bright bits of news. When it came to conversation, I followed my mother's cue and said nothing. I had already caused enough problems and if something was going to go wrong, I didn't want it to be because of me.

When Socorro served caramelized bananas after dinner, my grandmother pushed hers away untouched and lit another cigarette. She blew a ring of smoke up toward the chandelier. The circle's center grew wider, then the edges dissolved.

"There's a dress shop for rent in Burlingame," she said.

Frank scooped up a bite of dessert, considered it, then enveloped the spoon with his upper lip and tongue. He looked at no one. My mother was finishing her second glass of wine, something I'd not seen her drink, ever. She motioned to Socorro for a refill.

"Nothing fancy," my grandmother said. "I thought it might be a good way for Linda to get back on her feet."

Frank took another bite.

"She and Cinnamon could live here while things get up and running. Or over the garage if that were more appropriate."

I nodded to anyone who looked at me. Anything that would keep me clean, fed, and in a house where heat came from vents in the floor, I was willing to do.

Socorro started to clear plates, but my grandmother waved her away.

"I know what I promised, but they're here," my grandmother spoke like my mother and I weren't at the table. "What am I supposed to do? Leave them like urchins in the street?"

Silence. No one but Frank ate.

"Pierpoints are hotel people," Frank said finally laying his spoon on the saucer. "Linda doesn't know how to run a dress shop. I've always been clear the only person I keep in your family is you."

My grandmother blew another ring of smoke. She stood, yanked my untouched dessert plate and smashed it on top of her own.

"Sit down, Elaine. The dishes are Susie's job."

Socorro stepped forward to clear but Frank waved her away.

He swiveled his neck toward my mother. "I've gotten where I am because I watch for people like you."

"You can't . . ." I started to defend my mother, forgetting for an instant how hard I was trying to fit in, how much I wanted this to work, but my mother grabbed my hand and shook her head no.

My grandmother ground her cigarette into her dessert plate and left the table, her heels hitting the stone floor hard as she climbed the stairs, then, slam! Frank followed her a moment later, turning off the lights on his way out. My mother and I sat in the dark room as her eyeliner ran in streaks down her face.

The next morning my mother lay in bed, sniffling and letting out little half-sobs. After my mother missed breakfast, my grandmother told me she'd be taking me on some errands. I went in to check on my mom before we left, but she turned her back to everyone who came in the room including me. I tried to not think about her as my grandmother drove us into San Francisco in her big silver Cadillac, but I knew something had already been decided the previous night, and it didn't bode well for my hope of us staying in Hillsborough.

At a shop off Union Square my grandmother gave a little velvet bag to a man with a jeweler's loupe and got a roll of cash in return. Then we went to the Metropolitan Club and she made phone calls in a private booth while I peeled leaves off a half-dead potted palm. After, we went to *I. Magnin's* and she bought me four cotton dresses all with Peter Pan collars and smocking across the chest.

"She'll need shoes and a coat, too," my grandmother said to the salesgirl helping us.

I looked in the three-sided mirror that hung outside the dressing room, admiring every angle of the starched navy-blue cotton dress, with a bow that tied in back, grapevines embroidered on the smocking. My grandmother approved and the saleslady hung three more dresses, a green, a red and a brown gingham neatly by the cash register. They were the first new clothes I'd ever had, but they were more than that. Wearing them I felt like I had the right costume to make me a part of the world where tidy girls held their mother's hands on the sidewalk. In these dresses I no longer had to scamper about, not knowing where I should be or who I was; these dresses were a ticket to belonging.

"Thank you, Grandma." I threw my arms around her waist.

"Grandmother, please," she said, pushing at my shoulders until I released her. "Grandma is vulgar. And I'm buying these for myself. I can't have you dressed in rags."

We were in Hillsborough six days more. My mother and grandmother talked behind closed doors, while I peeked and peered around the grand mansion, catching the scent of Joy perfume in my grandmother's rooms, coveting the bronze cherub that Socorro dusted daily.

During the hours Frank Ferguson was at work, I pictured myself princess of that castle. The cherub pointed to the queen. My mother became my sister and the three of us lived in a kingdom of roses. But when Frank Ferguson's car pulled into the motor court, the summer castle became a brumal fortress, clogged with briars, the pink stucco turning to gray, wet stone. Frank was the mouse king, the troll, the one who knew the password from five o'clock on, and the queen was under his spell. She mixed him as many cocktails as he wished. At night we gathered around the mouse king's table where he cut his meat with a serrated knife.

Frank's attacks over dinner, our time of forced togetherness, were virulent, spreading from my mother and my grandmother to me. I learned to be careful, to make the smallest possible target of myself, and watched my mother matching my grandmother glass for glass of Campari, then red wine, then brandy. My grandmother, a better subject changer than most, spoke of her day, not allowing any pauses, but I knew when Frank was about to strike; his chewing grew more deliberate as the volts accumulated.

I looked at my beautiful grandmother and wondered how she could have married such a bad man. One night my grandmother tried to deflect Frank by taking us all to a restaurant, but whiskey could be had anywhere. After three drinks, Frank would say things that nice people wouldn't even think.

"Money, Elaine, is the only reason you stay. The only reason you even give an ugly bastard like me the time of day. But I won't keep you," he leered at my mother, his voice rising, "unless you're gonna put out, too."

Conversation at the tables around us ceased.

"Frank," my grandmother said as if he'd returned from the store with the wrong kind of milk.

My mother tried to reply, but all that came out was a clicking sound, like her tongue had come apart from the machinery of her mouth.

Right then, I felt like I left my body. Some part of me floated up above and saw that no matter how pretty my mother was it wouldn't save her, no matter how pleasantly my grandmother made conversation it didn't matter. Frank was like the wicked characters from my illustrated fairy tales, picking on those weaker than himself. My mother and my grandmother were afraid of him, but the weapon to fight him was hanging within my reach. I was going to tell the truth.

"Frank's mean," I announced.

I sat to his right; he turned and gave a look that chilled me in my seat.

"What?" he asked, leaning in so I could smell him, his eyes hazy from drink.

"I said you're mean," my voice quavering, losing a little conviction, wondering if it would have been better to keep my mouth shut. I could see the soft, white towels, the heater vents, the clean sinks and toilets of the Hillsborough house slipping farther away.

He held out his hand, like he wished to take mine. I looked from my mother to my grandmother, neither would meet my eyes. I didn't offer it, but he took my arm anyhow, gathered the nip of skin underneath my elbow, and pinched.

The sting shot up my arm into my shoulder and then my forehead. But my resolve returned. Although I would pay for it, I knew I must not flinch; I must not look away. Against his sour mash breath, the pain, his pronouncement, I met his gaze with a solid stare, my body sweaty, trembling.

"Say you're sorry," he said.

"I won't," I said.

We locked eyes, him pinching and twisting my arm, until Frank decided he wanted to call the waiter over and looked away first.

After he let go, I held the bruised part close while my mother drained her sweet Chablis and ordered another. The queen busied herself with a cigarette. Although a blood blister formed where he'd pinched, I knew I'd done something important, something brave. I'd faced the evil king and stood my ground, not let him break me like he'd done to my mother, my grandmother. And the truth was a powerful weapon, I learned, for Frank left me alone for the rest of the night.

Our last morning in Hillsborough, my mother, pouring herself a cup of coffee from the credenza buffet, knocked a ceramic box to the floor. The lid broke off and shattered into a dozen pieces.

"The Capodimonte!" my grandmother said.

"I'll get it," my mother answered. She knelt down and gashed her hand on the first shard.

"Susie!" yelled Frank.

Socorro came running and hustled my mother to the kitchen with promises to stop the bleeding. Frank resumed reading his paper.

I knelt down. The box was beautiful, with roses and cherubs floating about a rim of gold. I knew it was something from the Pierpoint side of the family, bought on Jasper's grand tour of Europe, coveted by my grandmother and kept from the pawn shop until Frank came along and offered her a shelf to put it on.

This box was rare physical evidence of a time before my family had lost its money and reputation. And now my mother had broken it. I had to find a way to make it better.

The pieces were jagged, sharp, but I handled them with care, putting each into the basket I'd made of my skirt. I'll save you, I promised. I'll save you and Socorro will help me put you back together.

My grandmother came back into the room with a broom and dustbin.

"Leave it!" she said.

My hand jerked with surprise. I sliced my palm and blood flowed over the white porcelain. I wanted to bawl, there was a river of shame pushing against my eyes, but my grandmother had already told me she hated crybabies. I tried to hold back, but in the end, I couldn't.

"I wanted to save it, to fix it for you," I sobbed.

"Stop making such a racket," she said emptying pieces into the dustbin. "There is nothing you can do to make it whole."

Chapter 7

When my grandmother stopped paying for Napa Meadows, Dr. Falk asked my permission to contact Sam Gladstone. Although he'd never acknowledged my thank you, he had called Dr. Falk when I first arrived and told her he'd be interested in helping me any way he could. I shrugged my shoulders when Dr. Falk asked, thinking how unlikely it would be for a stranger to help me when my family wouldn't. But to my surprise, my honest and desperate request for help was granted: Sam agreed to pick up the tab for my last months at Napa Meadows. Why would he do such a thing? Dr. Falk said I should write him and ask. I did. This time, he replied immediately.

Dear Cinnamon,

You ask a good question. I wasn't sure myself until I sat down and thought about it. The first reason is when I found you in the vineyard I couldn't feel a pulse and I made a promise that if you could be okay that I would do anything. You pulled through and I wanted to make good.

Secondly, it seemed right to me that I should care for someone who needed a second chance (like I myself once got in spades).

Sam Gladstone
Proprietor
Trove Vineyards, LLC.

p.s. I'm a lousy letter writer, but I've been wondering how you are doing.

Sam was a wiry man in his sixties with ruddy skin who reminded me of a diminutive Clint Eastwood. The first time he came to visiting hours, we sat with Dr. Falk and talked about how he'd found me. I didn't know he'd ridden in the ambulance on the way to the hospital or stayed in the waiting room until they told him I'd make it. My face burned as I heard the story. I was ashamed to know how much trouble I'd caused.

Dr. Falk tried to explain to Sam how Napa Meadows worked, how it was different than a twelve-step program, why it took longer, about my progress.

Sam seemed baffled by the rehab jargon. "You tell me she's getting better, Doc, that's good news."

I asked him if he sent the flowers.

"Seemed like the right thing to do." He looked embarrassed. "Hospital rooms can always use some cheering up."

After that, I put Sam on my visitors list and he came every Tuesday. I'd show him my row in the garden or we'd walk the two-mile loop through the forest of curly-bark madrones and drink lemonade after in the courtyard. He was curious about my progress, didn't ask too many questions about my past and told me about the vineyard he was bringing back from abandonment, how he had dreams to make great Zinfandel from the hundred-year-old vines on his property.

He called me Cinnamon. I called him Mr. Gladstone. I thought of him as Sam, he wanted me to call him Sam, but every time I tried, the more formal name came out.

"Hot diggity," Sam said when I earned my first off-site outing. He wanted to celebrate that milestone with dinner in St. Helena. I'd agreed, but then panicked when we pulled up to the restaurant, which was ivy-covered with tuxedoed valets. I'd not been to such a fancy place since dinners with Frank and my grandmother. I knew I was underdressed in my faded cotton skirt and second-hand sandals, but Sam didn't seem to care and the maître d' didn't blink. I tensed when the waiter approached to take our orders. Frank enjoyed verbally torturing anyone in a subservient position, and waiters were a prime target, but Sam and he ex-

 46 *The Angels' Share*

changed pleasantries about the evening and then Sam ordered a vintage Rafanelli red Zinfandel.

"Pour her two fingers," Sam told the sommelier in huge violation of Napa Meadows policy, one he had read and signed before I was released into his care.

"I don't think . . ." I said. Wine, alcohol even, had never been my problem. I thought it tasted bad and took too long to work. But still I'd made a promise.

"This abstinence thing is bullshit," said Sam. "How are you supposed to be able to live when you get out of that place if they don't teach you to moderate?"

I was petrified. Sam drank his glass and polished off a small foothill of warm bread, while I sipped water. Sam had a second glass of wine with our appetizer and although I still couldn't bring myself to take a sip, I was curious. I had nasty memories of the wine my mother drank, the sweet stench of it on her breath; I'd never wanted a glass of it. That wine was a couple dollars for a two-gallon box; I guessed this small green bottle that had been filled with wine fifteen years ago cost a whole lot more and tasted different. I smelled the Rafanelli. It didn't remind me of my mother's quaff, but rather of the blackberry and currant jam Socorro made from the brambles that grew along the fence at my grandmother's house.

I wanted to try it, to taste it like I had the fresh butter and walnut sourdough on our table. But the heroines in my novels kept their promises, didn't they? I thought of Anne Elliot in *Persuasion*, of Jane Eyre. They had not always. They were careful and moral, but they pursued personal freedom, happiness. I could never, ever put myself in the same social circle with meth makers or users, that I knew for certain. But I was willing to bet that a sip of wine with dinner might not be the end of me.

When Sam started his third glass, I watched him, waiting for a slobbery drunk or a Frank-style monster to surface. It was something I'd have to have my guard up for, but Sam remained jovial and in control, telling me about how they'd had to replant a section of the vineyard because the roots had been destroyed by a pest no bigger than a grain of rice. He didn't mention I'd not tasted the wine he'd ordered.

When dinner arrived, I took a tiny sip. I was right about the berries and the currants, mingling with something else, maybe leather. Maybe grounds from an espresso machine. I swallowed the drops and the layers of memory the wine uncovered in my mouth went on and on, filling my palate and my mind for a good minute.

"Tell me," Sam said, "what's the most planted varietal in California?"

"You mean kinds of grapes?" I said between bites of potato. "Chardonnay?"

"Nope. Some think Chard, some think Cab, but it's Zinfandel. It's been here since the Gold Rush, hit hard times when all anyone cared about was chasing the French, but it's making a comeback."

Sam held his wineglass up to the light, swirling the red liquid around the bowl. On the table, I copied him, releasing more of the intoxicating berry, which smelled baked now, like a late summer dessert.

"Cabernet may be Arthur, the one everyone thinks is running the show, but Zinfandel is Lancelot, the one who wins the battles, the one who gets the girl." Sam looked at me intently when he said "girl." I felt a little confusion, then familiarity. Of course there was a cost to the favor Sam had done me, he wanted something in exchange for everything he'd paid to Napa Meadows. I'd been naïve to think otherwise. No one ever helped you just because. It just took him two and a half drinks to let on.

But instead of following up with a rude comment or insinuation, Sam pulled a small notebook out of the inside pocket of his jacket and wrote down the producer, vintage and tasting notes. I saw him scribble "baked currants" and I got a little zing of joy. I'd been right, I'd tasted right!

"This one's got a few years left in it." He tucked the little notebook and pen back into the pocket of his sport coat. "Let's drink it again next year." He motioned to the sommelier and ordered another bottle to take home and cellar.

The waiter went to refill my wine but I covered the top of the glass with my hand. I was taking a risk, but I wasn't going to be an idiot about it. The waiter lifted the bottle and set it on the table.

"How did you get the name Cinnamon?" Sam asked.

"I was born with red hair like my mother, and my father wanted to name me Cinnamon. Cinnamon Umbriel Monday. Cin-Um-Mon, get it? C-U-Monday, get it? My name's a laugh riot."

Sam didn't smile.

"What's an Umbriel?"

"Moon of Saturn."

Sam pushed his lips together, looking confused. "But your hair's not red."

"Right after they named me, all the red hair fell out, grew in black, and stayed that way. But my dad had already filled out the birth certificate and he said the name made him laugh so why change it."

"What about Monday? Were you born on a Monday?"

"No. My dad's real name is Stephen Monday. He's from Cleveland."

"What's he do?"

"He plays guitar in a band," I said. "He was trained as a machinist, but when he needs money he sells pot."

"Where's he been this whole time?"

I shrugged.

Mr. Gladstone did one big nod and ordered a bottle of Sauternes to finish the meal. I protested, but he insisted I take just one sip. The gold-sweet liquid coated my mouth; heavier and more lush than the Zinfandel. It tasted of honey, ripe peaches off the tree in the small orchard at the Hillsborough house, the thick juice dribbling down my elbow. I had forgotten those peaches like I'd forgotten Socorro's current jam. I closed my eyes to feel the finish of the d'Yquem once I'd swallowed.

"From rot," Sam said. "It's rot on the grapes that makes this taste so damn good."

Although Dr. Falk's frown became a little more pronounced each time she signed my evening release, Sam took me out once a week to a new, wine-focused restaurant.

After introducing me to Zin, he guided me through Bordeaux blends and Napa meritage, the difference between an oaky California Chardonnay and stainless steel fermented white Burgundy. Through his tutelage, I began to sense nuance again, to recover the use of my taste buds that had been fried from years of pot, coke and speed. I was careful to only have a few sips. Drinking the wine didn't bring back the burning on the inside of my elbows, the ache at the back of my throat for the acid trickle of a bump of meth and I didn't crave it during the week. Still, I didn't tell Dr. Falk. On Tuesday visits, Sam brought me dime bags of dried cherries, roasted figs, a bit of green tobacco.

"Learn these, Cinnamon." And I did. Walking the grounds at Napa Meadows, I explored the herb gardens going beyond the lavender to the rosemary, the sage. The Madrone forest was dotted with bay trees. I rubbed the leaves between my fingers and drew in the smells, building an encyclopedia of scents in my head to compare against the wines I tasted.

I poured over the books Sam brought me on vineyard maintenance, California winemaking, American vs. French oak, issues of the Wine Spectator with the pages he wanted me to read dog-eared. I was fascinated with the science of wine, the intricacy of details in its planting, tending and manufacture. I read all that Sam brought me, interspersing them in the tall stack of novels I read and re-read on my bedside table.

Chapter 8

After Socorro had bandaged my gashed palm and changed my bloody dress, Jorge packed our few bags into the black Fleetwood and, after a cold goodbye from my grandmother and no acknowledgement from Frank, he drove us away from the Hillsborough house, north across the Golden Gate Bridge and into Marin. We followed Sir Francis Drake Boulevard toward the coast, the road twisting first through a dark, mossy forest, then a rolling cow pasture before we turned north and Tomales Bay came into view. There, white shorebirds picked their way around the tidemark and a faded boathouse stood on eroding pylons. A few minutes more and we hit Inverness, a two-block town as foggy and cold as Bolinas but farther from San Francisco. The two blocks consisted of a post office, a bar and a grocery. Everything else, even the gas station, was shuttered. North of town, Jorge smoothed the Cadillac to a stop in front of a white peaked-roof farmhouse with a wide front porch and two upstairs windows like sad eyes watching the water. A standard red and white 'For Rent' placard was taped over a faded B&B sign on the roadside. Jorge carried our two small bags up to the porch, handed my mother a single key, and waited while she jiggled it in the lock.

The front door opened into a furnished parlor and dining room separated with broken pocket doors. The rest of the first floor was one chilly bedroom with a clawfoot tub and sink in the room and kitchen in a lean-to attached to the back of the house. Up the sagging staircase were three more bedrooms and one toilet for all to share. Behind the house, a forested hill rose straight into the fog.

"You want fire?" Jorge asked, motioning toward a tiled woodstove in the front parlor.

"Yes, please," my mother said, sitting down on the couch and patting the spot beside her for me.

"Your grandmother paid a year's rent on this place, Cinnamon, giving us a head start. It's up to us to make it a success, to show Frank Ferguson he's wrong."

Smoke started backing up into the room. Jorge opened two windows and shook his head at the flue.

"We will have to work very hard," she said, her voice tired, watching me. I knew my mother was frightened, and I was too, but one of us had to at least pretend this was all going to work out.

"We're going to do great, Mom," I said, nodding with what I hoped was enough enthusiasm for the both of us.

The next morning, I scrubbed the porch floor while my mother repainted the peeling sign on the road. I suggested she stencil in the letters, but she insisted freehand was more inviting.

"What do you think about calling it Monday's?" my mother asked.

"I don't think people will want to get away for the weekend at a place called Monday's," I answered, scrubbing.

"Right," said my mother and she painted the sign to say "The Pierpoint B&B". She ran out of room at the end, though, and the last B was half-scale.

The first weekend we had guests, my mother burned the breakfast and gave them half their money back to go eat in town. When it rained, the roof leaked in two of the three upstairs bedrooms, the ones with a view, of course. The landlord told us maybe next winter he'd fix it and for now just use buckets to catch the drips.

So, we rented the leaky rooms out only on sunny weekends. My mother hauled laundry to Pt. Reyes Station and back on the bus. I cut wildflowers from the hillside, put them in a coffee-can vase, and set it in the picture window you could see from the road. We got a few guests. We found wild blueberry bushes behind the house and started serving fresh fruit with our pancakes. We set out ant traps and roach traps and rat traps. By mid-July we'd not made enough to cover our rent, but could buy food and had a supply of wood in the shed curing for winter.

The San Francisco *Examiner* heard that Linda Pierpoint, of the once great hotel family, had opened a B&B and paid us an undercover visit. I still hadn't learned to read, but my mother read aloud:

As close to the road as it is, you'd suspect the Pierpoint B&B to be full on a Saturday night. But on our visit, we were the only guests and with good reason. Linda Pierpoint, despite her lineage, has not yet mastered the art of hospitality. The mattresses were musty and filled with what felt like soft-balls. Our breakfast was two parts burned and one part tasteless. We have reason to believe the establishment was infested with four-footed vermin. This B&B is the last stop on a train to nowhere for the once magnificent hotel family.

Despite the review, we did get a long-term guest. Bari DeGarzi, a zaftig transpersonal psychology student with greasy black dreadlocks, took the bedroom on the first floor. Bari paid for her first week, and we never saw any money after that. She could cook, however, and our breakfasts improved. Cruising around our kitchen in a long gray t-shirt, black sweatpants, and bedroom slippers as big as calzones, Bari cracked eggs with one hand between drags on her joint. I wanted her to teach me how to make breakfast, but Bari didn't like me around.

"You're underfoot," she said.

Bari DeGarzi and my mother liked to stay up late. Bari on the couch with her roach clip and my mother with her glass or three of Gallo. When we didn't have guests, they put Janis Joplin or Jefferson Airplane on Bari's turntable and danced. If I woke and wandered downstairs, Bari would give me a less-than-welcoming glare, but my mother would cover me with a blanket on the couch while she giggled and Bari did her stoned version of the shimmy.

Grandmother Elaine didn't invite my mother back that year, but did take me for a weekend when my mother needed to rent out my room to accommodate a group. Jorge picked me up on Friday afternoon and I spent two anxious, glorious days in Hillsborough, trying to anticipate my grandmother's every need and desire and dodge Frank's presence. I helped her cut roses in her garden. When she seemed tired of seeing me, I stayed quiet and out of the way. I tiptoed inside the house so my footfalls wouldn't bother anyone.

She and Frank had dinner guests on Friday and went out on Saturday, leaving me to happily eat pozole and Socorro's yummy caramelized bananas in the kitchen.

"You were less trouble than I would have guessed," my grandmother said as I kissed her cheek goodbye Sunday afternoon.

After that, Jorge would pick me up about once a month on a Friday afternoon and drive me down to Hillsborough. I spent those weekends terrified I'd spill something on the white carpet, irritate my grandmother, or attract Frank's bad attention, drawing a pinch or shove or sting with words. Shivering away the nights in mildewed, foggy Inverness, I longed for the starched sheets and warm blankets at my grandmother's. But once I was there, I bit my nails to the quick and couldn't sleep from the anxiety. Nevertheless, when I waved goodbye to my grandmother and the black iron gates swung closed behind us, I choked back tears because I didn't want to go home.

For the first few days after visits to my grandmother's, I was exhausted, emotional, easy to set off. My mother blamed it on too many of Socorro's desserts, but what closed my throat and made my eyes fill was the thought that I didn't fit in either world, there was no place where I was at home.

When we'd been in Inverness for six months, our upstairs toilet overflowed, running through a loose second-story floorboard and dripping onto the front porch. My mother called a plumber from Point Reyes Station who came out and snaked the lines. Then he produced a tool that, when stuck into our drains, would clear out the knots of my mother's red hair, intertwined with black strands that Bari said must be mine that strangled our pipes. The plumber was young, looked like a rugged version of Prince Charming from my illustrated fairy tales, and had an ancient red Dodge with 'D. Hammond, West County Plumbing' painted on the door. I nudged my mom and said, "Dinner." He checked our septic line free of charge while Bari DeGarzi made spaghetti and meatballs.

Dwight Hammond blushed when my mom sat next to him and must have mentioned five or six times what a powerful thing a home-cooked meal was.

"She didn't make it, Plummerman," Bari DeGarzi said, using the nail on her pinky finger to clean between her front teeth. "She can't cook."

When he left, he and my mother lingered at the door, and I heard him tell her that parking cars on a leach field was going to give us more trouble than it was worth.

He called a few times after that, to see if we needed any more help. Bari intercepted these calls and told him no thanks, we were fine, and hung up.

"Bari, don't be so mean. Cinnamon enjoyed him. I shouldn't keep her away from nice men. That's what your books say. The positive male role model is important in the development of a young girl."

"Positive is the key word," Bari said. "This guy has a black aura, Linda. Do you know what that means? Do you have any idea?"

"He didn't seem like he had a black aura," my mother said.

"What do you know about auras?" Bari insisted. "It's so black, it's nearly purple. Do you want another controlling man in your life?"

My mother guessed not.

"I don't think you should see him again," Bari said that night after two joints and the rest of the Gallo box. "Negative energy is contagious."

Then Janis started really screeching and Bari turned it up.

In the forested hills above Inverness, footpaths connected the houses built up in the ravines with the elementary school, and eventually all paths led to town. Where three paths intersected, I made a new version of the playground I'd had in the Bolinas graveyard. This spot was near the school where I could crawl into the bushes and peer through the chain link at children playing foursquare or tetherball until the bell called them back to class. I'd tried again in Inverness to bring my imaginary friends to life, but I had no better luck, so I watched the real children on the playground and made up stories about them. How they suffered the atrocities of my mother's description of her own school days: sitting in the corner with the pointed cap on their heads for giving the wrong answer, nursing bloody knuckles they'd gotten from the whack of a ruler. But the children on the playground seemed to be having a good enough time. I watched, my fingers woven into the cool steel of the chain link, until the final bell rang and the lines of children disappeared inside.

I wandered home slowly that day knowing the house would be empty when I got back, as Bari had taken my mother to San Rafael to do a big grocery trip and see a movie. It was nine months into our B&B experiment. I didn't like Bari or how cold my room was on foggy mornings, but it seemed like my mother was starting to learn the business, and if we kept at it maybe we could make it work. I came through the last trees and saw the emerald velvet hills across the bay and the fogless blue sky. I skipped down the hill to the B&B, and sitting there on the front steps, holding a folded copy of the *Examiner* article, was my father.

Chapter 9

The spring I was going to graduate from Napa Meadows, Sam threw a party at his vineyard. He invited neighboring vintners, journalists, Zinfandel advocates, his small staff and me to a barbeque celebrating the first warm days of the year. The gravel driveway curved up the hill from Dry Creek Road, and after we passed under the drape of several giant oak trees, Sam's low-slung whitewashed farmhouse came into view. I felt the muscles in my shoulders relax like I was coming home. Weird, I thought, I'd never been here, but then I remembered that I had seen it before; this was the house I'd fixated on when I was stumbling through the vineyard. This was the house that had encouraged me to keep going.

We passed a few whitewashed outbuildings and a massive pair of oak doors set into the hillside.

"The caves," Sam replied when I asked him. "That's where we make the wine."

Sam wanted to show me around but just as we parked, the first guests arrived. He motioned and I followed him toward the lawn that sloped from the porch of his house down to the start of the vineyard where the first hint of green was unfurling from the dormant vines.

Long trestle tables, their front legs supported by bricks against the hill's slope, held the trays of roasted vegetables, lamb chops and rounds of Sonoma County cheese. The caterers poured Zinfandel, from Sam's first unreleased vintage. Sam introduced me around as his friend from Calistoga. I forgot everyone's names seemingly a second after they were spoken. At one point, I noticed some of the vintner's wives, uniformly worked out, sucked in and done up, eyeing my long-sleeved shirt, jeans and cheap tennis shoes, amusement apparent on their faces. My first thought was to bolt out of the party. I couldn't stand the idea of being stared at and ridiculed for what I couldn't help. But, me leaving would upset Sam, be rude to the man who had done so much for me, so I comforted myself with thoughts of my favorite heroines. They were often poor and plainly dressed, but with time their character outshone the fanciest of girls. Take a picture, I thought at the last one I caught side-glancing me, it will last longer. Then I refilled my glass of water.

Sam had hired a bluegrass band and, between swigs from his glass, danced with anyone willing. I shook my head when he asked me. I'd never danced with a man in my life. After I'd begged off for good and Sam jigged with a pretty blonde, I sat on a bench, alone, under an arching oak, my dinner plate balanced on my lap watching the rest of the sport-coated and pashmina-wrapped crowd circulate. I was near a small pond and the frogs were beginning a tune-up. Their gentle croaking, the temperature of the air and the smell of the earth lulled me into a dreamy trance. I sunk into the comfort of one perfect, safe moment and released a sigh I didn't know I had. It came from the backs of my knees and neck, the insides of my wrists, leaving my body in a wave. I felt lighter, different, better.

As the sun slid behind Mount Jackson, Sam grabbed the mic and welcomed the crowd.

"All this for a little grape juice!" Sam said, chuckling at his own joke. "I'd also like to thank my foreman, Pedro, and his wife, Alma, who keep this vineyard running." Sam raised his glass to an older couple that stood not far from me. Pedro smiled, Alma did not. Neither held a glass of wine, so they only nodded to Sam's toast in their honor.

"And, ladies and gentlemen, Pedro and Alma are also the reason for my next announcement: their son, a boy who used to work the fields of this county, graduated last June from UC Davis. I apprenticed him in Bordeaux, which turned out to be an expensive proposition, because he's now so good, I had to hire him to be my winemaker."

A polite murmur spread through the crowd.

"I'm proud," Sam choked up. "I'm so proud that we can watch the generations grow here. Eduardo, we are glad to have you, welcome to the Trove family."

I stood and turned with the rest to watch the new winemaker's entrance.

He was no taller than I—jockey sized, really—with a thin face and high mestizo cheekbones. His hair was black in a long, thin braid down his back. He wore the same work boots as his father and climbed the little hill toward us, making his way between tables of glassware and cases of wine. Alma was smiling now, she and Pedro clapping along with everyone.

As Eduardo passed me heading toward the stage, we locked eyes. He had already taken another step, but he was fixated on me. He looked confused, frightened, like he'd seen a ghost, and his foot hooked the brick under the trestle.

Before I could reach out to catch him, he fell face-first, taking the whole table of dirty plates and glasses with him.

"Are you okay?" I asked kneeling down.

Eduardo did not answer, but picked himself up and dusted off his jeans. Pedro tipped the table back upright and I gathered the scattered wine glasses. Mortified for the new winemaker, I concentrated on the ground where dribbles of wine had made veins of mud in the soft vineyard dust.

"Folks, he makes a better wine than an entrance," Sam said.

Eduardo Delgado made a half-wave toward Sam, his dark skin unable to hide its crimson hue, and scooted back behind the cover of the vines, favoring his left leg. Pedro followed. I watched them go, my hands filled with dirty plates and stemware, the crumbs and crusts of the party mingled with lipstick and dried saliva.

The band started up again and I scanned the darkening edges of the vineyard, waiting for Eduardo to return. He didn't.

At twilight, the caterers lit glowing lanterns between the trees. I still stood on the sidelines nibbling a cookie from a platter of desserts. Partygoers that had seemed so stuffy when they'd arrived were swinging around to the music.

"D'ya have a good time, Darlin'?" Sam asked as he put me in a car for the valet to take me back. I had been looking forward to the drive with Sam to find out more about the new winemaker, but despite my curfew, the party was still going full steam. The *Chronicle* wine critic, who Sam had pointed out to me earlier in the evening as the person at the party with the most potential influence on Trove's future, was drunk and getting chatty. After Sam gave the valet overly detailed directions back to Napa Meadows, he leaned in my window.

"I bought the land," he said.

"What?"

"The land. The place where you got hurt. I bought it. I'm gonna make it into a vineyard, a good one."

I must have gone pale.

"Don't worry," Sam assured me. "All the bad stuff is gone. It's just waiting to show us it's potential."

I didn't know what to say. The trailer. The greenhouses. Kevin's lab. It was hard to believe it wasn't all still there, suspended in time, waiting for me to come back and set the whole nightmare back in motion.

The Saturday before I graduated, Sam took me back to that first restaurant in Saint Helena and reserved the same booth to celebrate.

"What's your plan after Wednesday, Cinnamon?"

We'd talked about this a few times. Sam knew the answer. He was just hoping I'd changed my mind.

"After the halfway house? I'll live with my mother or my grandmother," I said. "Get a job. Save up money for a deposit on a place."

I'd sent them both a note telling them I'd be leaving Napa Meadows. My mother had responded with a letter saying she was proud of my progress and would come visit me if Phil would let her use the commune's car. My grandmother sent a fifty-dollar check with the word "graduation" written in the memo.

"That's a terrible idea," Sam said, as he had before, crunching away on a bread stick.

"I know, but it's the reality I have to face and make work."

"Why don't you come work at Trove and live on the vineyard? Pedro needs help, he'll teach you how to run the machines, you've already read half my library," he said.

"I don't think someone coming out of rehab should go and work at a winery," I said.

"And I don't think someone coming out of rehab should live with family members who are crazy as polecats. I think you can beat this if you have someone there to make sure you don't slip."

"What would you know about slipping?" I asked.

"Enough," said Sam. "The people that work for me, they all live on the vineyard. I'll fix up one of the places for you."

"How much is rent?" I asked, stalling.

"I'll make you an offer you can't refuse," he said, leaning back. "Besides, that Alma's a sourpuss. I need a friendly female around."

I wanted to say yes to let Sam spare me from what was surely going to be a rough re-entry. But I was wary of generous offers. I knew Dr. Falk wouldn't approve of this plan and although wine and old men had never been a part of my downfall, I couldn't blame her.

Sam drummed his fingers on the table. "It's a starter position, a way to learn everything about the vines, the crush, the bottling."

I wanted to ask for more time, find a way to turn down his offer without offending him.

"Go on, say yes or no. I feel like I'm on bended knee here," he said.

But why would I turn down someone who had been the kindest person I'd ever known? It didn't all add up, but if I didn't say yes now maybe the offer wouldn't be there in the future. Dr. Falk, who had never met my grandmother, thought staying in Hillsborough would be my best chance at recovery. I had to admit staying in a halfway house with other people just like me, most of whom were going to start using again, followed by trying to convince my grandmother who had disowned me to let me come and live with her seemed like a plan without much promise.

"Okay," I said, "I'll do it."

Sam put one arm around my shoulders and held me tight. "Welcome to the Trove family, Ms. Monday," he said.

My first instinct was to hold firm against Sam's hug, to be rigid and hedge his affection. But he held me tight while he laid out his plan for my first week at the winery. He'd clearly been thinking about this for months, creating a safe place for me to land, to grow and grow up. Whether or not I knew all of Sam's motives, whether or not going from rehab to working at a winery was complete insanity, I knew he was the one person I had in my corner and I knew that I'd need him. I let myself collapse a little into the pressure of Sam's squeeze. He told me about one of the cottages he was having renovated so I could live on the vineyard but have my own place.

"I want it cheery. Yellow or blue paint on the walls?" he asked.

I exhaled, closed my eyes and rested my head on his shoulder.

Chapter 10

"I'm seeing a nice lady," my dad said as we bounced over Point Reyes-Petaluma Road. He left a note on my mother's door saying he'd return me Sunday.

"This is her truck."

It was a yellow Chevy Luv with a queen of hearts playing card and two eagle feathers dangling from the rearview. He had a paper sack on the seat between us.

"Sunflower seeds," he said. "Did you know they are nature's best source of Vitamin K?"

We chewed and spat out our windows as we drove over the hill that divided Marin from Sonoma County, my father extolling the benefits of a tablespoon of brewer's yeast, wild mushrooms, and raw beet juice instead of coffee.

"It's like liquid energy; there's so much iron in there," he said.

I scooted close to him. I'd forgotten how much I liked him when he was in a good mood. He had dirt smeared on the inside of his elbow, lots of welding scars, little and big, scattered in constellations across his forearms.

We pulled up to the Sebastopol Mobil station and out of the garage came a woman in a grease-monkey jumpsuit with a Dorothy Hamill haircut.

She walked up to the Chevy and put her head into the open passenger window. She didn't say anything for a minute—her chin rested on her crossed arms while she looked at me. Her eyes were the color of toffee. I didn't think she was that much older than my mother, but her skin was freckled and wrinkled from smiling around her eyes. Her teeth were white, crooked.

"Hello, Cinnamon. Your daddy has told me lots about you," she said after a while in a voice sculpted by cigarettes.

"This is Nancy, Cin. Can you say hi?" my dad prompted.

"Hi," I whispered.

"Let's go get us a drink," Nancy said and she punched the side of the vending machine until three cold Cokes came out. We walked to the little white aluminum-sided house behind the gas station, which I took to be Nancy's place, sat on the stoop, and drank.

"What grade you in?" Nancy asked, skipping stones across the dusty yard.

"I don't go to school," I said.

"Humph," Nancy said and gave my father a narrow-eyed look before she took another swig of soda.

That night after they thought I'd gone to sleep, Nancy started in on my father.

"No school? Shit, Steve. She's eight, right?"

"Linda handles that stuff. She thinks school is bad for children."

"Oh yeah, Dad? How long are you going to let her stay illiterate? A truant? You want kids to make fun of her?"

"Course not," my dad said, and I heard one of them kick their work boots bam, bam to the back of the closet. I'd gathered that through Nancy, my dad had found a tool and die job at the auto body place.

"Then sign her up. Tomorrow would not be soon enough."

My father grunted.

"She may have me beat in the beauty department, but that lady's got shit for brains," Nancy said.

"She doesn't have you beat in any department," my dad said. "C'mere." Then he and Nancy started making so much noise that I crept down under my covers. My dad moaned and Nancy screeched, but when they stopped, they started talking and laughing like they'd had the biggest relief. When he and my mom had been together, every night ended with my dad pissed off about something and sucking on his pipe to escape. The smell of pot was my lullaby, but at Nancy's he hadn't lit up once.

The next morning my dad said, "There's a park down the street, Cinnamon. You can take off right after breakfast."

"Forget it," Nancy said. "We didn't have her over here so she could be alone. You ever play softball?" Nancy asked me.

I shook my head.

"Well, there you go. We'll play softball." Nancy took the aluminum bat from beside her bed, sweet-nagged my father into the truck, and with me in the middle, drove into town to play at the elementary school field.

"Watch the ball, Cinnamon. Connect the ball with the bat."

I missed the first three pitches. My dad, groaning, annoyed, looked up at the sun.

Nancy was patient. She must have pitched to me twenty times before I hit the ball ten feet.

"Great bunt," my dad said. Nancy stuck her tongue in his direction and blew.

"Okay, Cinnamon, watch the ball and when you hit it, think of someone or something you don't like. Don't take your eyes off that ball and swing as hard as you can."

I hit the ball in a long drive past my dad. He threw his head back and laughed.

"That's it, that's right. Now, let's work on your fielding," Nancy said.

We played until lunch and then got burgers and ice cream at the Tastee Freeze.

"This is the best thing I ever ate," I said, sitting on the same side of the picnic table as Nancy. My dad walked to the 7-Eleven and got two beers. Nancy popped the caps off on the edge of the table.

"What does your shirt say?" I asked Nancy.

"It says 'I'd rather push my Harley than ride a rice burner.'"

"What does that mean?"

"It means I like my bike," she said, her smile toothy. She rubbed the top of my head until my hair stood up on end.

At the end of the weekend, Nancy hugged me goodbye. She smelled like engines and leather and garlic.

"Come back real soon, Cinnamon Monday."

And she looked over at my dad and mouthed the word 'school' before we drove away.

My dad and mom fought for a while when I got back. Bari DeGarzi and I sat in the kitchen.

"What's your dad's girlfriend like?" Bari asked.

I told her about Nancy.

"Sounds like a dyke to me," Bari said.

Then she stood up because it had been quiet in the living room for a few minutes, and I followed her out there to see my parents facing each other on the couch, my father twisting a piece of my mother's long red hair between his fingers.

He stood when he saw Bari, said bye to me, and left.

"Don't look at me like that," my mom said to no one in particular, and passed us going back into the kitchen where she banged pots around trying to sound busy.

"What's a dyke?" I asked that night as my mom snuggled in bed with me instead of going down to dance and drink wine with Bari.

My mother jumped. "Who said that?"

"Bari did. She said Nancy sounded like a dyke."

My mother nodded for a bit, then smiled.

"It's an ugly word, Sweetheart. Don't use it, okay? Now you've got to get to bed because you've got school tomorrow."

In the morning, my mother registered me at Inverness School. Because I couldn't read, they put me in first grade, even though I should have been in third. My teacher, Miss Debbie, instead of fitting dunce caps, thwacking rulers and poisoning my independence, played the old upright to accompany our songs and served us cloudy apple juice at snack. She sat with me at lunch and we worked through the Dick and Jane readers, then second-grade primers. I burned through every book in Miss Debbie's room by Thanksgiving and after Christmas break I got moved to second grade.

Nancy put a library card in my stocking and each time I was in Sebastopol I'd take out enough books to keep me for the weeks in Inverness. By the end of the year I was reading Rudyard Kipling and Roald Dahl. Although these stories took place in exotic or make-believe places, I could see the glint of Shere Khan's eyes in the stalk of an Inverness tomcat and shades of the sadistic Trunchbull in Bari's heavy sashay. Then I discovered *Little Women* in my grandmother's library. I had to have a dictionary by my side to read it, but I made it through.

"You remind me of Jo," I told Nancy, who bought me my own paperback copy.

Weekends I didn't spend with my grandmother, I went over the hill in that yellow Chevy Luv. Sometimes, if she didn't have to work, Nancy would come and get me herself. After we mastered reading, she helped me with math and spelling so that I could skip third grade and go into fourth in September, with kids my own age. And, despite my late start, I was now reading ahead of everyone.

Nancy also taught me tetherball. Her 'round-the-worlds' were unstoppable.

"Don't let me get goin' on you, Cinnamon. Once I get the right orbit, you're done for. When you see me start to wale on your ass, then do whatever you can to take me down. Jump for the ball. Punch it. Whatever you have to do. Because otherwise you're dead meat at the back of the line."

One Sunday after tetherball, we returned to Nancy's to find my mother there. She'd borrowed Bari DeGarzi's car and had driven over. She and my dad were sitting an odd distance apart and were as still as feeding ticks when we walked in, my mother's cheeks flushed as though she'd been running.

Nancy looked them over, dropped the keys on the table, and walked out.

"Let's go darling," my mother said to me, her eyes sparkling like she'd won something.

As we drove back over the hills to the ocean, my mom told me that the year of my grandmother paying our rent was over; we would have to leave the inn.

"We can't get enough guests to make it work," she said.

"Why doesn't Bari start paying then?"

"We'd have starved over the past year if she hadn't cooked for us."

This wasn't untrue.

"What are we going to do?"

"I'm not sure yet," my mother said, downshifting, "but we might move closer to your father."

"Is Bari coming with us?"

My mother said she didn't think so and that was fine by me.

We did better than get close to my dad. He left Nancy and moved with us to a ramshackle hut he'd built when he was high with some carpenter friends on the highway between Sebastopol and Bodega. It sat right off the road and shared a driveway with an empty lot up the hill.

From the front, our house looked like a recycled wood sculpture, pieces of various lengths and colors overlapping to form the façade. Our front step was a wood pallet on cinderblocks, and my feet were little enough where I'd have to be careful or I'd twist my ankle in the gaps. Our door, complete with porthole, had come from a ship. The entire place shook in the wind.

The house was built up against a rocky cliff, lean-to style. Inside was only one room but big, like a cavern. A long counter on the right defined the kitchen; a utility spool turned on its side was our table; the bed—a bunk with a double on the bottom for my parents— was against the left wall and in the middle was a faded sofa, its burgundy velvet dusty and shredded, facing a rabbit-eared TV on a milk crate. On a second milk crate next to the TV was my father's stereo, a shiny, black-knobbed anachronism in our homemade hovel. The floor underneath everything was rough concrete with unpolished quartz stone mixed in. My father had poured it himself.

"Yuck," I said when we walked in the dusty place, my dad still out at the car carrying in our boxes.

"Shhh," my mother said, holding my head close to her. "Don't be critical when your father provides."

The bathroom did not have walls or a door, but my father welded some metal army trays together to make a divider about four feet high, which provided visual, if not auditory, privacy.

When I cried because I didn't have my own room, my dad strung a wire and hung a curtain around my bed and nailed a long shelf into the wall for my books. He also came home with a clip-on lamp so I could close my curtain at night and read while they watched TV a few feet away.

Although I stopped seeing Nancy, she'd drop off new books for me in our mailbox. Soon, *Anne of Green Gables, A Tree Grows in Brooklyn, Are You There God, It's Me, Margaret* shouldered together on my shelf. I started the next year in the fifth grade at Orchard Elementary, part of a rural school complex that housed the elementary, junior, and senior high schools all on one campus. The original one-room schoolhouse was preserved as the main office at the front.

"I love this, all the ages learning together," my mother said.

I saw some kids from the high school hitching rides. They smoked, looked almost as old as my parents and twice as scary.

My mother took me shopping at the Goodwill. I found a pair of jeans without holes in the knees, a few faded t-shirts, and a brown corduroy jacket that I liked a lot. I schooled my classmates on the tetherball court and was picked first for softball.

Some nights, Nancy would roar up to our place drunk on her bike and scream for my father.

"Steve, you shitheaded son of a bitch! Get your cowardly ass out here!"

"Go away, Nancy, you're drunk," my dad yelled out the kitchen window.

"Don't call me a drunk, you stoner! Be a man, Stephen Monday!"

"We are calling the authorities if you don't leave the premises," my mother called out into the night.

"You don't have a fucking phone, you bitch. Don't lay your empty threats on me!"

"You're upsetting Cinnamon, Nancy," my dad said. "Go home."

She was upsetting me, and when my dad said that, she did leave.

I didn't see her again until a few weeks later. She was waiting outside my classroom when school let out. She wore her leather motorcycle jacket and pants like she always did before a big ride. In her hands, a present.

"I'm goin' away, Cinnamon," she said when we sat together on the bench outside my classroom.

"Why?"

"Because it's best."

"I don't want you to go."

Nancy looked away, and when she looked back at me, she was crying. "I don't mean to embarrass you," and she handed me the present.

I unwrapped the gift: a pink case with a dozen pink pencils inside, my name stamped on each in gold script.

"I know you say they don't make nothin' with your name on it, but I saw these in a catalog and I got 'em for you. I hope you like pink."

I grabbed Nancy and threw my arms around her neck.

"Don't leave," I begged, salty tears dripping in my mouth. All the other kids were staring at us now. The leather-clad lady and Cinnamon Monday, who never had a new thing, with a pretty pink pencil box on her lap, sobbing.

"I've got to," she said, putting on her mirrored aviators. "I'd like to stay, but I'm getting in the way of your mom and dad."

And then Nancy walked fast to her bike, started up the engine, and roared off.

Whenever I was in Sebastopol after that, I went by the little white house behind the Mobil station to see if Nancy's truck or Harley was parked outside. There was always some car there that could never belong to Nancy: a Ford Lynx station wagon, a beat-up Mercedes, a Mary Kay pink Cobra. The Mobil changed to a Chevron and when that happened the little white house was torn down to accommodate the new mini-mart. It was then I knew Nancy was gone for good.

Chapter 11

Before I left Napa Meadows, I renewed my driver's license and began running errands in Calistoga. I visited the used bookstore and bought paperbacks the storekeeper suggested—Larry McMurtry, Neal Stephenson, Maeve Binchy. I'd also gotten the first professional haircut of my adult life. The Quick Clips stylist snipped my thin, dark straggles into a pixie fringe long enough that I could tuck a wisp behind my ear and hide the scar. When she handed me the mirror to check the haircut, I inventoried myself. Other than a little darkness under my eyes, my face was healed. My skin was pale, smooth, and the new haircut made my dark brown eyes appear wide. I'd put on enough weight where my bones weren't so visible. My arms were still gross-skinny and badly tracked, but I kept them covered up. Memories were clearer, my thinking was sharper, I was getting well.

The downside of this increased brainpower was I couldn't stop analyzing my decision as an ex-addict going to work in the wine business. I knew I should start new and fresh on my own in a job that had nothing to do with potentially addictive substances. But I didn't have the means. I'd have to ask my family to help me, and if they would I could never be certain of how long their support would last and what strings would be attached. When I compared Sam's offer of job training and a place to live against trying to stay sober living with my mother or grandmother, I calmed myself knowing I'd made the best possible decision out of less than perfect choices.

To keep a cap on my anxiety, I focused on the fact that if the job at Trove didn't work out, I'd at least gain some skills to be able to find work at another winery. There had to be a hundred small wineries in Sonoma County alone.

But, still, mine was not a plan without flaws.

Dr. Falk thought the winery job was a bad idea and was, in her passive Socratic-therapist way, not supportive. She thought I was sabotaging myself by skipping a halfway house, which I could only picture as a sagging rancher filled with aging versions of all the druggies I'd known before.

"You'd make a great English teacher," she said.

"Maybe so," I countered, "but I have forty-six dollars to my name, which doesn't cover a security deposit, let alone expenses. I have no money to go back to school and I have no credit history to get a loan."

"Have you considered asking Sam to give you a loan?" Dr. Falk said.

"I can't do that. I can't take his money without working for him. Then I'd be . . ."

"Be what?" Dr. Falk asked.

I changed the subject.

Dr. Falk's concerns scratched away at my resolve, but when she led me in another required visualization, picturing my sober self in one, five, ten years, I wasn't standing in front of a classroom. I was sitting under the big oak in front of Sam's farmhouse, a piece of cellaring equipment in my hands.

On my release day, the way Dr. Falk pursed her lips together so they disappeared as I wrote Sam's address on my mail-forward paperwork made me think maybe I'd outgrown what Napa Meadows had to offer. Dr. Falk said that for the next year I'd still be considered an outpatient, eligible for weekly group meetings and three in-patient stays, "tune-ups," she called them. I thanked her, suddenly desperate to be away from the beige hallways, the enforced quiet, daily counseling sessions, and tedious process of sign-ins and sign-outs. I was bored of talking about my past, my problems. Sick of Dr. Falk asking how I was feeling in a detached voice. The cocoon of the last nine months had stopped feeling necessary and started feeling stifling.

She stuck out her hand to shake. No hugging between staff and patients.

"Good luck, Cinnamon," she said. "Please take it in the best way when I say I hope I never see you again."

I mimicked her tight smile and then I was free to go.

I left my room holding nothing but a nearly empty army duffle. Most of what I owned I was wearing. The box of paperbacks I'd collected and all my wine books had gone home with Sam on his last visit. I stopped while the nurse unlocked the last frosted glass door, took a deep breath in, and stepped into the lobby.

Sam was waiting and insisted not only on carrying my bag but also stowing it in the way back of his cavernous Expedition like it was luggage of consequence.

Sam reminded me to buckle my seatbelt as his wheels crunched the driveway pebbles and we turned onto the main road. As we slowed for the first stoplight in Calistoga, I gasped when a man I thought was Kevin passed in front of the car.

"What is it?" asked Sam.

I saw a ghost, came to my lips, but instead I said, "Just can't believe I'm out."

When the man turned his head I saw he had a flatter nose, a weaker jaw. He had the same hair color, but he was shorter, not skeleton skinny like Kevin had been. With each additional second, the doppelganger I'd swore I'd seen looked very little like Kevin at all.

The rest of the stoplights were green and soon we were climbing Calistoga Mountain on the road that separated the northern parts of Napa and Sonoma Counties. I pretended to look out the window, but my thoughts were back to whom I'd thought I'd seen in the crosswalk.

Kevin had never come to find me when he'd seen my blood leading from the trailer out to the vineyard, which was unlike him. Kevin's high brutality was always echoed with sober care, lavish and devoted. Was he in jail? Even so, the Kevin I knew would have written. Written pages of apologies and begged for me to forgive him yet again. The sheriff could probably tell me what happened to him, but as much as I thought about Kevin, I questioned why I should be worried about someone who had done his best to kill me. This had been the focus of several therapy sessions at Napa Meadows. Battered woman syndrome

Dr. Falk called it, and she was probably right. Everything he'd done should have cancelled my love out. But he'd been one of the few people who stepped up when I needed it and rescue was my heart's currency. I now remembered the extent of the horrors of living with Kevin, the destructiveness of my psychological complicity, and as sick as it made me, I loved Kevin still.

That did not mean I was stupid enough to think it could ever work between us. But letting me go easy was about as likely as him quitting crank cold turkey. And when I tried to picture him and what he was doing I could only see a dark space. A dead place. But why would he be the dead one? He wasn't injured like me and he had his parents to look out for him, hire him expensive lawyers, pay for rehab. Maybe they'd sent him away. Maybe he'd been at some other version of Napa Meadows, getting better. Maybe he was just like me, tiptoeing back into real life, seeing remnants of me in crosswalks, hoping none of his demons would notice.

"You there?" Sam said. "You look a million miles away."

"I'm fine," I lied again. "Just a big day."

One of the other subjects that had taken up the majority of my last session with Dr. Falk was how I was going to manage living on a piece of land where I'd nearly died. Sam assured me that all of Mitchell & Sons' buildings and equipment were gone, the eucalyptus trees removed, the topsoil around the garage and trailer replaced, and a new Zinfandel vineyard planted where it all had been.

"I planted it with the strongest rootstock they ship," Sam told me. "It'll withstand phylloxera, drought, and anything else that comes its way."

But no matter how he'd prettied it up, I knew I'd be able to find the Mitchell place from the undulations of the land, the newly planted vines. For me, the outlines of the trailer, the greenhouse and the garage that housed Kevin's lab would still be visible against the sky. The ghosts of us would be there.

Thankfully, Sam's house, the cave and the cottage I'd eventually call my own were on the opposite side of the Trove property. Sam convinced me to stay in his guest room until the refurbishment was finished, no more than a week of punch-list work by the contractors, he vowed.

"My house is so big, you'll hardly know I'm there," he said.

Upon arrival, Sam again insisted on carrying my duffel. It seemed more a charade of chivalry than chivalry itself, but it was his house and I was his guest and I wanted to be polite. We went in through the modern kitchen, new made to look vintage with a pristine farmhouse stove and a distressed farm table in the middle of the room instead of a fancy island. Over at the sink, Alma Delgado, the mother of the table-tripping winemaker, was peeling potatoes.

"Alma, this is Cinnamon, our new employee and my guest."

Alma nodded once in my direction, her dark eyes shining and sharp. She turned back to her work.

"Dinner ready soon?" Sam asked.

"Six o'clock, like always, Mr. Sam," she said.

"Good, we'll eat out on the deck," Sam said and continued through the kitchen holding my suitcase.

"Nice to meet you," I said, but Sam had left the room and Alma didn't bother answering.

The guest room at Sam's place had a view of the hillside and the dry creek that ran in winter. The room was decorated with blue chintz curtains and bedspread, feminine, compared to the rest of the house, like it had been done just for me. I didn't ask if it had.

Sam acted like a bellhop dawdling for a tip. He turned the hot water tap on in the bathroom and remarked how quickly it came out. I wanted to lay down on the bed and rest. Sam opened the closet door.

"Yes, hangers," he said.

I stood silent, waiting.

"You're sure you're going to be all right?" he asked.

"I'll just need to lie down a little," I said.

I lined up my stack of paperbacks neatly on the dresser, hung up my jacket on the back of the closet door, then, I lay on the bed, turned to my side, and watched the tips of oak branches scratch my window until it was time to eat.

Much like Socorro used to, Alma served us in courses: warm bread, then green salad, then steaks and scalloped potatoes. Also, like Socorro, she stood just inside the kitchen door in case we needed anything else. For dessert, Alma brought out a lemon meringue pie. I wasn't hungry and didn't like lemon meringue, but I still asked for a piece. I remembered how nervous Socorro would be when she thought Frank or my grandmother didn't like something she'd made. I wanted Alma to know I was an ally, a decent girl with manners who was not going to let those who were offering me a second chance down.

But she served the sunny-yellow pie with her same poker face, excused herself, and left the kitchen, letting the screen door gently bang behind her before she headed down the hill.

"She's going back to the ranch house to make dinner for Pedro and Eduardo," Sam said.

"Two dinners? Each night? That seems like a lot of work for four people."

"Five now," Sam said, savoring his last swirl of Hillside Select before pushing his plate aside to focus on Alma's pie.

I took a taste, the lemon custard perfectly tart against the sweet meringue. Alma may not have been friendly, but she could cook.

"You tired?" Sam asked. "I can give you a few more days off before you start."

I'd been looking out at the vineyard in the fading April sun. My eyes had closed without me noticing.

"No," I said, my lids flying open. "I want to start tomorrow. I need to start tomorrow."

I began to clear the table.

"Alma comes up and takes care of that," he said, motioning with his hands for me to sit.

"I'd be happy to do it so Alma doesn't have to come back up. I don't mind washing dishes . . ."

"You're my guest," Sam said. "Let Alma do the dishes."

Sam apologized for a DVD collection heavy on John Wayne. I

watched a movie with him, but my mind was back on Kevin, the first time I'd taken Kevin's dose and he and I had played baseball with lemons in the field between the trailer and Sam's vineyard. How he'd told me about the old guy who was making a go of winemaking, how we'd planned to come and find the closed-off caves someday. And now here I was, in the house of the winemaker, wondering what Kevin was up to.

After the movie, the mess of dishes and napkins left on the table was gone, the kitchen spotless. I knew Alma made him breakfast and would be back up here at six am. Her days were long days.

I asked about Eduardo.

"You want to know if he has a girlfriend?"

"I wasn't asking that at all," I said, embarrassed, thinking now that he mentioned it I did want to know.

"Workplace stuff never goes off right. It's too messy. Make me a promise you won't let something with Eduardo get in the way of you staying here.

Who I liked or thought about seemed like it should be none of Sam's business, but he'd proven himself to be doing nothing but looking out for my best interests since the day he found me in the vineyard.

"I promise," I said.

Chapter 12

The first winter my mom, my dad, and I lived in the shipwreck shack, it rained solidly January through March. When the elaborate system of tarps my dad had placed over the gaps between the roof and the cliff wall failed, rain poured in and created a network of tiny waterfalls. My father patched and retied the tarps, but the rain found ways in, making the inside air clammy and our woolen blankets and cotton-stuffed mattresses mildew. A few weeks into the Old Testament-sized downpour, my parents escalated from end-of-the-day crankiness to morning-to-night fighting again. My father blamed my mother for bad housekeeping and nearly homicidal dinners, and my mother blamed my father for spending what little money he made on stereo equipment instead of providing a watertight home. After each bout, my mother scrubbed at the floor or banged dishes around in the sink and my father sat cross-legged on the couch and smoked, the pot another layer of stink on top of the wool, the wet, and the wood. I lay on my top bunk, withdrawing under the covers as the rain poured down outside and my parents raged at each other in front of me.

Once the deluge ended, a construction crew began to build a house on the empty lot up the hill from us. I spied on its progress from my perch in an oak tree that bordered their property. The builder dropped in ox-eye windows, roof finials, and other ornate Victoriana into the huge house. I discovered the contractor left the back door open for deliveries and I took advantage, walking around after the carpenters had gone home, wondering if children close to my age might move there.

Other than school and watching the house on the hill take shape, my only escape from the shipwreck shack was weekends at my grandmother's. I was asked down about once a month and then left on my own. Before I could read, I walked the crushed-shell paths around the rose garden, trailing Jorge, who pushed a wheelbarrow of bright annuals in the spring and brown leaves in the fall. Back inside, I would trace my fingers along the folded wings of the bronze cherub while Socorro dusted the entryway, or lay on one of the twin beds in the red room where I stayed searching the toile landscape for something undiscovered. But once I could keep up with a book, I spent days at my grandmother's, reading.

One Sunday morning the library was all mine. Frank was at the Club, my grandmother had a hair appointment, and Socorro, back from church, was cleaning the third floor. Grabbing the brass rails on the bookshelf, I pushed myself along on the library ladder until it rolled to a stop in front of a new section, my eyes level with the highest row of books. Most of the titles were uninspiring—a primer on Chinese lacquerware, chronicles of the Peloponnesian War, a biography of Dwight Eisenhower—but then I saw it, gold embossed on green leather: *Jane Eyre*. Leaning my body against the rungs, I opened the book. Its spine cracked with promise.

"To Elaine" was scratched in sepia ink on the flyleaf followed by a date and an illegible signature. Doing the math in my head, I determined my grandmother had gotten the book as a gift when she was around my age. The pristine pages were stiff, like they'd never been read. I skimmed the first few paragraphs to see if the story had promise.

A small room adjoined the drawing room. I slipped in there. It contained a bookcase: I soon possessed myself of a volume, taking care that it should be one stored with pictures. I mounted into the window seat: gathering up my feet, I sat cross-legged, like a Turk; and, having drawn the red moreen curtain nearly close, I was shrined in double retirement.

While my grandmother's library's curtains were green silk, not red, a window seat beckoned and I went to it, reclined on the pillows with *Jane Eyre*, and read away the dreary February afternoon.

Socorro finished her cleaning and my grandmother returned, but not until they called my name did I realize I was not an orphan banished to Lowood School, but instead a girl whose weekend visit at her grandmother's was coming to an end. But, like Jane, I had no wish to return home.

"Cinnamon," my grandmother called at the library door, barely masking the impatience in her voice.

I put the book down and went to gather my things.

Jorge was lifting my duffle into the trunk of the idling Cadillac when I decided I could bear leaving only if *Jane Eyre* came with me.

Saying I'd forgotten something, I ran back to the library. Post-storm sun shone through the diamond-pane windows and kicked up a butterscotch light from the wood floor. I crossed to the window seat and slipped the book into the lining of my raincoat. On the long wooden table in the middle of the room, a philosopher's bust sat atop a stack of books raising an eyebrow at me. To leave now would mean I was stealing. If the book belonged to Frank, the theft would hold little moral penalty, but considering the inscription, I was crossing a line to take *Jane Eyre*, even if neglected and unread. My grandmother could be generous, shockingly so, when her whims aligned with the tilt of my universe. But I'd found that the average request, things honestly asked for, were denied. So I accepted her light kiss on my temple, cradled the concealed book in my right hand, climbed into the car, and shut the door.

She motioned to Jorge to roll down my window. I grasped *Jane* tighter. "The next time you're here," she said, "your cousin Julia will join us."

I turned around and looked back at her while we drove down the hill and out the gate, momentarily forgetting the book.

"Who's Julia?" I asked.

Jorge wrinkled his forehead. "No se, Pulgita."

Although I risked carsickness, I pulled the novel from its hiding place and read on.

"Is good, Miss Cinnamon?" Jorge asked as he navigated the Eldorado down Nineteenth Avenue.

"The best," I said, because typhoid had descended upon Lowood

School, a place more miserable than any I'd endured, and though Jane had slept with death itself, I knew she would survive.

Before Jorge dropped me back at the shipwreck shack, Jane had left Lowood for a job that would make her independent of her sadistic Aunt Reed and the tortures of being small, poor, and female. I slipped the leather-bound book onto my bookshelf behind the paperbacks from Nancy. When I couldn't sleep, I'd click on my lamp and pick a passage at random. *Jane Eyre* always had something new to tell me. In the pages of *Jane*, Charlotte Brontë renders an escape plan from the hedge maze of a forlorn childhood, a narrative blueprint for lost girls, a way to navigate dark dead-ends and come blinking into the peopled light.

"The daughter of Victor and that Foxworthy girl," my mother said when I asked her who Julia was.

"But Uncle Victor's a priest," I said.

"He wasn't always."

"What does Julia look like? What does she like to do?"

After much begging, my mother got the number from my grandmother and I called Julia from a payphone in town. After hellos, we were both silent. I mumbled something about seeing her at my grandmother's, corrected myself to say our grandmother's, but she'd already handed the phone back to her mother.

I trembled and fidgeted on my next drive down to Hillsborough, asking Jorge, who'd picked Julia up the night before, every question I could.

"Is she like me?" I asked. "Do you think we'll be friends?"

"Cousins are cousins," Jorge said. "Blood is beyond friends."

My grandmother stood under the porte cochère as I arrived. Beside her was a plump girl, a whole head taller than me with bulging blue eyes and hair the color of old corn.

After kissing my grandmother on her cheek, the act that code-switched me from shipwreck shack to Hillsborough manners, I stuck out my hand and asked Julia how she did.

"Pleased to meet you," she answered. I saw she had splotches and hives on her neck, chest, and arms. Her eyes were swollen and pink like she'd been crying. She was rubbing the fabric of her skirt between her fingers hard and fast.

"Entertain yourselves until Susie calls for lunch," said my grandmother, leaving us alone outside.

I worked the riser of the steps with the toe of my shoe.

"Would you like to see the rose garden?" I asked.

She didn't answer but followed me around the back path, still rubbing her fingers together like her ability to breathe depended on it.

"What's your house like?" I asked her.

She shrugged.

"Mine's a Victorian. Painted yellow with white trim."

I watched to see if this impressed her. I couldn't tell, so I went on.

"And we have a maid. Just like Susie."

"Isn't her name Socorro?"

"That's so hard to say, so I say Susie." I hoped this new and more grown-up tone would help Julia see that I was worthwhile.

She looked like she was afraid I'd bite her. I tried again.

"Did Grandmother show you my rosebush?"

Julia shook her head.

"It's this orange one, here." The Cinnamon rose covered the trellis with buds, a deep copper color that would burst into fiery orange blossoms, dripping from the vine.

Socorro called for us and we went into the kitchen where I washed my hands, sat on a barstool, and took ladylike bites out of my ham and cheese on white. I told Julia about how many times our grandmother had taken me clothes shopping and how she'd promised me the bronze cherub on the foyer table, the one her grandmother had given to her, would someday be mine. Julia looked at her plate and took gulping bites of her sandwich.

"It's something grandmothers pass down to their oldest granddaughters," I said, parroting my grandmother.

"Shhhhht," Socorro shushed me, drawing air across her teeth.

I stopped eating. How dare Socorro tell me to be quiet. I glowered at her for embarrassing me in front of Julia, but she hovered around my cousin, paying no attention to me, clucking and giving her more chips and a second sandwich, which Julia promptly stuffed in her mouth. I excused myself, leaving my dirty plate for Socorro to clear, and went to the library. I could hear sniffling then sobs coming from the kitchen. I closed the heavy door to shut Julia's sad sounds out.

Later I heard Socorro and my grandmother talking in the foyer. I opened the door a sliver and peeked out, listening.

"You've got to find a way to stop her from crying. She's been in tears since the minute she got here. I can't stand it," my grandmother said.

"She's homesick, Miss Elaine. Maybe it is too much for her to be away."

"Well, Cinnamon manages."

I smiled.

"Miss Julia and Miss Cinnamon are different girls."

"Julia's been spoiled," my grandmother replied. "I'd send her home, but her mother is off with some boyfriend this weekend. I can't be rid of her until tomorrow afternoon."

Socorro curtsied to my grandmother and went back to the kitchen. I pictured Socorro comforting her, taking Julia upon her lap. I again shut the library door and moved myself to the window seat farthest from the sounds of the kitchen.

Socorro sent Jorge into town and he came back with bags full of games and toys. Julia and I played *Sorry!* that afternoon, and though my irritation with her had subsided and I made mistakes on purpose, swapping my players for hers closest to base, Julia moped through the game. I handed her a win to make her feel better, but she didn't even lift her chin from her knee.

My grandmother had put us together in the red room. When she thought I was asleep, she sniffled into her pillow. I waited for her to stop. She didn't.

"What's wrong with you?" I asked.

"I miss my mother," Julia choked out. "Don't you?"

I thought about that. My mother sitting on the couch, stinking of wine. The coldness of the shipwreck shack, the weekend of arguments between my parents I didn't have to hear.

"No," I said. "I don't."

She got up and crossed to the door.

"Where are you going?" I asked.

"To get Grandma."

"Don't," I said. "She hates crybabies."

She paused, then went into the bathroom, shut the door, and muffled her sobs into a towel.

I turned over and tried to sleep. Her noises, while quieter, were disturbing. I should have gotten Socorro, but I was still miffed at her for shushing me at lunch. Besides, this crying was probably Julia just wanting attention and Grandmother wouldn't like that at all.

I knocked on the bathroom door.

"Can you stop it?" I said, working a huff into my voice. "Because I hate crybabies, too."

Julia went quiet.

Frank didn't play golf the next morning and sat with us at breakfast. Julia hid her swollen eyes by looking down. As she took a second helping of French toast from the warmer on the credenza, Frank winked at me.

"Haven't you had enough, Porky?" he said to my cousin.

Julia froze. Our grandmother gave a disapproving, "Now Frank."

I snickered because someone else was at the bottom of the heap instead of me. I tried to catch Frank's eye, to smile, to think that now we had something in common. But he only looked at the paper as Julia returned to the table with an empty plate. She excused herself and went up to the red room. I sat for a minute longer, not hungry anymore, and then I excused myself.

"Wait a minute," Frank said.

I turned to him, still willing to share the joke, get another friendly wink from my old enemy.

"Susie's got the morning off," he said. "Take the plates to the kitchen."

I cleared the table, placed the dishes in the sink, although the empty dishwasher was right there, and climbed the stairs. Julia was sitting on her packed suitcase staring out the window.

"You wanna play *Sorry!?*" I asked.

"No thanks," Julia said. "I'm leaving soon."

I knew it was several hours until she and I could go, but I didn't argue and went down to the library where no book interested me, then out to the garden where I lay on a bench and watched the puffy white clouds float over the coast range. My eyes ached in the sockets and my throat hurt, but I didn't know why. It was Julia that was unhappy; it was Julia who was the butt of Frank's jokes now.

I went home and told my mother about the weekend. While I was telling her about Frank calling Julia a pig, I started sobbing, my hands wiping at my eyes in surprise. My mother held my head on her lap as I lay crying on the couch. She stroked my hair and I told her how Julia had kept me awake all night, how I'd tried so hard to be friends, but Julia made me miserable, and I never wanted to see her again.

My mom, for the first and last time I remember, suggested we go into town and get ice cream. My dad didn't want to go, but said if we brought him some back, he'd be happy to eat it.

We did, bringing two banana splits and one brownie sundae home in plastic bowls, the cherry-stained whip cream smeared against the transparent tops. After we finished off the treats, my dad asked if we'd like to go for a walk. He took us across the road and up into the forested hills where he foraged for purslane, morels, and miner's lettuce. When we came out at the top of the ridge, we could see the fog bank out at the coast. My dad leaned against a boulder and my mother joined him, reclining into his chest, gazing west as the sun hit the tip of the fog and lit up the middle of the sky with pink and orange.

I watched them together, my dad fingering a strand of my mother's hair, the setting sun making their skin look like it had the same rich, golden hue.

Everything can start over now, I thought.

Walking home, my mom caught sight of the confectionary roofline of the Victorian up the hill. There was now a 'For Sale' sign by the road. The three of us walked up to the house holding hands and stood and looked at it.

"This is a nice place," my mother said.

"Sometimes they leave the back door unlocked," I offered.

My parents followed me up inside. The house had been staged to look like people lived there, down to a tray of plastic T-bone steaks on the dining-room table.

"I love this window," my mother called from the living room with the big bay.

"Basement's big enough for a workshop," my dad hollered from downstairs.

"Come and see upstairs," I said.

They came up behind me and we looked at the bedrooms one by one. One set up for a girl, one for a boy, and a third as a nursery. The master bathroom had a view over the woods in back of the house. My dad climbed into the sunken Jacuzzi tub.

"Imagine after a long day just sinking in," my dad said from the tub and my mom climbed in and joined him.

He turned the spigot, my mother shrieked, but no water came out.

"There's room for three," my mom called to me and I climbed in too, giggling, nestled in between my parents, each of us taking turns, talking about the kind of life we'd lead in this house. How my father would have to sleep in a suit and tie and my mother would have to take gourmet cooking lessons to live in such a fine place.

"Can't we?" I asked.

"Can't we what?" my mom said.

"Live in this house for reals?"

"We're fantasizing, Cinnamon," my dad said. My mother's laughter trailed off.

"But can't we stop fantasizing and try and make it real? If you both got jobs and Grandmother helped us out . . ."

"Let's enjoy the moment," my mother said.

But I didn't want to fantasize, and I could only enjoy the moment if there was hope of it being more than just pretend. I wanted to live in that house. I wanted them to get along and wear suits and take cooking classes. Couldn't they see this was serious? Couldn't they see I was desperate?

"Time to go," my father said, shoving me out of the tub enough where I stumbled onto the floor.

"C'mon, Cinnamon," my mother said, holding out her hand to help me up.

I didn't want to touch her.

"I'll come home later," I said, and after they left I went to the staged girl's room, flopped on the bed, and held a fringed pillow to my heart.

Out the window of that room I could see the perch in the oak tree where I'd sat watching this house being built. The oak had a perfect view into this window and the girl's room had a perfect view of the oak. My hot tears spilled out again, dripping onto the rented sheets.

Chapter 13

The caves that ran under Trove Vineyards were a hundred years old. Excavated by Chinese laborers with pick-axes and shovels, the chalky earth had been carried out by wicker hand baskets and dumped where the grapes now grew. During Prohibition, when Trove's vines were abandoned, the caves were forgotten. Sam's lawyers found mention of them nestled in the deed, told him of the liability, and advised him to seal them shut with concrete blocks.

But Sam reopened the caves. He put in pillars and shotcrete where necessary, leaving the old brickwork and packed earth walls to guard his precious barrels, his progeny, his wine. All of the machinery and our offices were also in those caves. In the hillside, winter or summer, the temperature at my desk was a constant 58 degrees.

You entered the main cave through heavy double doors and immediately had two large anterooms, one to the left, the other to the right, filled with crushing equipment and fermentation tanks. Continuing on was a long, straight tunnel with barrels stacked two tall into the distance. Two smaller tunnels branched off the main, also lined with barrels, each ending in a room with a vaulted ceiling. One was a smaller room with a large conference table where we held our meetings and tastings, the other was a larger room where Pedro, Eduardo, and I had our office. Pedro used his desk only as a resting place for rusty screws and the black rotary telephones we used because the sleek cordless system that Sam installed was nothing but buzz and hiss underground. My desk, which in alignment with the Napa Meadows pretend-who-you-want-to-be-and-you'll-be-it theory was tidy, organized with a clear space for working. Eduardo had less of a desk and more of a long laboratory counter along one wall.

Keeping in mind my promise to Sam, I had hoped that when we

started working together, Eduardo the table-tripper and I could be friends, allies.

No chance.

He was even less outgoing than Alma. She had to speak to me: Did I want something dry-cleaned or pressed? Did I need more towels? But Eduardo, while the proximity of our desks would have allowed us to chat all day about winemaking, the upcoming harvest, or what people our age did for fun in Sonoma County, acknowledged me only when it would have been intolerably rude not to. At first I thought it might be because he was embarrassed about being so clumsy at the party, but weeks into the job I doubted that his embarrassment could have lasted so long. Then I thought Sam might have had the 'no fishing off the company pier' talk with him that he'd had with me, but even if that were true Eduardo's daily dismissal of me seemed extreme. Even passing me in the halls of the cellar, I would get at most a nod, like he didn't want to meet my glance, like it caused him physical pain to look me in the face. But then I'd catch him scrutinizing me when I worked at my desk. He'd stare, thinking I couldn't see, like he was sizing me up, figuring me out. I began to think the Delgados were all watching, waiting. I suppose they knew at least a little of my background and thought I was preying on Sam.

And I guess I was. I didn't have much to give—the majority of the giving at that time just went in one direction and I knew what people might think of that. So, I gave up trying to become close with Alma or Eduardo and concentrated on Pedro who was by far the most friendly. He'd praise me when I fixed a stuck valve or when I showed him I could train a row on the bud break. Pedro's accent was thick and when he said Cinnamon, it came out sounding more like Smart One. But training me was more work for Pedro; he was taking time to teach me to do the things he already knew by heart. Maybe Alma and Eduardo were afraid I'd replace him and that's why they were so unfriendly. But there was more than enough work for the both of us and Eduardo at least could see that, so I didn't get it.

One afternoon, after we'd been working together for over a month,

Eduardo was barrel tasting the last fall's harvest in the same far nook of the caves where I was taking inventory. Out of the corner of my eye I watched him work. He removed the barrel cork and slid the wine thief, a glass syringe that holds maybe a glass of wine, into the barrel of young Zinfandel. Using his thumb for suction, he half-filled the thief with ruby liquid and with a tap of his finger released it into the wineglass he held in his other hand. I knew he had to taste the barrels in order so I worked toward him, and he toward me, like an ultra-slow-motion game of workplace chicken. He didn't acknowledge me until we were side by side, but then, like we'd been talking the whole time, he offered me a taste not by asking but by holding his glass out.

"Rough, I know," he said, "but beneath, what's really there?"

I took a small sip that gnawed on the inside of my mouth. The tannins were fierce, and turbidity made getting a sense of what would emerge difficult, but I got the gist of it, spit my taste on the gravel floor, and took another.

"The fruit is strong," I said, all of the books and wine courses Sam had provided coming into play. "It'll balance the tannins out."

"Ripeness isn't my concern," Eduardo said. "This is California. We've got enough sun. What about the acid? The structure? Will it last?"

I took a second sip and pulled air across the wine as I'd been taught, and ran my still-healing memory across the catalog of masterpiece Dry Creek Zinfandels Sam had poured for me. Then I swallowed and waited for the wine's resonance in my mouth. From the long finish, I worked forward. Had they harvested the grapes in time? Was there enough acid left to form a lasting backbone?

"It's a keeper," I said.

Holding the pen tight, he wrote a few dark, messy lines on his note-pad I couldn't read without being obvious. Then, he dunked the thief in a jug of water to clean it and moved on to the next barrel. This time, he hadn't shaken the thief quite dry and the wine's red tendrils mixed with the water, like blood and liquid meth in the chamber of a syringe. In a rush of memory, Eduardo vanished, and instead I saw Kevin pulling back the stopper, my red blood mixing with the clear drug, making the same patterns as the water in the Zinfandel. My head went light and I steadied myself on the side of a barrel.

"Cinnamon?" Eduardo asked, dumping the ruined contents of the wine thief onto the gravel floor. It was the first time he'd called me by name.

"I'm fine," I said. But then I wasn't. The darkness of the cave was the same darkness of the trailer and my past mingled with my present until my head spun and my knees gave out on me.

I hit the ground hard. Eduardo put his hand on my shoulder until I stopped hyperventilating. When I was ready, I looked up and the thief was just a thief, the wine was only wine. Eduardo was kneeling in front of me, peering into my face.

"What happened?" he asked.

"Would you believe transfiguration?" I said, leaning my head back on the cave wall.

He felt my cheek for heat. "We should get you to the doctor," he said.

"I'm not sick," I said, pushing his hand away.

"Great," he said, abruptly turning back to the barrel, drawing up a vein of undiluted wine.

"Does it make you nervous?" I asked him, after a few minutes, feeling better, still sitting, not knowing why I'd pushed him away and snapped at him.

"Does what make me nervous?" he asked, not turning around.

"Your first vintage. That you'll fail?"

He took his time swirling the taste he had in his mouth before spitting it out.

"I fail at the little things, Cinnamon Monday. On the big ones, I get it right."

I hoped he might hold out his hand again to help me up from the floor. This time I would take it and thank him. But instead he gathered up his things and went back to his desk, leaving me to dust myself off and finish my barrel ledger alone.

That evening, I got a call from my mother telling me Phil had died.

"In Sacred Ceremony with a new convert," she sobbed. I didn't know what Sacred Ceremony was, but I had a decent guess. "The men are meeting to discuss who will lead us."

"Do you want a place to stay?" slipped out of my mouth before I really thought about the practicality of it. Sam wouldn't like it, but he might tolerate it if I asked.

"Oh, that's nice," she said in her zombie commune voice. "But I'm not allowed to leave the Mountain while we are mourning Phil."

Of course not, I thought, the men up there scrambling for alpha position want to keep their harem and income streams intact.

"I want you to know I'm in a place where I can help you now," I said. I wasn't sure if I was well enough to help her. Probably not, but I wanted to offer her something. She was my mother.

My mother broke into a fresh sob and then lowered her voice. "I called your father," she whispered. "He's on his way."

"Dad?" I said. "He hates Phil."

"Oh, no honey," she said. "He's coming here to be at Phil's side during the soul transition. Ascendance is what we are all striving for."

"Are you and Dad getting back together?"

"Your father and I will always be together. What's together in the eyes of God, Cinnamon, cannot be broken."

After I hung up, I went and lay on my bed in the guest room looking at the swaying oak tree branch. I thought for a while about offering to help my mom. It had been a crazy thing to do, but I was doing well at Trove. With the exception of the unfriendliness of Alma and Eduardo, my transition from Napa Meadows to my job on the vineyard had gone smoothly. Sam asked me to take classes, I took them. Then I came back and with Pedro's help, which I needed less and less, I was beginning to carve out little bits of work that were mine: all the ordering and inventory, the fermentation chores, side projects for Sam. Soon, I'd move into my own cottage, my own home. I'd been given a huge gift, and I felt I should reach out to people in my life that needed help, like my mother, like Kevin.

Kevin.

I still had the address of his parent's place on River Road. Although I'd never been asked, sometimes when Kevin would go to dinner there I'd follow him. I would park by the side of the road and look up toward the house on the bluff, wishing I'd been included.

I started to wonder why I couldn't go drive by Kevin's. Maybe I'd see the motorcycle, or him working in the yard, a little something to prove he was all right. Without telling Sam where I was going, I took the Explorer and drove south on 101 then out River Road. I passed more vineyards, then fields and houses. Getting closer, I slowed and turned up an asphalt drive to the low-slung ranch house on the bluff halfway between Santa Rosa and Guerneville. There was no sign of Kevin. No boy, no bike, not even one Mitchell Brothers' truck in the driveway.

I was already there. How big of a deal would it be to just go knock on the door and ask politely after an old friend of mine? Before I could think too much about what I was doing, I parked in front of their house and killed the engine.

Beside The Mitchells' front door, a plastic goose in patriotic dress, maybe left over from the Fourth of July, looked up his beak at me. I rang the bell.

A dog's paws clicked up to the door and Kevin's mother opened it. She was tall, in a tennis skirt with the same reddish-blonde hair and faded freckles as her son. The dog, a Rottweiler, was showing his teeth at me, growling. She held him by the collar.

"Mrs. Mitchell, I'm Cinnamon," I said, sticking out my hand, "a friend of Kevin's."

"Wait," she said, hauled the dog back inside and shut the door behind her. We stood outside, just her and I, taking each other in.

"You're the girl?" she asked.

Up close, I saw the broken bits of mascara nestled in the wrinkles under her eyes, like she had applied it long ago and been too tired to clean it off.

She grabbed my arm, hard. "Were you the girl?"

I shook my arm free. "I was Kevin's friend," I said. "Is he here?"

Her eyes narrowed. Then she looked aside and laughed.

"I hope you're happy," she said.

"What did I do?" I asked.

"You ruined his life," she spat. "You ruined our lives. The state seized all that land and auctioned it off. We lost our business."

"Kevin almost killed me, Mrs. Mitchell. He was into drugs before I ever knew him. I begged him to stop. The only times he was sober was because of me."

"Get off our property," she said, turning away and opening the door.

I heard the nails of the dog sprinting down the wood floor toward us. She was siccing her Rottweiler on me.

I ran toward the car, the dog closing the distance. I shut the door and he slammed up against it, all his bared teeth in my open window, growling, lunging, wanting to tear me apart. I fumbled for the button that would close it.

"You make him call me, you hear! You tell him to call his mother!" Mrs. Mitchell screamed at me before I could get the window closed. The Rottweiler chased the car back down to River Road, lunging and yelping at my tires while I waited to make the left turn. Make him call me? I thought. Did she think I still talked to him? Knew where he was? How long had it been since she'd seen him? Other than his parents, where else did he have to go?

That night I dreamed Kevin was on my left side and Phil was on my right, each with a vial they wanted to shoot into my veins. I tried to move, but was tied down, gagged. They leaned closer, in unison, the needles glinting. I knew if I got that stuff on the inside I'd be finished. I screamed into my gag, struggled to get free, and woke in a sweat to find Sam standing in my doorway, illuminated in the moonlight. I looked at the digital clock beside the bed: 2:25 am.

"You were crying for help," he said.

"Bad dream," I said. "It's over."

When the contractor said we were waiting for final inspection on my little cottage, Sam asked me if I'd be afraid living alone, but I said no. I'd lived in every kind of hovel, what could be scary about a tidy white cottage? Eduardo lived catty-corner down the lane, and the Delgado's modest ranch and the farmhouse were within screaming distance. I wanted to make my own meals, clean my own dishes, do my own laundry.

"Please, Mr. Gladstone," I said. "I need to have my own place."

"I'll see it's finished by the end of the week," Sam said, and it was.

What was once a laborer's dormitory with rope-frame bunk beds and no indoor plumbing had been transformed. Sam's contractor had installed wide-plank flooring, insulation, central heat and gigantic double-pane windows where there had before only been rough-framed wall. He'd built in bookcases along one wall and shelving and drawers in the closet. When he showed me the finished place, I threw my arms first around the contractor and then around Sam, thanking him for making this place so perfect.

I was giddy with love for my new house.

"Now promise you won't be a stranger up at my place," Sam said.

I promised.

When they left, I went back outside, climbed the sturdy wood steps, and walked over the threshold into my first real home. I put my yellow toothbrush and favorite jasmine lotion on the bathroom counter, hung my few clothes in the closet, and stowed my collection of paperbacks on the bookcase.

After, I sat on the living-room floor, my feet in a rectangle of sun, propped up by my elbows, and dreamed about the comfortable reading chair I'd put in the corner, about curtains and dishes.

When I was ready to head back to work for the afternoon, I locked the door behind me, although there was little need to do so, just for the feeling of dropping the key into my pocket. It was near two o'clock and instead of going directly back to the caves, I walked down the lane of six whitewashed cottages that ended in an orchard that supplied the

farmhouse with fruit for apple butter and pies.

Of the six cottages, mine was the first in the row on the right and Eduardo's was the last on the left. I climbed his steps and peered in his windows. His place had no bedroom partition and the walls of his cottage were unfinished and un-insulated. A kitchen had been added, but not recently, the white sink stained by the iron-rich well water. His bed was made, but the kitchen table was covered in newspapers, breakfast plates, and a French press with the dregs of morning coffee at the bottom. Above the table, there was a poster of a Flamenco dancer, ripped at the edges, tacked to the beams in the open wall. Sam had put no big picture window, no new flooring, no central heat for Eduardo's cottage.

"Why isn't Eduardo's place as nice as mine?" I asked Sam at dinner.

"How'd you see the inside of Eduardo's?" he asked.

"Looked in the window. Why didn't you fix his up?"

"Eduardo's lived in worse." Sam said.

So a college graduate, someone that Sam trusted with making his beloved wine, was getting nothing, while I, a high school drop-out and all-around loser, was getting a sparkling renovation. Sam was no Frank, but this was too much injustice for me to keep quiet.

"It's not right," I said.

"If Eduardo has a problem with his place, he can tell me himself," Sam answered, the first bit of anger I'd ever detected in his voice. For him, the subject was closed.

So now I had a bit more insight into why the Delgados didn't accept me as one of their own: I wasn't. Alma, who cleaned Sam's toilets, had to watch as Sam gave me something special while her own son got something substandard.

The next day I sat at my desk in the cellar while Eduardo laughed on the phone with a friend from Davis. Guys from the viticulture program called his line all the time and dropped by Trove to check out their former classmate's good fortune: they aspired to someday be named winemaker, the job Eduardo had gotten right out of school. I eavesdropped, listening to him tease, then laugh hysterically when he was teased back, discuss weekend plans, old friends, current events. When he hung up and it was just he and I again: silence.

He approached my desk that afternoon. I looked up from orders I was filling out for corks and bottles, put my pen down and waited for him to speak. He was staring at my desk. I'd pushed up the sleeves of my sweatshirt just a little, but enough where you could see the end of my track marks. It was nothing compared to how the skin looked closer to my elbows, but still a lot of scars and redness. Slowly, I moved my arms to my sides.

But he had seen. He had opened his mouth again to say something, but turned and walked away.

"Wait," I said, going after him, grabbing his shoulder. "What were you going to say?"

"I forgot," he said, looking at where my fingers touched him like I was holding a knife.

He'd known I'd come from rehab. The track marks couldn't be total surprise. But his face had been so stunned and held a look I could only guess was disgust.

"You didn't forget. Tell me."

"It was nothing," he refused.

The next day he had a visitor. A girl, with blonde hair and blindingly white teeth, who dressed like a model in the Ann Taylor catalogs I'd started getting in the mail. It was Friday afternoon and she dropped by for a tour of the cellar. She had the high-pitched voice of a little girl and gave me one of her business cards that said she worked corporate sales at Mondavi. She called Eduardo *Edward*. I listened to them walking deeper into the caves, her giggle echoing, and became infuriated. So I had a nicer cottage than he did; all he had to do was see the shipwreck shack to feel superior. So I was an ex-druggie; I was clean, I worked hard, I didn't ask him for anything, and I'd taken a load off his dad now that I'd been trained. Why was he so unfriendly?

Eduardo and Mondavi Girl returned for her to pick up her purse, clearly heading to lunch, without a glance in my direction as they passed.

I waited for the invitation to be extended to me. I was their age, sitting right before them with no lunch on my desk. But it didn't come.

And Eduardo didn't come back to work. When I went to bed that night, music was on at his cottage and Mondavi Girl's Jetta was parked next to Eduardo's truck. Saturday morning it was still there.

Chapter 14

My fifth-grade teacher saw her profession as a subversive act.

"Do you know what a nuclear winter is?" the teacher asked, guitar in hand, one cork-soled sandal up on a stool. I didn't know what a nuclear winter was, but when we'd lived in Inverness Bari DeGarzi talked about it. Bari went on marches and chained herself to things. She must have been popular with her protest group because once she chained her large frame to something, she'd be there to stay.

"We are going to spend a few weeks, children, on the horrors of nuclear war," my teacher said. "We've got two crazy leaders, one in Washington, one in Moscow, each with his finger on the button. Any day now, tomorrow even, we could be living under a mushroom cloud. Some would try and hide Armageddon from you, but I think you must be prepared."

We, even the hyper boys, sat ramrod straight, barley breathing.

She stuck a bootleg tape into the classroom Betamax and let us watch *Testament*, the story of a Northern California town much like ours in the aftermath of a nuclear attack. The children and grandparents, those most vulnerable to radiation, die first, wasting away in agony. I learned that a forest or a valley with a microclimate could lessen your exposure to radiation, that little will grow in contaminated soil, that nuclear winter is not a season but a description of the earth's climate after an atomic holocaust. Everything you rely on will be in ruins.

I couldn't sleep that night or any night that week.

"Is it real, Dad? Could it happen?"

"With that Hollywood cowboy in the White House, World War III is a distinct possibility," my dad said.

"But don't worry," said my mother. "If Russia bombs us, we'll die right here in our bed, together, as a family."

I took survival into my own hands.

On Saturdays, often after reading one of my favorite books over again, I stole away from my house and searched for a place to hide come WWIII. The Victorian up the hill was still for sale, but now locked up tight, so I traveled the fields that backed up to the shipwreck shack. I tried burrowing into a large thicket and found it already occupied with my dad's marijuana plants. He'd crawled in, hollowed out the center of the grove, and grown a crop. I backed out of the hole he'd created and kept going.

The moor-like field sloped downward until it ended in a wood. I slipped between two mossy, rotting fence rails into the unexplored trees. Keeping low, I crawled along an animal's path under the oak brush and heather scrub. The ground was moist, although it hadn't rained for months. I came to a clearing and stood up.

Leaves floated down from a circle of branches as the sun's light, but not heat, slivered through. Could this be the spot where I'd survive a nuclear winter? Worried I wasn't far enough from the road where post-apocalyptic scavengers would pass, I pressed on, descending into the forested ravine. I passed a rotting log, dotted with red mushrooms so beautiful I wanted to pick them.

Pretty, I thought, but poison, and passed them by. I pushed forward through the thick forest and the earth sloped further. I attempted a controlled slide down the incline on my bottom until the cliff ended in the damp, cool hollow of a creek bed.

To my right was a round gully, the bottom filled with coat-button sized pebbles. To my left, the dry streambed twisted out of sight. The opposite bank was steep. Roots stuck out like a ladder, but instead of climbing up and seeing what was on the other side, I went downstream.

I went less than twenty yards then froze. A boy sat on the bank watching me. He must have heard my thrashing through the underbrush, but it hadn't frightened him off.

"Hello," I said.

He didn't answer.

I got goose bumps. There were never any children around; I was

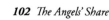

always alone at my bus stop. "What's your name?" I asked, ready to run if he became transparent or flicked a demon's tail.

He shrugged and opened one of his fists showing me a handful of green, plastic toy soldiers. He had high cheekbones and eyes like quick darts. Maybe he was a surviving member of a local tribe who'd hidden in this creek for a hundred years. But then how would he get a hold of plastic soldiers?

We were still, watching each other, the forest muffling all the sounds of the outside world. Who could he be? His skin was coffee colored, like the men who picked apples. I knew they spoke Spanish like Jorge and Socorro—maybe this boy didn't speak English and that's why he wasn't talking. He lined up his soldiers on the ground and lifted his hand, palm open, like he was willing to take an oath.

"Will you join my survivalist movement?" I asked, my voice crisp, proper, like Jane Eyre or one of the many noble heroines from my favorite books was speaking through me.

His forehead wrinkled.

"In case of nuclear war?"

At 'war' he perked up and nodded.

"First we have to decide where our settlement will be."

When Frank Ferguson spoke to Socorro or Jorge, he talked louder, but this boy seemed to understand me, although he didn't answer. I kept talking properly, slowly.

"I have an idea," I said. I lead him back to the gully. "It's cool here. Good to store food. Things to eat," I motioned like I was eating soup. "We'd have to hunt and gather." I motioned a bow and arrow.

He nodded and pulled a package of Nabisco crackers out of his pocket and laid it in the gully.

"Yes!" I said. "We must prepare! The Soviets will bomb us and then invade."

"We have to camouflage our provisions," I said, climbing up the bank to a bunch of broken tree limbs. "Otherwise the bad people will come. People get desperate in a nuclear winter."

The boy had a switchblade. He seemed young to have one, but I didn't question people with knives, and he cut, with two swift whacks, a leafy branch. He dragged it over the gully, hiding whatever was inside from view.

The boy understood our situation perfectly.

"How old are you?" I asked.

Pointing to myself, I held up ten fingers.

"Nine," he said in good English, looking down. "Ten in April."

He'd been shy, not mute.

With our food stash camouflaged, we set up a hospital. We marked the four corners of the infirmary with stakes, carved by the boy with his sharp blade. In a nuclear winter, I told him, you get sick from the fallout. We practiced how we'd handle patients. I put one hand to my forehead and one to my stomach and lay in one of the leafy beds. At first, the boy hovered over me looking concerned. Then he touched his hand to the pulse point in my neck. The tips of his fingers were calloused and warm.

"I'm going to be very sick," I said.

"I'll save you," he answered.

A wolf whistle broke through the trees. He heard it and looked up at the sky. We'd been so involved in our game we hadn't noticed the daylight was almost gone. He touched my hand and said, "Tomorrow?" I nodded and then he ran in the direction of the whistle, opposite from the way I'd come.

I picked my way back up the creek to the gully and then crawled on all fours up the hillside, back over the old fence, and crossed the wide moor toward the shipwreck shack. I scampered home in the near-dark, afraid of the invading Russians who might skulk through these fields at night.

My mother stood at the stove stirring a pot of something that smelled burnt, and my dad sat at the kitchen spool, rolling a joint and reading a newsletter. He had a gig later that night and was dressed in a wrinkled paisley shirt and jeans. His damp hair held the neat rows of the comb. His guitar leaned up against the door.

"Did you know, Cinnamon," he said without a hello or asking me

where I'd been for the last ten hours, "that doctors can keep you hooked up to a ventilator for years?"

"No," I said.

"I'm thinking about joining," my dad said, reading further. "If you get sick, this organization will send you some natural stuff to eat and you take the big sleep. No medical intervention. No doctors keeping you alive for their own benefit."

A Gideon on the sidewalk outside the grocery co-op had given my mom a New Testament and she'd started reading it. "Suicide's a sin," she said from the stove.

"If you're dead, what does it matter?" my dad said, annoyed.

"Your soul goes to hell," my mother said, "and then you're separated forever from the ones you love."

My mom served us chewy, undercooked beans on burnt rice. My dad spit his first bite into a napkin.

"It's rice and beans, for Christ's sake," he said. "How hard can it be?"

My mother stared at her plate, her shoulders up near her ears. "If it's so simple, Stephen, next time why don't you make it?"

"I wasn't raised to cook," my father said. "I don't ask that much of you, Linda," he added.

"I wasn't raised to cook either," my mother answered.

I expected him to pound the table or give my mother a knuckle whack on the side of her head; he didn't like it when she or I talked back. But he didn't. He ate around the blackened grains; his pre-dinner high had been enough to amp his appetite and suppress his temper. Starving as I was, I could still only eat the unburnt bits of rice.

When my mother and I were washing dishes, he went back to his newsletter and ripped out the reply card.

"You in, Linda?" he asked.

"On what?"

He waved the newsletter at her.

"I'd rather plan that trip to Baja you promised me," she said, leaving me to dry as she switched on the TV. My dad left the blank reply card on the table and lit his pipe.

The smell of burning resin filled the shack again.

Oh, how I hated that smell. My clothes and my hair reeked of it. On the rare occasion I was invited to play at the house of a classmate, the mother sniffed my jacket and never asked me back. Having someone to my house was out of the question.

The nuclear winter game went on. I met the boy at the creek every day that summer. He'd be there when I came, sitting still, like he'd been waiting hours although I got there as early as I could. He brought little things: red-checked oilcloth for our table, a glass dish, a frayed deck of cards missing the seven of spades. I loved our game, partially because I finally had a friend and partially because I thought he might really be my best hope in an apocalypse. But when the days got shorter and colder, without saying goodbye, he didn't come anymore. Picking the produce of California required a large, roving workforce: oranges down south in the winter, apricots in the summer, apples in the fall. Whole families lived in their cars, moving from one seasons' wages to another. By the beginning of October, the apple harvest was finished. The boy and his family had moved on and I was left to survive the nuclear winter all by myself.

Chapter 15

After Phil's death, my father moved back in with my mother at OHM.

"This time, I think it's for good," my mother confided on the telephone. She had that giddy, girly tone that accompanied their romantic upswings, but I ignored her enthusiasm. This honeymoon would end like all others.

"If you can make it a month, I'll give you both a Scooby snack," I said.

"Come see us," my mother asked ignoring my snark.

I had promised myself I would never go to OHM again, but what I'd really been avoiding was Phil. Now that he was under a ton of marble, and could not bother me, I figured myself safe. When I talked to my mom again a few weeks later, and my father was still there and she still sounded happy, I relented and went to visit.

When Phil was alive, and had forbidden my father and me to see Mom, we'd taken a forest path in from the state park that bordered the back of the commune. While I doubted Phil had lifted the ban on me, OHM was still without a new leader and no one would stop me from coming in the front this time.

I came across the cattle grate, drove up the steep grade, and parked under the redwood trees. Avoiding the Holy House, I walked the path toward my mother's dome. When the path made its last turn coming out of the forest into the meadow, I saw my parents outside on a swing my father must have concocted out of old railroad ties and wooden movie theater seats. They swung back and forth, my father sticking out his leg and pushing them off the tree trunk to keep them in motion when they began to slow. I was about to call out, show myself, but instead I stood behind a cover of redwoods and watched.

My father, who looked thinner and less shaggy than usual, was explaining something to my mother, drawing it with his index finger in the space before her. She was laughing.

He put his arm around her, and she lifted her hair from underneath it and fanned it over her shoulders. They seemed younger than me. The air of the meadow popped with the bright orange wings of Monarch butterflies.

My breath caught in my throat. The two of them, together in the swing, in the golden light of late afternoon was the most beautiful thing I'd ever seen.

I had come to introduce the new and finally improved me as another necessary step in my progress, but this vision of them, together, happy, healed something in me better than a thousand counseling sessions. I considered sneaking back to my car, to keep this vision of my parents crystalline, undisturbed by what might happen if I showed myself. I was afraid my arrival would burst the bubble around them and in fifteen or twenty minutes I'd hear my mother's voice go up an octave when my father displeased her, and hear the slam of the door as my father went to grab his pipe or his jacket to get some space away from the harpy he'd had the bad luck to impregnate.

But my mother turned and saw me first.

"Cinnamon," she called, waving. They made room between them on the swing, but I declined, standing against one of the anchor trees, my hands behind my back, while they heard about the drive up, my job, and my new life.

Then my dad told me foraging stories, how he'd found a grove of chanterelles and sold them at the Ukiah farmers' market, pound for pound, for more than pot.

"And I didn't have to hide them or worry about the narcs," he said. "People just handed me cash and thanked me right out in the open."

My mother told me OHM had gotten a loom and she was learning to weave on it, making rough blankets she also hoped to sell at the farmer's market in Ukiah. She had one on her lap, the rough oatmeal-colored weft intertwined with mulberry-colored weave. It was rough, chunky, and beautiful.

"I'm thinking of getting some gold thread and putting just a little in to give some sparkle," she said.

We stayed in the meadow until rivulets of fog tumbled in from the coast. My mom shivered, my dad held her tighter and said, "What do my girls think about going to town for dinner on my mushroom money?"

I was glad I hadn't left. Even if the night's chemistry was short-lived and nothing about my parents was fundamentally improved, I felt different. We made it through dinner without arguing, my dad telling stories at such a clip he barely touched his meal. He had us in stitches.

Afterward, they wanted me to stay the night.

"The roads are really dark, Cin," my mom warned.

I was tempted, but I'd pushed my luck far enough. Eventually it would run out, and I wanted to keep tonight's happy snapshot in my head. So they walked me back to the parking lot. Instead of the usual scenario of me upset, hurrying to the car amid their complaints, we walked silently the last little way on the path illuminated by my father's flashlight. I kissed them goodnight and they stood, arms around each other's shoulders and watched me go.

I savored my drive, cars passing me on 101 south, shiny tire rims appearing to spin backwards, darkness everywhere but the freeway's exits.

Turning in the gravel driveway of Trove, I realized that I'd driven the last ten or so minutes on autopilot. I didn't have to think how to get from the highway to the vineyard anymore.

Because it's home, I thought.

I saw lights on at the farmhouse when I parked the car, although it was near midnight. I thought about checking in with Sam and letting him tell me about his day, but I didn't want to risk having my reverie interrupted, so I walked down the dirt lane back to my cottage. The lights at Eduardo's were on, and a Latin-polka beat was coming out the window at so low a volume I could barely hear it. No Jetta this time. The vineyards, heavy with new grapes, knit our cottages, the caves, and the farmhouse together. I stood on my little front porch and waited for the crickets to start up again before I went inside and latched the door behind me.

Chapter 16

My father quit his job at the auto body place, but he wouldn't join a machinist's union and never found steady work. He sold a little pot, but he was smoking so much that what he had left didn't cover our meager expenses.

In an attempt to make ends meet, my parents tried one glossy-brochured scheme after another: a llama farm, soap-free laundry detergent, chinchillas. The animals escaped or died en masse; soap-free detergent didn't get clothes clean and people wanted their money back. After every failure my parents scoured the want ads for another income opportunity.

What stuck was breeding cats. My dad traded a full Ziploc of buds for a breeding pair of papered Siamese.

"Your grandmother didn't let me have any pets," my mother said. "Not even a bird. Not at The Pierpoint. I swore when I grew up I'd have as many as I wanted."

At the peak of our cat-breeding years, when I was eleven, we had thirty cats and kittens. My father welded makeshift cages out of bicycle spokes, chicken wire, and metal oven racks. They never closed right and the kittens escaped into the brush, where I commando-crawled to pull them back to saleable territory.

It was late May, and Sylvia, who had been a kitten last fall, was pregnant.

"We should take her to the vet," I said when I saw Sylvia's distended stomach. She was still only half the size of a full-grown female and drug her belly around, looking confused, like she was waiting for an explanation.

"God wouldn't let her get pregnant if she wasn't ready," my mom said. The Gideon Bible was now a fixture in our house. "She'll have the kittens when we are in Baja and we'll come back to a new litter to enjoy."

"Baja?"

"Daddy and I are taking you whale watching next week."

"But it's the last week of school. Games and ice cream on the last day. I'm getting an award at assembly. I can't go."

"I thought you'd enjoy getting out of school. I couldn't wait for school to be over."

"I never want school to be over," I said.

I was reading my way through the school library, burning through Beverly Cleary and Judy Blume. When I told the librarian I loved *Jane Eyre*, she brought me more Brontë and Austen and introduced me to Thackeray and Dickens. *Wuthering Heights* was a disappointment; a false happy ending. Austen entertained with manicured perfection, everyone getting what they deserved, but I didn't trust it. What happened to Lizzie Bennett when she was alone with Darcy and his darkness returned? Dickens, *Bleak House* especially, came the closest to Charlotte Brontë's impact on my soul.

"Okay," my mother said. "But you're going to have to stay by yourself."

"Fine," I said.

They left the Sunday before the last week of school in a borrowed Dodge van with nonsense words and numbers spray-painted in silver on the sides. My dad, dressed like Jimi Hendrix on laundry day, handed me twenty dollars in wrinkled ones, my mother hugged me once tight, and they were off. Before the van sputtered to the crest of the driveway, I'd already turned my back.

I opened all the windows in the house, took my dad's ashtrays and white five-gallon buckets of pot out to the spider-infested shed, and shut the door.

The last week of school was better than I'd expected: shaving-cream fights, a barbeque, water balloons. I felt a part of the group, not hiding in the library or sitting on the fringe at lunch.

"See you next year in Junior High!!!" we scribbled in each other's yearbooks. Nobody mentioned the unglamorous detail that elementary, middle and high school were only across the playing fields from each other.

And then school was out, and my parents were still gone. For two days, this was fine. I read all day and kept the lights on at night.

Then on the morning of the third day, I woke to the throaty sound of a cat's cry. Outside in my nightgown, I saw three little mounds on the driveway, spaced a few feet apart. Sylvia was at the front, dragging herself toward me.

She'd about gotten a fourth kitten out. I stroked her on the head and told her everything would be okay, but I was worried. Experienced mama cats found a spot hidden in the bushes to have their kittens, and by the time my mom could track them down they were already days old. But a cat having her babies on the driveway in the open I had never seen. I knelt at the first bundle. It had burst through and was moving a little in the dirt. The other two were dead in their sacks, their mouths open, gasping for air.

I ran into the house, lined a shoebox with a dishtowel and ran a washcloth under a trickle of cold water from our faucet. Then I raced back outside, picked up the first kitten, wiped it with the washcloth, and laid it in the shoebox. The fourth kitten was dead, also suffocated.

I burst the sack of kittens five and six with my fingers, moaning in horror as I pulled at the membrane until it gave. After six, Sylvia lay on the driveway, panting. I hoped that was all the babies she had. Three dead, three alive, for now. They had to start nursing, I knew, but Sylvia wouldn't fit in the shoebox. I put the shoebox in the one real cat cage we had and went to get Sylvia, but when I rounded the corner to the driveway, she was gone.

I called for her. Nothing. The kittens began to cry.

We'd once had a kitten before that my mom had to hand feed. Eyedropper, I remembered; some mixture of milk, or maybe condensed milk. I had no condensed milk, so I heated some regular on the stove and fed those greedy little babies. They fell asleep and woke with green diarrhea all over the towel, scream-crying to eat again.

I set food out for the adult cats and wondered what I should do. The babies wouldn't last without Sylvia. I wondered if I should call the animal shelter? I knew I shouldn't be there alone when I was only eleven, and what if they wanted to speak to my parents? I sat on the pallet steps, my fingers in my ears so I couldn't hear the kittens' screams, until I saw Sylvia at the edge of the yard, watching the other cats eat from the big bowl.

I jumped up, moved the big bowl inside and shut the other cats in. Then I filled a new bowl with food, set it inside the cage, and waited. Sylvia paced the periphery, flicking her tail back and forth. She came a few steps closer, then a few more. After an hour, the kittens mewing the whole time, Sylvia stepped into the cage and hunched over the food dish, unaware when I slid the latch closed.

The babies attached to her underside. She looked up from her food, narrow eyes flashing me a malevolent glare.

"You're going nowhere," I said. "Get used to it."

But I still had a problem: I was low on cat and people food and it was three miles to town.

My parents should have been back by then, but they'd called from Rosarito Beach. The clutch in the van had failed.

"Mexicans," my mom said, the connection staticky and delayed. "It's mañana, mañana, mañana. I mean, when is mañana going to get here? You'll be okay, right?"

I considered calling my grandmother's—Socorro would answer the phone—and begging Jorge to come and help me. But I was two weeks away from my next visit and without the excuse of picking me up, Jorge would have to ask for permission to be gone the whole day. I knew it would irritate my grandmother to be inconvenienced and I didn't want to get Jorge or Socorro in trouble.

Instead, I hitched a ride with the PG&E guy who'd been up at the Victorian inspecting the meter.

"Your parents know you're hitching?" he asked.

"Sure," I said. "They're sick. Our car's in the shop."

He dropped me at the 7-Eleven, but I couldn't ask him to stay and drive me back. I had to walk three miles with the heavy bags. Walking the weedy path between the two-lane highway and the reflecting guardrail, I had to stop and rest every hundred yards or so. It was getting dark, but I kept on, trudging, switching the heavy bags between my hands, resting, then going on again. When I'd gone less than halfway, the last bit of light disappeared completely and cars whizzed past me in the darkness.

One slowed behind me, its beams bright on my back. Please don't let it be the cops, I thought. When it coasted to a gravel-popping stop, I saw it was a green Volare, not a police car.

"Do you need a ride?"

I peered into the open window, the green dash lights illuminating the passengers: a woman about the age of my mother and a girl my size in the passenger seat holding a red and white striped Kentucky Fried Chicken bucket.

"Thank you," I said. I opened the back door and got in. A little boy, two or three, sat in back holding a matchbox car in each hand. He stared at me.

"Where do you live?" the mother asked in a light, sweet accent, like Melanie in *Gone with the Wind*. Her hair was in soft curls around her face. She wore a collared cream silk shirt under a navy-blue v-neck sweater. Her smile was cheerful and I relaxed. I wouldn't have to make it back on my own in the dark after all.

"About a mile up, on the left."

"That beautiful Victorian?"

"Right next to it."

"I'm Mrs. Ranzetta, this is my daughter Marjorie and back there with you is Joey. We moved from Atlanta on Tuesday. Are you at Orchard?"

"I'm starting junior high."

Marjorie turned around in her seat and smiled at me.

"Oh, Marjorie is, too. How nice to meet a friend on our second day in town." Mrs. Ranzetta looked in the rearview. "What's your name, honey?"

I hated this question. Adults often thought I was kidding. I wished I had a different answer, a different name.

"What do you want to change it to?" my mother asked the last time I'd begged her.

"Jane."

"Jane?" she said. "Where did you get that idea?"

"A book."

"Plain Jane," said my father, singsongy.

"Exactly!" said my mother. "All those other kids at school are just jealous that you have such an interesting name when theirs are all so boring."

"I don't think anyone's jealous," I said.

"Changing your name would not change you, Cinnamon," my dad said.

Always a chance, I thought.

"I knew school would strip you of your imagination," my mother said.

"How about a nickname?" I asked.

"Like what?" my mom said.

"Cindy. Short for Cinnamon."

"Cindy?" my mother said. "That's common."

"That's why I like it. I want to be like everybody else."

"Sometimes I think we should ship you down to Frank and Elaine Ferguson and see how you like being like everybody else," said my mother.

"My name is Cinnamon," I admitted to Mrs. Ranzetta, waiting for the laugh, the comment.

"Well, nice to meet you Cinnamon," she said. Good sign. I pointed her down my driveway, where the shipwreck shack stood dark in her high beams.

"Are your parents home?" Mrs. Ranzetta said, her voice quiet. "I'd like to talk to them."

"Uh, no. They went to San Francisco to pick something up, and they must not be back yet."

I could smell the bucket of fried chicken on Marjorie's lap. All I would need was one piece. I'd eaten canned soup for a week. Maybe they had some of those biscuits, too.

"They're coming back tonight, you're sure?" she asked.

I sat for a moment and tried to make myself sound a little afraid. "They said they would be."

The Volare's engine rumbled, almost like it was saying chicken, chicken, biscuits, biscuits. I could tell Mrs. Ranzetta was deciding.

"Would you like to have dinner with us?" she asked.

I ran inside, stuck the milk in the fridge, changed the food and water in Sylvia's cage, and sped out again.

"I left them a note," I lied, hopping into the car.

The Ranzetta's house had a front porch filled with moving boxes. We sat on the floor of their empty dining room and ate the chicken, the biscuits, and the peanut butter parfaits. Mrs. Ranzetta nibbled on a turkey sandwich and I realized she'd given me her share of dinner.

Mr. Ranzetta was an airline pilot and was gone on a trip. Once Mrs. Ranzetta got Joey to bed, she found the box with the turntable and her stack of 45s. We twisted the night away putting spoons, forks, and knives into the drawers Mrs. Ranzetta had already lined with fresh white contact paper.

"Do you want to spend the night?" asked Marjorie in a whisper. "My mom will say okay."

I dialed the number for time, talked and listened for thirty seconds and hung up.

"They didn't want to talk to me?" Mrs. Ranzetta asked from the other room.

"I told them you were busy unpacking. I just need to be back by ten tomorrow," I said, thinking that if I made up a rule it would sound more plausible that I'd actually talked to a parent.

I coveted all the beautiful things Marjorie had: a frilly white bedspread, a ballerina music box, pink towels with an "M" embroidered on them. When I spent the night that first time, Marjorie let me borrow a Strawberry Shortcake nightgown. It was polyester, faded, pilled. I never wanted to take it off.

"That fits you," Mrs. Ranzetta said. "It's too short on Jorie, why don't you take it home?"

"Thank you," I said, knowing that a junior-high girl should not like Strawberry Shortcake anymore, but thrilled just the same.

My parents came home married. They'd stopped in Nevada on the way back. My dad welded my mom her ring, and she declared it would always be on her hand; without it, she'd feel naked. In the picture of them in front of the chapel, part of the $19.95 wedding package, my mother clutched her New Testament.

"We're bound by God now, Cinnamon," my mother whispered in my ear when she hugged me hello. "We'll be together for eternity."

"Look, Mom," I said, holding her by the wrist and dragging her to the yard. "Look how good I took care of Sylvia and the babies."

My mom and dad praised my work, told me how wonderful I was, and sold the Siamese kittens for fifty dollars each.

I spent most of that summer at the Ranzettas'. Every day I was there, I loved Mrs. Ranzetta more. Being around her, I had no trouble remembering my manners, not because I was afraid of her disapproval or temper, but because around her I wanted to be a better person, I wanted to be like her. Her goodnight kisses were manna to me and flowed from my forehead down my spine, coaxing my body to sleep.

"Sounds like a priss," my mother said when I told her about Marjorie's mother.

"She's not," I insisted. "She's pretty and kind and a really good cook." My mother winced and went to the fridge for another refill of her wine.

It was an empty feeling when Mrs. Ranzetta would bundle me into the Volare and take me home. She had only been inside the shipwreck shack one time; after that she just waved in the direction of the kitchen window before she drove away whether my mother was standing in it or not.

In addition to Marjorie, I made another friend that summer: my cousin Julia. A year after that first, bad visit, my grandmother invited Julia back. During that year, nobody mentioned her; like she'd never existed. Then one Saturday, when I arrived, Julia was there. She stayed one night. She didn't cry. She brought Old Maid in her suitcase and we played it at the kitchen table while Socorro put away groceries, each of her spices marked with a date for freshness, the bananas and lemons always in separate bowls, she told us, because citrus and bananas would rot each other if they touched.

After that visit, Julia was invited every time I was. We spent a weekend together almost every month, staying together in that same third-floor room. My grandmother never called it my room or Julia's, it was the red room, with a suggestion in her voice that it could be used by anyone at all, we just happened to be there at that particular moment. But we called it ours. Julia was sometimes still homesick on these weekends, but now when I heard sobs from her twin bed, I'd call her over, and she'd put her head on my shoulder to sleep while I lay awake staring at the blood-red ceiling.

Julia and I never spoke or visited with each other outside of the trips to our grandmother's. And when we were there, little else existed. I never talked about the shipwreck shack and Julia didn't mention stepfather three, then four, then five. Instead we went the direction opposite of where the cherub pointed, kept our eyes in our laps at meals, and tiptoed when Frank was home so as not to be noticed. When we escaped a cocktail hour or dinner without being humiliated, we'd hold hands and giggle as we ran up the stairs, thrilled with the feeling of coming out ahead.

I didn't like to think about the end of summer. I'd see less of Julia, spend more time with my parents, and the girls who would befriend Marjorie would be unlikely to take me as a part of the package. I was still a good ball player, but now it was only the boys that played; the girls stood in little circles and talked. And that never went well for me.

I could never say the right thing. I lived in that weird thrown-together house right off the road. I never had any new clothes. I shared a bunk bed with my parents.

So I held onto the last days of August. Marjorie, Mrs. Ranzetta, and I had a running game of Monopoly, the game left out on the otherwise never-used dining room table. My grandmother planted a "Julia" rose-bush, which was orange, too, but a lighter, peachy shade, in a corner of her garden next to the burnt umber "Cinnamon." Julia and I stuck our thumbs on a jagged thorn and mixed our blood.

"Weekend sisters," I said.

"Sisters, period," Julia answered as we linked arms and walked up to the kitchen to get Band-Aids from Socorro.

The week before school started, the Victorian sold. The mother and father were doctors in San Francisco and they had two boys, only a little older than I, who'd be starting school at Orchard. I daydreamed about having Marjorie as my best friend, weekends with Julia, and two older neighbor boys who might look after me. Julia, Marjorie, and the neighbors, a double set of my imaginary friends made real.

Chapter 17

A mid-September heat wave had Eduardo testing sugar levels in the vineyard. After the third ninety-degree day, the brix came in at 24 and the harvest began. All of us—me, Sam, Pedro, Eduardo, and the laborers we'd picked up in front of Healdsburg Hardware—worked in a fever, picking all night because another sunny day might convert a great wine with perfect balance to a flabby, mediocre one.

When you think of the wine harvest before you work at a winery, you think of grapes crushed by the feet of cherubic peasant girls, a leisurely afternoon, perhaps an accordion player in the background. Not even close. We pulled grapes in the pitch black until my muscles shrieked and my fingers were stained like Lady Macbeth's. As dawn broke, we realized how much more we had to go and worked with the devil behind us to finish before the Indian summer sun got high enough to beat its rays upon the vines.

We filled the last tractor before nine. Sam slapped everyone on the back, handing out cash to the workers while Alma carried steaming plates of Chorizo and eggs to the picnic tables. Plate in hand, Eduardo walked past plenty of open seats to sit next to me.

"Congratulations," he said. "You made it."

Despite every muscle below my chin already stiff and aching, I had made it. And after a few minutes of rest and some protein, I was euphoric, volunteering for the first shift amongst the sorting and crushing machines. Eduardo went home to shower and nap. Pedro drove the laborers, exhausted but desperate for more work, back to Healdsburg in hopes of getting another night's job pulling grapes before the harvest was done.

Later that morning, I stood in the caves watching the crusher-destemmer mangle a half ton of grapes at a time. Then, with a long hose,

I filled the tremendous tanks with the juice and bits of the skins. As I worked, the tank room warmed and filled with good organic stink. I'd spent the last five months at Trove, cleaning and repairing the three thousand-gallon oak tanks in wait for this. I hoped that if I did my part carefully, methodically, there was a chance that something good would come of it. I was part of a team and, at last, a positive contributor to the world.

I had filled the last tank to capacity, pulled off my purple-stained gloves, and come out of the darkness of the caves into the oppressive heat, when I saw the sheriff's cruiser.

My stomach sickening, I watched it kick up a dust cloud as it closed in. Although every guy pulling grapes was probably illegal, the sheriff didn't handle immigration. Besides, if he had business with Sam, he'd have gone to the farmhouse. The sheriff wanted me.

Irony. After ten years of doing every single thing wrong, it was now, now that I'd been sober for months, that they came to get me. Little glimmers of a life—my collection of books, having an appetite, writing checks that I knew wouldn't bounce—what I'd worked so hard at pretending had started to become real. But what I thought was progress was only a joke and the punch line had arrived. Now I cared about what I had. Two years before, you could have done whatever you wanted to me and it wouldn't have mattered.

Going to the Mitchells' house, I thought. That had to be it. His mother had called and told them every incriminating detail she knew. Set the police on me because she blamed me for whatever happened to Kevin.

The deputy got out of the car, his black boots already mocha-colored with dust, and walked toward me.

"I'm looking for," he checked his notebook, "a Ms. Cinnamon Monday."

I sunk back against the thick cave doors, my hand on the iron ring.

"That's me," I whispered.

The deputy took off his mirrored glasses and I realized he wasn't much older than I was.

"Is there somewhere you could sit down?" he said.

"What do you want?"

It came out sounding wrong—too rude, too confrontational.

"Ma'am, this is my first time and I thought it might be easier on you if . . ."

"Easier?"

"Your mother," he blurted out, "was found dead this morning."

Wrong joke, I thought, wrong punch line.

The deputy cleared his throat. "She'd been deceased for a while," he looked at his notes, "a Mr. Pilgrim found her, knew she had a daughter, directed me here."

A familiar muddle fogged my brain; my mind started wobbling. Disjointed questions came to my head: had I set the hydrometer in the third tank? Why had Eduardo walked past a bunch of empty spots and sat next to me at breakfast? How long was a while?

Then I noticed the sheriff had taken my elbow and was guiding me toward the car.

Another thought: "How did she . . . ?"

He dodged the question. "Mendo sent a detective. He'll talk to you about it after the ID."

I nodded and let him lead me. Pedro, walking toward the caves, caught sight of the deputy and called out, "I get Mr. Sam?"

"Keep an eye on the temps," I said. "I'll be back."

The deputy offered me the front seat, but I sat in the back and watched the rows of grapevines fly past on Dry Creek Road.

"Is there anyone else I should notify, Ms. Monday?" he asked after radioing in.

My grandmother, I thought, but no one should call her until I knew this was for sure. My father, but I had no idea how to get ahold of him. My uncle, the priest, who had taken a vow of silence and wasn't allowed to talk on the phone or receive personal mail. Other than that, nobody.

When had I last talked to my mother? After that one magical visit when I saw my parents happy and together at Oh Holy Mountain, I called a week later, hoping to keep that good spark alive, to let her know how much I loved seeing them together, to tell her I was enjoying my job more than I'd thought possible, that maybe we were finally all pointing in the right direction as a family for once. But before we were on the phone for one minute, I knew something had gone wrong.

"You're still at the winery? Phil wouldn't approve," she'd said, her voice garbled with drink.

"Phil's dead, Mom," I said.

"Don't say that," she whispered. "God's children never die! They cross to heaven and wait for those who are bound to them. Besides, is a winery the best place for you to work?"

This was a reasonable, even necessary question. I could have answered it or changed the subject, but either the bad in me that wanted to see her snap, or the good in me that wanted us to be honest with each other, pushed again.

"I'm the druggie, you're the lush, remember? You're the one that shouldn't be working with wine."

"You are talking about a woman who no longer exists," she slurred. "I accepted Jesus into my heart and He has washed clean my sins."

On that last visit, the good visit, my mother had not mentioned Phil or Jesus the whole evening. Something had gone wrong. But instead of treating her gently, I kept on.

"You've got to get out of there, Mom. Get away from that idiot commune and Dad, and start over."

"Your father and I will be together forever," my mother said, sounding suddenly clear.

"You and Dad don't work," I said. "Everything about our family is a failure."

"Oh, Cinnamon. There's so much you don't know." And then my mother's clarity ended and her voice went back to its vodka mumble. "And you really better change your ways and accept the Lord into your soul. Phil saw your end days on this current path. He prophesized you'd be alone, always."

I'd slammed the receiver down and threw the phone across the room, making a dent in the paint of my closet door and breaking the antenna off the handset. I was stupid, stupid, stupid for ever thinking that good visit could possibly be anything but an isolated event. For the rest of the summer, I'd not called her and she'd not called me: my mother and I in a standoff that had now come to a tragic end.

Chapter 18

The Naughton boys were in eighth and tenth grade. Norman, the older brother, had gotten into trouble in the city and was the reason, my mother had heard, that Mr. and Mrs. Naughton had sold their place in Pacific Heights and moved up to Sonoma County. His brother, Matthew, only a year older than me, was bigger than Norman, but slower, denser. They both had white-blonde hair that Norman buzz cut and Matthew grew in ringlets to his shoulders. Both had small eyes in the palest blue. Norman wore an army jacket over his Polo shirt and jeans; Matthew preferred black concert t-shirts. Their parents were surgeons and commuted to the city; I rarely saw them. A housekeeper named Luz lived in.

Norman sat behind me on the bus home that first day of school. I was gathering my courage to say hello, introduce myself when he leaned over the green vinyl seat and said, "Your parents smoke out, huh?"

The color rose into my cheeks. It had already been a very long, very bad first day of seventh grade. Marjorie sat with me at lunch, but she'd asked me about who the other girls were and by the end of the day had found a locker partner that wasn't me. And my new English teacher, Mr. Wilton, sat me at the back of the class and hadn't called on me once although I'd raised my hand for every question.

"You heard me," Norman prompted.

"None of your beeswax," I said, not turning around.

"They do, then," he said.

"How would you know?" I asked.

"I can smell it on you," he said.

I ran from the bus stop. At the shipwreck shack my mother slept, an empty glass of wine on the floor beside the couch. This was her habit now, to go to Bible study in the mornings, then come home and drink herself into a nap. I paced, looking out the windows, afraid Norman would follow me. Usually I avoided my mother until she shook off her post-nap stupor, but today I jumped off the top bunk the moment she stirred and threw my arms around her.

"How was your first day?" she mumbled, rocking me slightly.

"Not good," I managed.

"I was always worried about sending you to school," my mother said, still groggy.

I held her tight and squeezed my eyes shut. Her long hair fanned around me like a shroud.

At Orchard, Marjorie drifted toward the girls I knew she would. I tried to keep her interested in me.

"I've got a secret—meet me at my locker at lunch," I said in a passed note.

"You wanna eat together?" I asked when she arrived.

Marjorie shrugged. "What's the secret?"

"No secret, I just thought it would be a fun way to ask you to have lunch."

"I've got student council," she said.

When Mrs. Ranzetta invited me over, Marjorie would stare off into space while I talked. Marjorie never asked me to sleep over anymore. I tried to impress her, re-told or made up stories about the grandeur of weekends at my grandmother's: Socorro in her black dress with the white apron, lavish dinners at the Club. I would finish one story and start with another, more embellished than the last time I told it, while Marjorie fidgeted and Mrs. Ranzetta poured us more milk or unloaded the dishwasher.

Once when I excused myself to the bathroom in the middle of a story about how my grandmother was going to treat me to box seats at the Nutcracker, although it was already November and she had mentioned no such thing, I heard Marjorie's voice through the walls.

"Do I have to listen to this?"

"She needs to be heard," Mrs. Ranzetta said, her tone barely audible from my spot in the hall.

"She's boring, and a liar," Marjorie countered. "I think she's weird."

Weird. Clearly, I was weird. I thought we all agreed on that already and they liked me anyhow. But I had gotten too weird for this house. I left without saying goodbye and walked the mile home.

My mother was watching *Days of Our Lives* when I came through the front door. "Mrs. Ranzetta called," she said.

"I already got the message," I said.

The Naughton boys infected the land. They hung out around the base of the road where our driveways split, waiting, watching, pushing each other from trees. I had no idea how rough brothers could be. At the bus stop, Norman threw a rock as big as my fist and hit his brother in the head. When I went to help Matthew, who was bleeding from a gash above his eye, Norman shoved me to the dirt, ripping the knees of my Goodwill jeans. Ignoring his bleeding wound, Matthew kicked Norman in the crotch and Norman doubled over into the ditch along the road. But by the next afternoon, they were comrades again, picking on a fifth-grade boy with headgear.

They liked to destroy things. The beautiful white fence that ran along their driveway was missing boards by their second week. They hung like monkeys on their driveway's black iron gates until the hinges bent. They crowed and screamed when I drove by with my mother. With my father, they were silent, their gestures visible only in the rear view.

"Those boys look like they need someone to play with," my mother announced.

"I'm scared of them," I said.

"Boys act like that when they like you, silly. Why don't you wander on over?" my mother asked as we unloaded groceries into our wheezing fridge.

"No way," I said.

In my top bunk, I slid the curtain closed and picked up a book from my expanding shelf: I had smuggled Harold Robbins and Jackie Collins from the adult section of the Sebastopol Library. I hid behind that curtain and read like it would save my life.

But the next time I went down to the creek to check on my nuclear-winter hideout, Matthew jumped out from behind a bush and blocked my path. I turned and Norman stood between me and home.

"Get us some pot," he said, kicking one rubber toe of his Chuck Taylors into the ground, spraying dirt on me.

"It's not mine to give," I said.

"You could make money."

"I don't need money," I said, thinking of the travel-sized shampoo bottles and toothpaste tubes I shoplifted from the Rexall because my dad thought baking soda and vinegar were good enough to clean my teeth and hair.

"Everybody needs money," said Norman.

Thick heather bushes blocked all sides of the path, but I tried to run anyhow. Norman stuck out his leg and tripped me while Mathew grabbed my ankles and sat on my stomach.

"I'm going to spit all over you unless you get me some weed," Norman said.

"Off," I said with the little air I had left, but I could see the teardrop of spittle forming at the edge of his mouth. It dripped and hit me on the cheek when I turned my head.

Matthew hocked a loogie and Norman said, "Get us some pot or I'll hold your mouth open while my brother spits inside."

I shook my head no, and Norman grabbed my chin and forced my mouth open. Matthew leaned over: close enough to kiss me, close enough to spit.

I thought to spit right back at him. But I remembered their pummeling fists on each other, the gash above Matthew's eye, how much smaller I was even than Norman. Against both of them I had no chance. All they wanted was a bag of pot. I would get it for them and then they'd leave me alone.

"Okay," I tried to say, my mouth held open, "I'll do it."

They walked me back to my house, where my mother was taking her afternoon nap on the couch. I grabbed a handful of weed out of my father's stash in the cigar box beside the ashtray, walked out to the boys who sat at the picnic table, and dropped it in front of them.

"Holy shit," said Norman scrambling for all the tiny pieces, "all buds!"

He and Matthew stuck every speck into a worn plastic baggie that had been hiding in one of the pockets of Norman's army jacket and they scooted out of my yard.

From then on, Norman told me I was to supply them every morning before the first bell. My dad harvested enough where he never seemed to notice the amount I'd take. When I mentioned the money he promised, Norman laughed a chicken laugh. My only consolation was being allowed to join the stoner table at lunch and hang out with them after school. I hated the stealing, the deliveries, but it kept the peace between my neighbors and me, bought me some friends. I traded my father's drugs for little shreds of acceptance, a chance to join a group behind the equipment shed at recess, but it kept costing me. In order to fit in, avoid the group's heckling and suspicion, I had to smoke some, too.

While I had never had an easy time getting to sleep, with the heavy secrets of stealing and smoking inside me, it was impossible. I'd dealt with my insomnia in the past by clicking on my bedside lamp and reading, but by the fall of seventh grade I couldn't find the energy to even open a book and would instead stare at the dark place where my curtains didn't meet, awake until the first light. I complained of headaches and stomachaches and stayed home from school. On the days I made it to class, I lay my head on my desk and let red-marked assignments float to the bottom of my locker like dead leaves. My grades slipped, especially in English, where Mr. Wilton went from ignoring my exuberance to mocking my apathy. All his praise, his good attention went to the Marjories of the school. He read aloud a poor short answer question from my *Of Mice and Men* test as an example of what one needed to do in order to earn a failing grade. I hated the first three books he assigned, I hated him and soon I hated English class altogether. With the bit of money I got for Christmas I bought an army jacket at the flea market and huddled in it while I sat at break and lunch with the rest of the smokers, biting my cuticles bloody and laughing at everything Norman said.

"Those boys seem to be taking a real interest in you," my mother said once when they came over after school wanting more weed and I had to turn them away with promise of a delivery later.

"Doubt it," I said, lying on my bunk, staring at the ceiling. My mom gave my dad a knowing wink. I'd not opened a book in a month.

Then, on a summer weekend with Julia at my grandmother's, I woke to a rusty stain on the back of my nightgown.

"Did you hurt yourself?" Julia asked, rubbing her eyes when I was on my way to the bathroom.

"No," I said, looking back and down. "Get away from me," I added, although she'd not moved from her bed.

I'd already been pulling out my pubic hair as it grew, like quills from my skin leaving a bloom of blood behind. Now this. Part of how I made the visits with my grandmother work was by ignoring everything I came from: dirt, stink, Bari DeGarzi and the girlfriends of my dad's musician friends, whose armpit hair leaked out from their tank tops. Pubic hair and periods were associated with them and had no place in my grandmother's mansion on a hill.

Socorro scrubbed and bleached, but the stain was set. If it had happened at home, I could have hid it, but I'd made a mess of the bed and I saw my grandmother and Socorro whispering later that morning. Socorro gave me a box of bulky pads to catch the flow and my grandmother never mentioned it to me, never mentioned it to my mother, and neither did I. I added Kotex to the list of things I shoplifted from the drugstore.

As I became withdrawn and miserable, Julia blossomed. Her awkward tallness grew into statuesque beauty. Her sun-streaked hair fell like silk over her shoulders. Her blue eyes and upturned nose in a thin face became classic, serene. The balance of my grandmother's interest tilted toward my cousin—my grandmother began to criticize and ignore me as she had once done to Julia. She escorted Julia to dancing class and etiquette lessons. She'd never once driven the hour and a half to see me—not that I'd ever been a part of anything to be seen. I was so afraid of losing my grandmother's love, Julia's friendship that I made every snub, real or perceived, into something huge and weighty. My only weapon against this hegemony of the beautiful and poised was a bad attitude. I pierced my ears and stuck safety pins through. I gave myself a spiky and uneven haircut perfect for the girlfriend of Sid Vicious. I wore ripped jeans and a scowl. My grandmother was disgusted.

"You've never been beautiful, but you could give the illusion if you worked harder," my grandmother said as she rearranged a vase of roses Socorro had placed on the breakfast table.

I felt the tingle-burn in my cheeks. Yes, I wasn't gorgeous like Julia, but on good days I would stand at the mirror and admire the clearness of my skin and my delicate bone structure.

I could give the illusion? I wanted to make a sneer back, something sarcastic, witty, but it was too early in the morning to come up with something good. What I did muster was, "Don't you love me anymore?"

"That's a stupid question," she said, yanking the stems from the vase. "But you make it difficult to show any affection."

I took my hurt out on Julia. When I was angry, hunched over my cassette recorder listening to treble-heavy music, smarting from something Frank or my grandmother had said, Julia would try and cheer me up by commenting about the weather or a funny story from when we were younger. My response was, "A superficial comment from a superficial girl."

"What's that supposed to mean?" Julia asked.

"Look it up in the dictionary, Einstein," I'd say as I rolled away from her to face the red toile wall.

I went from considering Julia a sister to branding her a phony. She went from trailing my heels to treating me like something poisonous, explosive. That Christmas my grandmother took Julia to the Nutcracker but didn't invite me.

"You've outgrown that kind of thing, haven't you?" my grandmother remarked when I'd asked why. But she never asked what I'd grown into, not that I could have told her if she had.

In eighth grade, my first semester's report card was so bad it had to be taken home and signed. My mother shook her head as she picked up a pen.

"I would have gotten a slap across the face for grades like these," she said.

"Do it then," I said dully. "Do something."

But she did nothing. I took the signed paper from her, smashed it into a little ball, and tossed it into my backpack.

There was a girl, Tori, a ninth grader, who hung out with the Naughtons. She had stringy blonde hair and an army jacket like mine. There were two other stoner table regulars: Chad, small-eyed and as mean as Norman, and Alex, a quiet boy who had the face of an English noble and long, delicate fingers. I worked hard to be like them, tried to fit their ever changing definition of cool, but no matter what, I was an eighth grader who was allowed to hang out with the high school kids for one reason only: I supplied the drugs.

Mr. and Mrs. Naughton had built the boys a treehouse in their backyard. It was shingled and painted in the same colors as the Victorian, yellow with white gingerbread trim.

"Why don't you come over, Cinnamon?" Tori said at lunch one day. "I hate being the only chick."

So I stopped checking on the nuclear winter infirmary, the camouflaged larder, to see if that ghost of a boy had come back and instead started going to the tree house. It was the same thing every day: smoking, listening to music, making fun of the kids who did well at school, of the teachers. Once, I tried to convince the group to go down to the creek with me.

"Where?" asked Tori, confused.

"It's in the woods, across the moor," I said, borrowing a word from my favorite books. Books that I'd not read in a while, but their words

and stories, read so often, took up as much space in my brain as real life.

"The what?" Chad laughed, throwing his head back. "What's a fucking moor?"

"What do you call it?" I asked.

"A waste of goddamn space?" Norman suggested.

"A meadow? Grass?" Tori said, passing the pipe to Matthew.

"Grass!" Chad screeched, already with his hand out.

I didn't like smoking. I felt very little going up; I knew I was high only when I became ravenous and would eat boxes of Stouffer's frozen French bread pizzas from the Naughton's freezer. But the coming down was horrendous. I'd sink into a puddle of brain-murk and sit there for hours knowing that my life, in the grand scheme, meant nothing, and that no matter how I struggled, it was unlikely things would improve. I knew it was the pot that put me in these funks and I knew I should stop, tell my parents what I'd been doing, ask for their help in getting the Naughtons to leave me alone. But I didn't trust they'd help me or that I'd be safe since I had disrupted the pot supply, so I kept going, kept stealing little baggies worth, bringing them to school and putting them in my locker, and kept smoking in the tree house after school.

One post-tree house afternoon, I came home to a note on the table. "Out with Bari" it said.

Bari DeGarzi? I hadn't seen her since we'd left Inverness. How did she find us?

My mom came back about ten. Bari dropped her off, but didn't come inside.

"I wanted her to see how much you've grown, but she had to get home," my mom said.

"Bari's not welcome here," my dad said.

My mom and Bari started going out weekly. My mother loved movies. My father thought theater seats were uncomfortable. Bari became my mom's movie buddy. My mother stopped drinking on movie days, took a shower, and got herself ready to go out.

"Bari makes me dinner at her house, like old times," my mom said, pulling a fisherman's sweater over a tent-like flower print dress.

"Did Bari ever get her degree?" I asked.

My mother hadn't asked, but she did know Bari read tarot cards for a living. She added she was pretty sure Bari had gotten her degree.

"She thinks she may be ready for a partner," my mom said, full of excitement when she got home one night.

"A tarot-reading partner?" I asked. My father snorted.

"Don't make light," my mother said.

"With everything you think is a sin, doesn't tarot reading qualify as some sort of commandment breaker?" my dad asked, pulling his leather jacket off the coat rack.

"Where are you going?" my mother asked.

"The Toads have a gig in Oakland," he said to the outside air and shut the door behind him. He was lying, I knew, because he had rituals on nights he was going to play with the band: he'd always wash his hair, wear more colorful clothes, tune his guitar. That night he'd done none of them.

My father was gone more and more, taking off on his bike, staying over with musician buddies he claimed we didn't know. My mother was less bothered by this than I would have expected. One night she came home with her waist-long hair cut short.

"Do you think I look like Geraldine Ferraro?" she asked.

"Your hair does," I said. "Frank Ferguson thinks she's a whore," I added.

"That's a big surprise. Under Frank Ferguson's definition, even the Virgin Mary qualifies as a whore."

My father went batshit when he saw her hair.

"You look like a dyke!" he said after she twirled around to show him the haircut.

"I do not," my mom said, her hands flying to her head.

"I think she looks like Geraldine Ferraro," I said.

"Who?" my dad said.

"That's so typical, Steve, you don't even know a woman's running for President," my mom said.

"Vice President," I said.

"Stay out of it," my dad roared at me. "How could you do it? How could you cut off your hair?"

"Bari thinks it looks good. She thought I needed a change. She warned me you'd flip out." My mother put her thumb and index finger to her chin, as if she were considering the situation philosophically. "I wanted to give you more credit, Steve, but Bari was right. You are nothing but an establishment chauvinist in open-thinker's clothing."

"Bari would say that, because, news flash, Linda, Bari is a huge dyke!"

My mom lost her Socratic cool. "Always trying to blame someone else," my mom said. "Bari's not a lesbian. She just likes women. Something you wouldn't know about. Female power threatens you. I saw it in my Tarot. You came up reverse King of Cups. Twice!"

"Great," my dad said, "fine." He grabbed his canvas bag and in it he threw his cigar box of buds, Zig-Zag wrappers, and the latest issue of Down Beat.

"Dad," I said.

"Stay out of this, Cinnamon," my mom said.

"How can I stay out of it when our house is just one room?" I yelled, but no one answered.

"Where do you think you are going? Back to Nancy? Talk about dykes—you love 'em. I would think this haircut would turn you on."

"Nancy was ten times the woman you are," my dad said.

My mom grabbed a plate and threw it. It clipped my father's head, and he lunged at her. She ran behind the kitchen table, keeping a chair between them.

He wiped the bit of blood off his ear. "Cunt," my dad snarled at her before he thundered down the loose front stairs toward his bike. My mother followed him out the front door and threw a thick, white coffee mug that hit him in the back. He turned and charged my mother again, shoving her down onto the pallet steps. She pulled herself up and ran back into the house, slamming the flimsy door behind her.

"Get over here, Cinnamon," she said as she moved a kitchen chair in front of the door as a lame barricade. "I'll protect you!"

"Fuck off!" I said, clamping my hand over my mouth in surprise. Norman and Matthew told Luz to fuck off at least twice a day, but nothing that nasty had ever come out of my mouth.

There was silence between us as we heard my father roar off down Highway 12. "Where did you learn such language?" She blinked her wide eyes, like somehow I should be immune to all the profanity I heard from my dad's friends, when my parents fought, from my neighbors.

"Where do you think? From this wholesome upbringing you're providing!" I yelled kicking the chair away from the door, and running out into the night.

"Cinnamon. Don't go. You are all I've got!"

My bare feet pounded the dirt. I heard my mother calling for a few minutes, first sweetly, then angrily, then wailing sobs. Somewhere a dog barked. I spent a few hours in the tree house, shivering in my sweatshirt and jeans, and snuck back into the shipwreck shack after my mother had gone to sleep.

She gave me the silent treatment the next day, her head buried in her Bible, reading passages under her breath. At night she softened, told me the fight with my dad had been all her fault, that she hadn't been subservient enough as was ordered in Corinthians.

"I'm sorry for what I said, Mom," I told her. "I didn't mean it and I won't swear anymore."

"I didn't hear you swear," she answered brightly, pouring another glass of wine.

My dad was back in a week. He didn't say where he'd been, my mother didn't ask. I came home from the tree house and there were glossy Beefalo farming brochures on the counter. My parents nuzzled and cooed to each other on the couch.

"He called you a cunt," I said to her the next morning. "Don't you at least want him to apologize?"

 138 *The Angels' Share*

"Your father never says sorry," she said. "And don't use the C-word," she added.

In the fall of ninth grade, on a day that any nineteenth-century heroine worth her salt would have recognized as perfect for a solitary walk with a sketchbook tucked under one arm, we stoners from Orchard High School sat in the hazy smoke of the tree house. Norman climbed through the trapdoor and dropped a Ziploc of white powder on the table.

"What's this?" said Tori.

"Fuckin' coke," Chad said, his voice full of thrill. He dropped the joint he was rolling and took the bag in his hands. "Where'd you get it?"

"My dad. He does tons. All the doctors do."

"It's an upper," Matthew said to me, trying to sound wise.

"Maybe it will take some of the munchie pounds off Tori's ass," Chad said.

"Fuck you," said Tori.

"Save the whales, harpoon a fat chick," said Norman. Chad gave him a high five.

"This one's getting an ass on her, too," Matthew said, nodding at me.

"You want to snort it on a mirror, but anything flat will do," Norman said, like he'd done it a million times, although I saw his fingers trembling. He put his algebra book on the wooden crate and pulled a grimy one-dollar bill from his pocket. He cut a line—like he'd seen his father do watching Johnny Carson—and snorted it.

Norman turned pink, held the left side of his face, but soon straightened up and handed the dollar tube to Matthew. It made its way around the circle, the little pile of white powder getting cut smaller and smaller. Then it was my turn.

"Come on, Cinnamon." Tori said.

"I don't want a dirty dollar up my nose."

"Everyone in your house shits in front of each other, get over yourself," Norman said, but Matthew pulled a newer dollar out of his wallet and handed it to me.

Luz called the boys from the back porch.

"Shut up, you stupid spic! We're busy," Norman yelled.

I put the dollar bill in my nose, leaned down and noticed the cocaine didn't smell, not at all. I hated the cloy of pot, but this was something new and clean.

"Go," said Tori, annoyed.

And I took a snort of it and sneezed.

"What a fuckin' newbie," said Chad.

"Shut up, Chad," said Matthew.

"You shut up, fuckhole," Chad said, but Matthew was bigger than him and he left me alone.

Over the next few minutes, the bad, heavy feeling I'd been carrying for months evaporated. Happy rented a room in my brain and radiated out my fingers and toes. Every cell in my body felt spectacular. This was why my dad smoked and my mom drank; it vanished the bad feelings. Norman and Matthew jumped up and down on the tree house floor, shaking it so that I thought it might come loose from the branches. When they broke one of the floorboards, there was only laughter and more jumping to see what else might give. Later, we played tag on the scrub meadow below, bumping into each other at full speed. Alex had his shirt off, I wore a tank top and when we bumped into each other I could feel the ropey muscles in his arms dent my skin.

As the sun set, we settled into a spot on the grass. The moon rose, the first star came out. I put myself near Alex, but he turned to talk to Chad. Matthew sat beside me.

"You're a pretty girl," Matthew said.

"I'm not," I said, glancing over at Alex, his back to me. "I don't even give the illusion."

"I think about you," Matthew confided, leaning his heavy arm across my bare shoulders. I pictured him sitting on my chest, a loogie in his mouth, and shuddered.

Norman came out of nowhere and began to beat his brother around the head with cocaine-powered punches. Matthew sprang back and they tumbled down the slope. I inched over to Tori.

"Epic," she said, drawing out the C.

"Ummmm," I replied. Tori began to play with my hair. She pulled on the uneven chunks, making short braids, massaging my scalp.

In the last of the light, I saw a girl just my age with a sketchbook tucked under her arm watching from the edge of the woods. Tori told me to stop jerking my head around otherwise she couldn't braid. I kept still but craned my eyes and could see her in my peripheral vision. She stayed watching until Tori finished plaiting my hair, and I turned to see her straight on. The girl and I looked at each other for a long moment before she slipped behind the oak trees, disappearing into the forest beyond.

Chapter 19

I assumed the sheriff would make me identify my mother's decaying body, and I was bracing for it, that familiar ache nibbling at the veins in my arms, worming its way into the back of my throat, but instead he showed me only a picture.

"Let's see if you can get it off of this one here," the Mendocino detective, a Matlock type, Sgt. Tully engraved on his nametag, said. I was gripping the sides of the chair. They'd said at least three weeks dead. I wondered what a person looked like three weeks dead. He told me I'd rather not see.

The photo was only of her wedding ring, no body, no hand, against a blue background. A brassy gold band with rough ridges my father had made himself. The ring always snagged her clothes and caught in her hair, but she never took it off.

"It shows our twists and turns, and I think he made it that way for a reason, for me to keep faith. Our bond will never break. We'll be together on earth and in heaven."

"Whatever," I'd said.

I don't know how long I'd been looking at the photo when Tully cleared his throat.

"Yes," I said, "that's her ring."

Tully opened his pad with deliberation. He had none of the nervousness of the younger deputy.

"When did you last see her?"

I thought about that visit, when I'd seen my parents giddy in love, when we were happy together. "Late May," I said.

"Three months ago?" he asked, watching me again.

I knew I should have had a shaky voice, teary eyes, but I was steady, my hands church-and-steepled in my lap. I waited for a tsunami of grief to break over my head, but nothing came. What was wrong with me? Maybe Phil and my mother were right. I was an unfeeling person destined to be alone. "I talked to her last in June."

"Did she say anything unusual? Was anything troubling her?"

"I troubled her, I suppose, but that's nothing new."

"What about your father?"

"What about him?" I asked.

"Haven't you seen enough crime shows to know I'd be interested?" the detective said. I thought he might be trying to be funny, but his voice was weary. He didn't smile.

"My dad is . . . nomadic. Sometimes he's with my mom, but they fight and he leaves. He crashes wherever. They were getting along in May, as good as they ever had. I haven't heard from him since."

He scribbled on his pad, asked me a few more questions about my dad's possible whereabouts, and offered to drive me back to the vineyard.

I didn't want to ever ride in a police car again. "No thanks. I'll call someone," I said. But when I went to use the lobby phone, Sam Gladstone was already waiting.

He strode over, addressing Tully in his gravelly voice: "I'm Sam Gladstone. Sheriff Gold is a personal friend of mine, and if I find out anything inappropriate has happened to this girl, this child, I will not . . ."

"It's all right," I said to Sam.

He pulled me aside and lowered his voice.

"What's going on here?"

"My mother died. They needed me to identify her."

Sam's forehead folded into accordion wrinkles. And then I saw what I took for relief. The druggie he'd taken under his wing was not in trouble he couldn't solve.

"Oh, Darlin'," Sam said, hugging me to his side.

He nodded to Tully, tipped his hat back on his head, and held the door open for me. He'd driven the Expedition; I had to vault myself into the passenger seat.

"You okay?" he asked after I told him as much as I knew.

"I don't know what I am," I said.

"You're in shock," Sam said.

"How'd you know to come?" I asked, changing the subject.

"Pedro. He beat feet to the farmhouse and let me know you needed 'looking after.' And if there is one thing I do," Sam said, "I look after my people."

Sam pulled off the road before Trove's driveway so I could lean out the window and pull mail out of his box. When I reached, my sleeve slid back to reveal my scarred arms. With anyone besides Sam, like that day with Eduardo in the cave, it would be a cause for panic, but Sam knew about my arms and didn't judge me. He inched the car forward and I took out my own few pieces, not junk to me as I still got a thrill by looking at my name and address on paper. I refastened my seatbelt and pulled my sleeves back down.

I'd forgotten about my mother. Then I remembered. A little jolt of surprise. Then calm. Nothing more.

"Why don't you stay at the farmhouse tonight, Cinnamon?" Sam said. "Not a good night to be alone."

"Thanks, Mr. Gladstone. I'll be all right."

"Say yes to supper at the very least. I'll have Alma make your favorite. Filet and grilled tomato."

"I need to get back down to the tanks and punch caps."

"I've got Eduardo on it. Do him good to get his hands dirty," Sam said.

"I'd like to check it myself," I said. After Eduardo had made the effort to sit next to me at breakfast, after so many weeks of unfriendliness, I didn't want to screw up by sticking him with my work, besides, I wanted to keep busy. Busy seemed like a good idea.

"I wish you'd let someone take care of you," Sam said.

"You do everything for me. You've given me a job and a place to live. You are the definition of taking care of me."

The Explorer downshifted at the steepest point in the driveway and Sam applied more gas to get us up the hill. I noticed his hands on the steering wheel. His liver-spotted skin, the veins prominent. I realized how precious Sam was to me, how much he had done and how little I deserved it. How I'd doubted his generosity, how I'd been suspicious of his motives of hiring me at Trove. I might have shot the moon with my entire family, but Sam had anchored me back to earth just in time. No matter what Phil prophesied, I wasn't yet alone.

Chapter 20

Norman and Matthew stole a lot of coke from their parents that fall. When it wasn't enough, Norman drove us down to the Mission in his red Jeep to use my dad's buds as currency for other things we wanted to try. I cut school more than half the month of October; I had gotten the shitty English teacher again, so I didn't care. Matthew fucked me against the side of their house our first time on X. I remember looking to the side, alternating between pretending he was Alex and just wishing it was over, and saw Luz staring at us from the kitchen window, her mouth open in shock, but instead of stopping us, she turned away and as far as I knew, she said nothing. I threw up after and limped home, but was back at the stoner's picnic table at school the next day. However false their friendship, however terribly they treated me, having a group to hang out with was better than being alone.

One afternoon soon after Thanksgiving, Mr. Naughton climbed up the ladder to the tree house, cuffed Norman around the neck, and dragged him out. The rest of us grabbed the bong and every other bit of paraphernalia and scattered like insects into the woods. I'd come away with a water-warped High Times magazine we used as a placemat for the bong. I hid in some bushes across the road from the Victorian and the shipwreck shack and read the High Times until the shouting and the cars coming and going stopped.

I stumbled home after dark. My father was at a gig in the city and my mother was watching *Dynasty*.

"Hug?" she said, holding out her arms not looking away from the TV.

Ignoring her, I looked through the refrigerator. I found an English muffin, scraped mold dots off, toasted it, and sat with her. I knew I reeked, and anyone else would know what I'd been up to, but in my house the smell was camouflaged. At commercial, instead of picking up her Bible and leafing through it, she turned to me and said, "Mr. Naughton came here looking for you."

I froze, every follicle chilled to zero.

"There was a gang up at his place this afternoon doing a bunch of drugs and he thought one of them might be you."

She'd caught me. I was quiet in my admittance, waiting for the punishment, the grounding, the chores.

"I told him I was sure you weren't doing all that drug stuff," my mom said. "You play in the woods after school by yourself." She looked at me for an answer, although she'd not asked a question.

I waited for her next move. The commercial ended.

She turned back to the show.

In the morning I had a rash all over my body. After three days home from school, I'd scratched myself bloody despite the honey poultice my mother said would draw out the toxins.

"It hurts," I said.

"Well, of course it hurts, you rolled around in God knows what," she said, rubbing the sticky cheesecloth into my blistering skin.

"Jesus, Linda, take her to the doctor," my father said when pus ran from my eyelids.

"Let's give it one more day," she said.

I itched and cried through the night, my fever rising, and we were on the steps of the Freestone health clinic when it opened the next morning.

The intake nurse did not let me sit in the waiting room; she gave me a scratchy gown and told me to wait for the doctor, who would be in shortly.

I looked in the mirror over the sink in the examination room. My lips were inflating and deflating in cycles, shredding a layer of skin each time. My arms, neck, and chest had reddened and darkened; the places I'd scratched the most were oozing, crusted, black. My hair stuck out in greasy clumps between scabs. I looked crazy, like someone who should be locked away.

The doctor prescribed antibiotics and gave the nurse an order to call them in before he even sat down.

"Don't you have any natural remedies?" my mother asked.

The doctor didn't answer, but sprayed icy calamine on my worst spots so I could stand to be in my skin.

"She's never had a problem with poison oak before," my mom said. "We live in the middle of fields of it."

The doctor was older, gray. He'd been in this town long before my mother and her type had arrived.

"Childhood immunities end without warning. Poison oak is a good example, bee stings another. You can have exposures with no reaction and then, bang. Keep your daughter out of the woods. And bring her in before she scratches herself raw next time."

The doctor asked to see me alone. I asked for another round of the cooling spray, which he handed to me. I applied it to my arms, reveling in the numbness.

He opened his manila folder, picked up a pen, and without looking at me began to ask questions.

"Are you sexually active?"

"No," I said.

"How many times a week do you engage in drug or alcohol related activities?"

Related activities? "Never."

"Do you smoke?"

"No."

"How about a seatbelt?"

"Of course."

"And sunscreen?"

"I forget some days. I'll try harder once this heals," I motioned to my face. The last time I'd worn sunscreen was when Socorro slathered it on me before I swam at my grandmother's pool.

"Great job," he said, signing the page and closing the folder. "Clear this rash and you'll be set."

My mother didn't like the doctor's scolding tone or the bill due upon receipt and huffed out of his office. I followed, wishing I could immerse my entire red and itchy self in a tank of whatever came out of that little spray bottle. My mother grumbled about waiting for the prescriptions and grumbled about the cost of the pills and the lotion. When we got home she banged her purse down on the table.

"Cinnamon is now allergic to poison oak," she announced. "I'd appreciate if you'd burn it off and plant something more respectable, like a lawn or a garden."

My dad didn't look up from where he sat on the floor shelling walnuts he'd gathered. "I can't burn it, Linda, the poison gets in the smoke. We'd have poison oak in our eyes and ears and throats."

"Well, can't you do something?" She slammed a pot into the sink, filled it, and put it on the stove. She took a sack of rice out of the cabinet and dropped it on the counter. "We live in a goddamn dump, a shithole without a proper yard, nowhere for Cinnamon to play," she flung her arms dramatically and the pot sailed off the stove, hitting the floor, the cold water splashing against my legs.

"I'm too old to play," I said.

"This shithole was good enough for you when you had nowhere else to go, wasn't it, Linda?" My dad's anger rocketed through his pot-haze. "When you had nowhere else to go, this place was good enough, and I was good enough. And my dick was good enough."

"I won't have that kind of low-class talk in front of our daughter!" my mother said. She went behind him and started shoving him with her foot, poking her fingers into his back like she was trying to motivate him to get up and go fix the yard right away. "Can't you do something right for once, lazy bastard?" she taunted.

I saw my dad look up, his bloodshot eyes glaring at her from under the darkness of his lids. I took a step back. He rose from the rug and knocked her to the kitchen floor, sitting on her and closing his hands around her throat. When they fought it got physical: she threw things and he'd shove or hit her, she'd scream at close range into his ear, but I'd never seen him as focused as he was now, his face white, his fingers red.

"Stop it!" I screamed, and my mother clawed at his wrists, but he

 150 *The Angels' Share*

straightened his elbows and locked his thumbs on her windpipe. My mother's eyes bulged from their sockets and fixed on me. I turned to the wall, braced myself, and began to kick my dad with my heels like a donkey might. I caught his head with a hard strike and heard her gasp for air when he released. I slid to the ground. My dad rolled away from us.

We all heaved together for a moment on the floor of the kitchen.

"The two of you now, huh?" he said.

He grabbed his jacket, cigar box and lighter and clattered down the stairs, shaking the house. His bike came to life and was already making space between him and us before my mother got enough breath back to speak.

"Marry a rich man, Cinnamon," she gasped.

I stared at the thumb imprints littering her collarbone. She sat up against the stove; I had my back to the cabinets. Only two or three feet between us. Eye to eye. The misty look she usually sported was gone, like the adrenaline from the fight had cleared her mind.

"I married your father for love, and he's as awful as Frank Ferguson. Any man you're with will make you miserable. So find a man with money, then get pregnant or whatever you have to do so that they marry you. It's better to be miserable rich, trust me."

I looked at her and shook my head.

"You didn't marry Daddy for love," I said.

"Of course I did."

"No, you used him to get yourself out of a jam," I said. "You were humiliated because you'd lost your money and your friends. He was your escape." I took a breath. "I'll never be like you," I vowed. "I'll never be like Grandmother."

I waited for her emotional deluge, the sobbing, the crawling to the fridge for the solace of her box of wine, the price for me saying what I thought, but it didn't come. No yelling, no tears. My mother patted her Geraldine Ferraro haircut back into place, pushed herself up to standing. On her neck she was rapidly gaining a necklace of bruises, a choker of amethysts embedded into her skin.

"This is the best advice I'm ever going to give you," she said, talking to me like everything was normal and she hadn't just been nearly strangled. She refilled the pan with water and set it on the stove to boil. "Find a rich man, Cinnamon, then marry him."

I went to her purse and found my pills. The itching had returned.

My dad didn't come back after the kitchen-floor night and neither did the Naughtons. It was a week before I would be able to return to school, a month before I looked like myself again. When I finally went back to Orchard, my rash still coating me in red, scaly bits, I found out both brothers had been shipped off. Chad, Tori, and Alex sat alone at lunch.

"What happened?"

"Dude, that fucking spic narced on them about the pot," said Chad. "And the dad didn't know they'd been stealing his coke until he saw we had some. Called some place to take them away in the middle of the night. They're like in Utah or something."

"Did any of you guys get busted?" I asked, looking for room on the bench, but there wasn't any. I sat on the pebbly concrete at their feet like a one-girl audience to the Greek stoner chorus.

"Naughton called all our dads. I got grounded for a week. Alex got a warning."

"My dad took me to Sizzler and didn't make me order the child's plate," Tori said, cracking her gum. "We 'talked,'" she said, air quoting.

I kept waiting for them to ask me about my rash, if I'd been caught, what had happened to me, but they didn't.

"Hey," Chad said, "when can you get us some more weed?"

My dad had come and collected his things, including his white five-gallon buckets. He didn't say anything to me, acted like my mother and I were invisible. My supply was gone. Even if he had left some stray seedlings, it would be months before they were ready to harvest.

"My dad left and took it."

"How about some coke?" Tori asked.

I had no money to buy them coke and no pot to barter for it. While I could still hover around their table, my lack of supply took away any

bit of feigned respect they'd had for me. I was nothing more than the butt of their jokes. And I laughed along because I had nowhere to go.

One afternoon, I passed Mrs. Ranzetta in the hall at school. Her shirt was crisp white and she wore navy pants with a deep crease.

"Cinnamon," she said. "Good Lord, what happened to you?"

"Poison oak."

She took my still swollen face in her cool hands.

"You are really allergic to that stuff," she said.

I loved how the chill from her fingers flowed into my enflamed skin. I wanted to slump into her arms and never let go.

"I ask Jorie about you all the time," she said. She didn't say what Marjorie had reported back.

"Yeah, I'm having a great year. Working hard. Thinking about college." I had no idea where this BS was coming from. Tori and I made fun of girls who talked about college.

"A good idea. I didn't go, but my Joe did."

I looked down at her dark blue Sperry Top-Siders. Sixty dollars a pair. In 1986, even the stoners wore Top-Siders.

The bell rang and Mrs. Ranzetta pulled me into a hug, scabs and all. "Call me if you need anything," she said. I thanked her and walked the other direction, away from my class and into the foggy, rainsoaked orchards behind school.

Come winter break, my father had been gone over a month, and it seemed to have rained the entire time he was away. The rock wall was soaked; everything in the house was damp and when we got the woodstove going, it smelled like we lived with a pack of wet dogs. My mother read her Bible almost without cease.

For Christmas, my mother and I got matching gilt-edged Bibles from the Assembly of God church she'd joined; a postcard from my father postmarked Puerto Escondido, Mexico; and a check from my grandmother my mom used to pay the most overdue of our bills. Socorro and Jorge gave me my only real gift on Christmas: twenty one-dollar bills. Each worn note was pulled taut and tucked in a card with a Precious Moments angel on the front.

Back at school from break, I took Socorro and Jorge's dollars and bought some pot from a senior who said I could have more if I sold to the junior high kids. I did. With my new status of dealer and the money and access to pot that came with it, Chad and Tori and Alex accepted me back into their circle. I was grateful.

At lunch on a sunny, sharp February day, Tori and Alex talked about *The Dark Side of the Moon*. I'd been wanting to save up enough money from my dealing to buy the tape and a cassette player.

"Cinnamon," Tori said, "when are you going to score us come coke?"

"I don't have the money to buy coke," I said, thinking it would take all my cassette player savings just for one afternoon's worth.

"You're useless," Chad said, carving into the wooden picnic table with a red Swiss army knife.

I pulled my feet onto the bench and zipped my jacket around my knees. A few tables away I watched Marjorie sit eating her sandwich and Oreos, drinking her chocolate milk. See me, see me, I prayed. She raised her eyes and looked in my direction. I sat up, hopeful, raised my hand to wave. But I was not who'd caught Marjorie's attention. She'd noticed Mr. Danvers, assistant principal. Marjorie and her friends watched as Danvers busted Chad for defacing school property and suspended us all for his destruction.

Tori and Chad wouldn't stop bugging me about getting them cocaine and I was starting to want some, too. I wanted to get back that good feeling I just couldn't get from smoking pot, so on my next trip to Hillsborough, I snuck into my grandmother's white-carpeted room while she was at her bridge game and opened the drawer of her vanity table. Whenever she wanted something that Frank would not allow, I saw her go there, take out a black velvet pouch, and get cash for what was inside.

This magic bag was going to solve my problems. A sparkling salamander brooch, a cold jade necklace, a blood-red ruby cocktail ring filled the rows of the jewelry drawer. Near the back my fingers touched

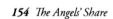

velvet and inside were a dozen loose diamonds. They sparkled in my palm like fallen stars. I stood, staring, until I heard my grandmother's heels on the stone entryway, the scrape of the cherub as she pointed it up the stairs, and then the soft thuds on the hall carpet. The smallest stone, still big, fit snug in the hip pocked of my too-tight jeans. I threw the pouch back in the drawer, shoved the other baubles and boxes back in at random, and slunk up the backstairs to the red toile room where Julia lay, reading, her back to me. I spread out on the bed and as my heartbeat subsided to its normal, sluggish, rhythm, I dozed.

I awoke from my nap to hear my grandmother yelling at Socorro. Julia was up on her elbow, her book down, looking at me with wide blue eyes.

"What did you take?" My grandmother's voice was angry.

"Nothing, Mrs. Elaine."

Julia crept down the stairs and I followed. We watched through the railing where my grandmother had backed Socorro into a corner of the foyer.

"You've been through my jewelry drawer. I'm missing a diamond. Did you think I wouldn't notice?"

"But Mrs. Elaine, I . . ." and Socorro's English failed her.

"Get out," my grandmother said.

"But please! Mrs. Elaine, I did not do it."

"I don't like thieves, Susie."

"I'm no thief."

Julia rubbed the fabric of her plaid skirt between her thumb and forefinger. Her being nervous made me nervous. I knocked her hand away and gave her a warning look I hoped would stop her.

"Leave the keys on the table. And don't think I won't get the locks changed," my grandmother said, her voice rising.

"Please, we have nowhere to go. Maybe someone else took it. Maybe . . ." but no one had been at the house that day except for Julia and me. Socorro let the comment die midair.

I crouched, frozen along the railing, feeling the pointy end of the little diamond in my jeans pocket.

I waited for my grandmother to pause, her reasoning catching up with her anger. Clearly the only person in the house who would have stolen anything was me. But either my grandmother's denial about the extent of my failings or her suspicion of her employees was deep enough that if my guilt occurred to her, it didn't matter.

"Get out!" growled Elaine Pierpoint Ferguson at the cowering Socorro. "Get out or I'll have you arrested!"

Julia and I watched, speechless, as Socorro and Jorge packed what belonged to them into their old Impala. Jorge shook our hands. Socorro, shorter than both of us now, gave us a hug and a kiss.

"Take care, Cinnamon, mi pulgita, and Julia. You are good girls," Socorro said, her face wrinkled up with suppressed sobs. She kissed us both on the forehead.

I hadn't taken the diamond out of my pocket. I could go and tell my grandmother I'd been playing around and made a mistake, but I'd never seen her that mad. She didn't like me as it was. If I went in and told the truth and she turned her wrath on me, then I wasn't sure what I'd do. So I let Socorro and Jorge back down the driveway in the sputtering car and turn left onto Ralston going toward nowhere. Jorge had worked as the groundskeeper for my grandmother since she and my real grandfather ran The Pierpoint. When she'd married Frank Ferguson and asked Jorge to garden at the mansion, he'd brought his new wife Socorro as the cook and housekeeper. They'd been with her for twenty years and known me since that first day my mother arrived in the rainstorm.

I slunk back upstairs, went into the bathroom, and sat on the edge of the white bathtub. The door was open and Julia sobbed on the bed. I rocked a little and then decided I couldn't stand any more blubbering.

"Can you shut up?" I called to her, still on the edge.

I went home via car service that Sunday and called Chad and Tori, who drove me right back to the city. On the corner of Twentieth and Treat I traded that one flawless little stone for a film canister half-full of cocaine that lasted the stoner table less than a week.

Chapter 21

At Trove, we held our staff meetings in what Sam called *The Bodega*, a room dug deep into the mountain that was at once a meeting place and where we kept the artifacts of the land. In glass cases along the walls surrounding the burlwood conference table lay a Chinaman's stackable lunch tin, arrowheads, antique metal batons, that looked something like a riding crop with a bent edge, we still used to stir the wine as it aged in the smaller barrels. And *The Bodega* was where we kept the real treasure of the caves: the old bottles of wine.

The original owners, an Italian family, fled to North Beach after Prohibition to run a bakery. For law-abiding fornaio, an excess of wine to hide during Prohibition was an inconvenience, so they left all their bottles behind, forgotten until Sam discovered them in the caves.

The grape variety and year harvested were written on the bottles with white grease pen that, after decades, had ochred. The unfamiliar names tripped off my tongue after drinking them: Taurasi, Fiano, Primitivo.

For a man who would open a '67 Stag's Leap like a jug of milk, Sam uncorked these bottles with a priestly deference. "It serves a dual purpose," he said, using a silver strainer over the mouth of each wineglass to catch the cork and sediment from the bottle as he poured, "of reminding us of the importance of tradition and expanding our palate."

Sam had urged me to skip this particular meeting, take some time off because of my mother, but I wanted to keep working, keep my mind occupied. I'd lain awake all night searching my memories, trying to tease out my grief. But, other than feeling a little weird, a little disengaged, I felt mostly fine. The best I could describe how I felt was that my mother had been dead a long time and the trip to the sheriff's office was no more than a reminder, an anniversary. My only panicky moment was when I realized I would have to be the one to tell my grandmother, who I was pretty sure never wanted to see me again, that her only daughter was dead.

Sam handed me my glass and I raised it, focused back on the meeting, the wine. A toast with these vintages, in the farthest reaches of the maze of caves, felt like swearing an oath. I touched Pedro's glass with mine and reached for Eduardo's.

When he clinked my glass, and I tried to catch his eye, Eduardo frowned. I knew I should give up on Eduardo's good opinion, but I couldn't. I wanted him to notice me, I wanted to see if my hunch was right and we were more alike than our surfaces might suggest, but Eduardo wouldn't budge. Since sitting next to me at the harvest breakfast, he'd gone back to acting like I didn't exist.

This week Sam had chosen a bottle marked *Primitivo, 1919*. At 76 years old, I could taste enough of the spicy plum against the frail backbone of tannins to sense the wine's stature. As we drank our way through the bottle, we were reverent, thinking of the Calabrian or Apulian immigrants who smuggled these vines across the ocean. Sam hoped they'd be our guides on how to plant, harvest, and bottle our way to the best wine, the truest terroir that could be made on these acres.

Eduardo considered the sediment at the bottom of his glass. "They are running some tests at Davis right now, thinking Primitivo is a cousin to Zin."

On our next sip, I imagined that the wine from the current year's harvest, what I helped craft, might be drunk well into the next century by people I'd never know, in this very room. That making wine bought me, and everyone working with these grapes, a few decades of immortality.

What life was left in the old bottle quickly faded. After ten minutes of simple air exposure, we tasted nothing but liquid dust.

Coming out of the meeting, I started on my next task: moving wine from the three-thousand-gallon vats to sixty-gallon barrels to start the barrel aging.

Oak is permeable. In Sonoma County's low humidity, we lost five to ten percent of our harvest to barrel evaporation. The molecules that comprise wine, always in random motion, would collide, transferring energy. Sometimes the transfer was so one-sided, the molecule shot up, ascending through the bulky, ill-fitting oak staves, escaping its confinement for a home with other effervescents. That evaporation, those escapees from the barrel's dark confines—the angels' share—is what perfumed the already earthy air of our wine cave.

I worked, draining the wine from the valve at the bottom of the tanks into the barrels. To lose as little as possible, I'd tap the bung in immediately with a soft mallet, but on hot, dry days, the angels' share multiplied enough to make me feel drunk just inhaling.

I was in the rhythm of scooting barrels under the valve, turning the giant spigot, filling the sixty gallons, then inching the trolley forward over a new, empty barrel. It was relaxing, hypnotic work, and I didn't hear Eduardo come up behind me.

"I'm sorry about your mother," he said, close to my ear.

I knocked the trolley too far forward and wine spilled on the floor. Eduardo reached over and turned off the valve.

"Thank you," I said. Neither of us acknowledged the spill.

"If you need time off, you should take it," he said. "I'll cover."

"Work helps me," I said.

"It distracts you, certainly, but if you never allow yourself to feel . . ." This was the most words he'd strung together when the two of us were alone. "If I lost my mother or my father, it would be unbearable."

I knew I should lie, that I should be vague and polite, but Eduardo was looking at me with such intent that I couldn't.

"I've been an orphan in practice for a while," I said. "So now, I'm half caught up with myself."

He stepped back like I'd slapped me. My black rotary phone rang. I left him with the trolley of barrels and picked it up. Detective Tully was on the line.

"We've got the preliminary autopsy back," he said. "Amatoxin."

I held the receiver to my ear and lay my forehead in my hand. "I don't know what that is," I said.

"Poisonous mushrooms, most likely. At the time of death she also had a blood alcohol level of one-point-seven and severe cirrhosis of the liver."

The cirrhosis I was expecting. In the time I'd had to think about it I'd decided the two most likely causes of death were my father or the alcohol. I'd been hoping it was the alcohol. But amatoxin?

"What kind of mushrooms?" I asked.

"Coroner says Death Cap or Avenging Angel could give us readings this high, but they aren't commonly mistaken for edibles," he said. "Had she spoken to you about suicide?"

In the fifteen years of her adherence to some form of the Bible, my mother had been unwavering in her belief that suicide was a damning sin. She'd also told me that Frank Ferguson's first wife, who'd died with her head stuck in the oven, would certainly go to hell for it. I'd said I hoped she'd get off on time served.

"She believed it was an offense against God," I said.

"Did she eat mushrooms she picked herself?" he asked.

"No," I said, not adding that my dad was a forager and an expert on telling the edible from the poisonous.

"Have you heard from your father?" Tully asked, reading my mind.

I could honestly say I hadn't. It had been the longest stretch I could remember without a postcard at least. He'd been radio silent and I had an awful feeling as to why: he was on the run. But Steve Monday was almost fifty, and living out of makeshift tents while he skulked toward the Canadian or Mexican border seemed improbable. More likely he'd found a new girlfriend and was shacked up in her mountain cabin. There was always some long-breasted Mendo chick ready to take in a craggy artiste.

"Did your mother have life insurance?"

"Not that I know of, the commune owns everything and she wasn't that into . . . paperwork."

No need to explain this further to someone who tried to mete out the law in rural Northern California.

160 The Angels' Share

"Was your father a violent man?"

He was, but I wasn't sure if I should say that.

"He could have a temper," I said, hedging.

"Paranoia?"

This was one area where I wished I could be more ignorant. My father had become more and more worried about the government, any institution really. He thought they were spraying Malathion on his pot plants, using fluoride to sterilize him, and grinding up chemical waste and putting it into bricks of tofu to make them carcinogenic. Each year he inched more to the left of libertarians and closer to the camouflage-and-bunkered-compound constituency.

"Yes," I told Tully. But even with his temper, and the paranoia, this amatoxin thing wasn't adding up. When my dad got mad, the attack was fast and physical. He would beat her, choke her, leave her writhing on the floor, then bolt. When he was angry he wouldn't have the patience to go out, pick mushrooms, and hide them in dinner. He couldn't even make dinner. My mother's death hadn't been violent, and therefore I told Tully, with the most convincing tone I could manage, that I did not believe my father was responsible.

The last time I'd seen them together, I told the detective, they'd been getting along. What I didn't tell him was that seeing my parents together that day had given me a jolt of happiness I wasn't willing to dispel, even now. When my parents were at each other's throats, it took away one of the few reasons I had for living. I'd blown my education, disappointed my relatives, and spent a lot of cash on drugs. I'd stolen from those who trusted me, gotten innocent people fired, fucked indiscriminately, and murdered thousands of my own brain cells. What did I have left to show for myself? Not even a high school degree, tracks up my arms, and a history of relationships that resembled Sherman's march to the sea. But when my parents clicked, I knew my father had a string tied to his heart that attached to my mother in the same place. He'd go away, but he'd always come back. My existence was evidence of that attachment. It made me worth something. I was the product of more than just bad judgment.

"Okay, Ms. Monday," Tully said. "But I'd still like to talk with him."

After we hung up, I sat at my desk, trying to think of the people I could call who might know where my father was. The list was short and I had no idea of where to start looking for any of them. I wrote my grandmother's name at the end of the list, thinking she needed to know and also that she might have been the last person outside of OHM my mother talked to. I decided to take Eduardo up on the offer to take the afternoon off. I stripped down to my long-sleeved t-shirt, preparing to leave the 58 degrees of the caves for the 98 outside. When I passed by the fermentation tanks, I saw Eduardo, who'd been in earshot of my conversation, sliding barrels under the spigot and finishing my job.

"I'll be back," I said. "Thanks for doing that." He nodded and kept working.

Chapter 22

I didn't last long at Orchard High once the Naughton boys got shipped away. Midway through sophomore year, Mr. Danvers searched my locker, found six joints—I'd had twenty but sold a bunch the day before—expelled me, and called the cops. I got fingerprinted and had to wait in a locked room until my mother came to pick me up.

Even before my arrest, she had replaced sweet wine with vodka and was drinking at least half a bottle a day. Other than two postcards from Rosarito Beach—"fishing is great," but never "wish you were here"— my father was absent and sent no money. Our telephone was shut off. We got our groceries from my mother's churches. The Sheriff had served us with a tax lien on the shipwreck shack. The cats still brought in some money, which paid for her liquor and sweets, but little else.

"No one hires the obese," my grandmother said and offered to pay for Jenny Craig.

My mother went to the motivational meetings and got the freeze-dried meals, but continued with a diet of mostly Smirnoff and ice cream. I ate the cardboard diet lasagna and frostbitten plugs of carrot. She tried working as a veterinarian's assistant, but claimed she was allergic and quit. She sent away for information about teaching at a Montessori pre-school and bought a real-estate appraisers test-prep booklet. Both went unopened on the counter.

Once I turned sixteen, I applied for jobs, but considering my lack of experience, my expulsion and the upcoming restrictions in my schedule due to court-ordered drug counseling, I wasn't that hot of a candidate.

Whenever we ran out of money, my mother would call my grandmother and grovel. But every time she had to beg, the volume of my mother's alcohol intake ticked up a notch and my grandmother sent a little less.

The percentage of the cost of my drug counseling at St. Jerome's Adolescent Treatment Facility—the part they called parental responsibility, in our case $200—was coming due and we were broke again. There were no kittens on the way, nothing left we could sell. I offered to make the call, thinking a fresh voice asking for a handout might be more effective. But my mother refused.

"You shouldn't have to," she said, as we hitched into town to make the call on a pay phone.

I was afraid asking this time might be the final straw, but my grandmother came through for us again. I knew she'd be hocking a dragonfly brooch or Limoges tchotchke for little ol' delinquent me.

She promised to send a check, but by the Monday I was due at St. Jerome's it still hadn't arrived. My mother and I walked up to the mailbox once we saw the rural-route delivery jeep pass by, desperate for Elaine's dove-gray envelope to be resting inside. It was there and contained a rare note:

"This is the absolute last time I bail you out," my grandmother scolded us on heavy cardstock. "You live in America! Stand on your own two feet."

"Between us," I said to my mother, "we've actually got four feet."

My mother looked at me, her eyelids heavy from the drinking she'd already done, her hair winging out in two side puffs like lightning bolts on the helmet of Thor, and smiled at the joke.

In our sputtering Corolla, we crossed the floodplain between Sebastopol and Santa Rosa with me in the passenger seat reminding my mother which of the two lanes was hers.

As we circled the cement block building that could as easily have been an auto-body shop as a teen rehab facility, I wondered if it was irony or poetic justice that my drunk mother was dropping me off. Irony, I recalled from the few days I made it to sophomore English, was associated with words or actions having the opposite effect of their intention, and poetic justice was a kind of sweet retribution. This was irony, I was pretty sure. Additional irony was that even as I was heading down loserville lane, ten-dollar words from all those books I'd read

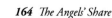

still roiled in my head. Even though I'd stopped reading, the habits and patterns I learned from novels were embedded inside me. A teenager who thought in the formal diction of a nineteenth century novel and yet who was on her way to a court-ordered institutional stay was a ridiculous contradiction, pushing irony to its bounds. And yet, there I was.

My first counselor, Joseph, was a short guy with black hair, in a sleeveless t-shirt. He had a cross tattooed on one arm, John 2:17 on the other; and even though he'd grown a goatee and flexed his muscles like a tic, I couldn't imagine he was much past twenty-one.

He asked how my detox was going. Honestly, now that I was away from the Naughtons and my father's stash, I hadn't done any substance in a while. Joseph seemed disappointed, like he was missing a chance to swaddle me in those blue polyester St. Jerome's blankets and yell that we'd get through it with the Lord.

I went through the motions of the counseling. I admitted I had a problem, but it was mostly a problem of judgment, of whom I hung out with. I had no cravings, not even for the coke. I was going to get my GED and head to the junior college as soon as possible. A couple of years there and I could transfer to a college with dorms where I could go away and start my own life. I just needed to hang on a little bit longer.

Then my mother met Phil. He'd been preaching in front of the same grocery store where she'd first gotten her Gideon's Bible. She took this as a sign and when he invited her up to Oh Holy Mountain, his spiritual commune, for a retreat weekend, she went. This happened during my two weeks of mandatory church camp in July, and on pick-up day my mother and father showed up together, holding hands.

My mother told Joseph how my father had come home repentant and she'd brought him to Oh Holy Mountain. My father had accepted Jesus. We were going to become a real family now.

"He's changed, Cinnamon," my mother told me. "Really. And I've changed, too. Things are going to be different."

My dad, his longish hair now trimmed above his collar, nodded. "You ready for a family, little girl?" he asked.

Every part of me wanted a family, but I wasn't so sure about this family. I remembered the string of bruises around my mother's neck. But my mother seemed sober and my father didn't smell of pot. Their eyes were clear and they were nice to each other and me for the entire lunch and tour of camp.

Oh Holy Mountain was more than just a church. Phil sold spiritual salvation, and just as she'd sunk every dollar into chinchillas or a crate of soap-free laundry detergent, my mother swallowed up to the sinker on OHM within a matter of days. The truth about my father's conversion is he had run home from Mexico to hide from the boyfriend of a woman he'd "borrowed" drugs from, was initially grateful for any means to cover his tracks, but told me he'd now found the first peace he'd had in years while praying.

Less than a month after meeting Phil, they were selling the shipwreck shack, my father's tools and all our cats. My parents signed over the proceeds to Oh Holy Mountain which, in turn, gave them a place to live with a view of the redwoods and access to the spiritual teachings of Phil.

"I don't think this is a good idea," I said to my mom as my father took cash from someone in the driveway for his machinist's equipment.

"It's our chance to start over. A new home, a new life. Trust us," my mother soothed.

And although I took care to nod impassively and said all the required cynical things to myself in the bathroom mirror, I daydreamed about starting sophomore year over at Ukiah high school where no one would know me and I could shed my stoner reputation. I imagined myself studying in a cathedral of sequoias near the comfortable Oh Holy Mountain bungalow my parents described to me. If I had to pray and murmur there like I'd done at church camp, I was willing to keep at it, pay that toll.

Two weeks before I was to graduate from St. Jerome's outpatient drug treatment program, and after we'd sold the shipwreck shack, my family went to visit our new home. My parents had been there for the retreat weekends and initiation activities, but I'd never seen it in person.

We drove north on Highway 101 and then west on the narrow 128, turned off onto a dusty driveway, crossed a cattle guard, and passed under an ironwork archway with OHM welded at the top like a ranch brand.

"Phil's on a mission today," my mother talked into the rearview. "I showed him some pictures of you, though. He had to make sure your aura was pure before you could join."

Auras.

"Does Bari DeGarzi live here?"

My father whipped a look at my mother.

"Goodness, no," my mother said. "What made you ever mention her name?"

I looked out the window as the A-frame Holy House came into view from behind the redwoods. Scattered across the burnt-gold hills were domes of gray weathered wood the size of small storage sheds.

"What are those?" I asked.

"That one there is ours," my dad said pointing.

"Ours?"

"Our living space," he said.

My father parked the car and they toured me through the Holy House. A hand-lettered poster on the wall advertised Vegan Agape, seven-thirty on Fridays. One pay phone was on the wall between the door and the couch of the Holy House, affording no privacy. In the kitchen were several women, all with their long hair in kerchiefs, preparing food.

"Sisters," my mother said, "this is Cinnamon."

The women nodded at me, bowing their heads. Before we continued on, I caught two glances from them at my mother's back that were biting, cold. Neither of my parents seemed to notice.

The chapel, with floor to ceiling windows that showed off the towering redwoods, was as majestic and peaceful as my father had said. A driftwood cross hung from the zenith of the A-frame but over the altar was a life-sized portrait of a bearded, graying man, his hand raised like the Buddha.

"Yes," my mother said before I asked. "That's him."

My dad trailed behind us on the way to their living quarters, examining new green shoots and flowers along the path.

"Phil has made your father the forager of Oh Holy Mountain. His job is to find us seeds and berries to sustain us when Phil needs our earthly resources for his missions."

I saw children, much too old to be home during a weekday, playing naked in the mud near a stream.

"Shouldn't they be at school?"

"They have no need for desks in rows," my mother said, taking my hand, leading me up the hill and into the woods. "Phil's children learn everything they need from the sun, the sky, and the Bible."

Their dome could not have been much more than fifteen feet in diameter with a narrow sleeping loft against one wall. There were faded maroon cushions on the floor and a milk-crate table with candles melted down to nubs on a plate. Where my parents thought we could all live was less than half the size of the shipwreck shack.

"Where's my box?" I asked. I'd carefully packed my books and few clothes a week before and seen them driven off in the OHM van.

"We've been relieved of our earthly burdens," my mom said.

"You gave my things away?" I said, attempting to keep my voice level, my good-girl act up.

"You haven't read those books for years now," my dad said.

That was true, but it didn't quell my panic.

"Everything already belongs to everyone, honey. OHM has just helped your father and I actualize that."

"But where am I going to sleep?" I gestured around the tiny dome. "It doesn't seem like there is enough space."

"I've strung up a hammock out front, and we can put you on the floor when it gets cold."

Idiot. I was an idiot! Why had I believed them?

My parents continued to look at, touch and speak to me, but none of it was real. I could feel myself retracting, folding, looking for a way out.

"Cinnamon," Joseph said at my second-to-last counseling session, "how did it go?"

Finally Joseph's endless proselytizing of the tenets of evangelism was coming in handy. I named a substantive list of how OHM differed from what he would find acceptable. The portrait of Phil hung over the altar was the ace in the hole, and I used it.

"I don't want to speak badly of my parents," I said. "I feel like a sinner telling you without them present. But I've come so far during my time at St. Jerome's. I want to remain . . . dedicated to truth," I said, bowing my head.

Then Joseph did what I hoped he would. He called my mother. He asked about what I'd seen. She, under attack, grew haughty. Joseph called her and my father sinners. She called him some choice non-Christian names and accused me of not honoring my parents by telling Joseph, who defended me and said I'd come to him in shame of doing just that thing.

To his credit, Joseph found me a spot in a group home and a sympathetic probation officer who drove me to job interviews and filed paperwork for emancipation. I wasn't in the group home two weeks before I'd gotten a job at the new Blockbuster at Coddingtown Mall and channeled Elaine Pierpoint for the family court judge who declared me a legal adult. Two paychecks later I found a studio apartment in a crumbly stucco building that the manager said was to be torn down as soon as a lawsuit with the city was settled. But until then I could afford the rent on minimum wage, as anyone who wanted a solid place to live had already moved out.

I had to attend Joseph's church both Wednesdays and Sundays while this was all working itself out. Once the emancipation was approved and I settled into the new apartment, I went less and less, giving up the church entirely by the time my probation ended. Joseph was saving a new group of kids by then, youth counselors and probation officers were overworked, new cases every week to replace the ones that had dropped off. Joseph left more and more angry messages for me, both on my phone and stuck in my door. He threatened to reverse my emancipation if I didn't come back to church. I knew he couldn't. He told me I'd deceived him and the Lord and would pay. I didn't care. I was on my own, finally, and didn't have to answer to anyone.

Chapter 23

After I left Eduardo doing my job filling barrels in the caves, I walked up to the farmhouse and took a set of keys from the rack inside the kitchen door. Alma was cooking at the stove. Sam was on the cordless at the table, negotiating the details of a tasting trip to Europe in a few weeks. He gestured for me to come and sit with him, to wait for the call to be over and keep him company.

I shook my head, thinking perhaps I should write him a note and tell him where I was going, but I was planning to be back in time to take the evening shift. No one would think I went farther than town.

I drove south toward Hillsborough.

The number on my grandmother's gate keypad hadn't changed. Parked under the porte cochère was a white pick-up with a generic security badge on the door and a siren slapped on the roof. Except for the truck, my grandmother's house looked deserted. All the drapes were closed. Not even the birds were making sounds.

A Sasquatch-sized woman in a security uniform answered the door.

"I'm Cinnamon, Mrs. Ferguson's granddaughter. I'd like to see her."

"Your grandma very sick lady," she said. "Two strokes and broken hip. Where you been?" She was Samoan or Tongan, I guessed, close to six feet with a radio on her belt. With her mass, she could waste me with one hard knock.

"I've been away, but I'd like to see her."

"You not on list," the security guard said, scowling.

What list?

She handed me a business card and shut the door.

The name on the card, Philbrech & Fitch, was familiar because they were the law firm that handled OHM's business. Of course, I thought. OHM had been expecting my mother's inheritance. That my mother had died before my grandmother must have been causing a logistical inconvenience. They were protecting their booty, no doubt.

I'd been nervous about going to my grandmother's, anxious about telling her the news, scared of what she might say about me, to me, but now, imagining her alone in the house, sick, and under the care of OHM's lackeys, I just wanted to make sure she was all right.

I guessed I had some kind of legal right to see her and that if I called the police or Sam for help, I would eventually gain entry, but certainly not today, maybe not even this week. The guard was big and wasn't going to let me in, but she also hadn't spent a hundred weekends of her childhood here learning every curve of the land, every niche in the house.

I drove down the driveway, parked on Ralston where the chain link fence didn't quite meet up with the stone fence that fronted the road. I sneaked uphill under the cover of pine trees, their soft needles a quiet carpet under my feet until I was against the retaining wall under the house.

I looked in the kitchen and saw the guard on a kitchen chair watching a TV on the countertop. The front door was out of the question. I tried the porte cochère entry. Locked. I sat down behind the camellias and thought. I could try to climb to the second floor and see if any windows were open, but that seemed foolish. However healed up I was, I wasn't in shimmy-up-a-drainpipe kind of shape. Hidden by the hedge, I walked around the perimeter of the house looking for an open first-floor window. There wasn't one, but the basement window, the window to where Jorge and Socorro's apartment used to be, was open just a crack. I worked it wider and dropped into the basement of my grandmother's house.

Julia and I had played hide-and-seek so much that I knew all the squeaky spots on the stairs. I passed the kitchen sticking close to the wall, noise from the game show muffling any sounds I made. I searched the second floor, nothing. All the rooms, including my grandmother's, were empty of both people and furniture.

Where could she be?

With a broken hip she certainly couldn't get up and down stairs. I slipped down the main staircase and into the grand foyer. Everything was wrong.

There were no fresh flowers in the vases that lined the hall. Some were filled with plastic daisies, which would have caused Grandmother an additional stroke. The cherub, covered in dust, pointed to a blank wall. I suppressed the urge to grab it and hustle back to my car, back to my cottage where I could care for it. But that would take time and I had to find my grandmother before Security Sasquatch found me.

I discovered her, in what used to be a ladies' sitting room off the first-floor bathroom. She lay in a mechanical hospital bed that took up half the space. The room was clean and her pill bottles were lined up in a neat row out of her reach. I approached the bed. My grandmother's body was so diminished that you could barely tell she was there. Until then, her presence had been larger than life. No longer.

"Grandmother," I whispered.

She turned her head toward me. Her dentures were out, her wig, which I'd never known she'd worn until then, was askew.

"You dress like a ruffian," she said.

I wore the same grape-stained overalls and long-sleeved t-shirt I'd worn to fill the barrels that morning and I did look terrible. She'd always included a critique of my appearance with her hellos, so for once upon seeing her, her comments were reassuring.

I wanted to reach out and hold her hand. Tell her the truth about Socorro. Apologize for my part in all of the wrong that had happened. Work my way slowly up to the news about my mother. But I was afraid she'd pull away, refuse to touch dirty, lying Cinnamon. Instead I listened for the sound of anyone coming down the hall. I heard a rattle in her breath.

"Grandmother," I said. "I stole a book from you once."

"What kind of book?"

"It was a novel, from the library. It had been a gift to you; your name was in it. But I loved the story so much I wanted to take it home with me. I'm sorry I did it. I'd bring it back to you but it's lost."

"I never read any of those books. You could have stolen half of that library and it wouldn't have affected me one bit." She laughed a little. "But thank you for telling me."

I wanted to tell her so much more, confess the worse things I'd done, tell her the terrible news I had.

She turned her attention toward the ceiling. I followed her gaze, but all I saw was dusty spider webs hanging from the light that would have never been allowed under Socorro's watch.

"Grandmother," I said trying to get up my courage to tell her about my mother, but she didn't answer. So I studied my hands in my lap and started tracing the ridged scars from my wrist to my elbow through the fabric of my shirt. I waited and listened. Far away in the kitchen, I heard the din of a Jerry Springer brawl.

"You've found a good husband," my grandmother said. "No thanks to me."

I'd been wrong about her lucidity. "No, Grandmother, I'm Cinnamon," I started.

She waved at me like she was swatting a fly. "And your cousin. I've kept you from her."

What was she talking about? "No you haven't. It's been my choice to stay away from Julia."

"I've kept you from both of them," she said. "All of it traces back to me."

"Now I've got to tell you something," she said, "so stop picking at yourself."

I pulled my fingers from the crook of my elbow.

I reached out and to my surprise, she took my hand, gripping it hard, hard enough that I wanted to pull it away, but I realized she was not trying to hurt me, only get me closer.

"Take the cherub, Cinnamon," she whispered in my ear. "Take it, use it better than I have."

Feet in the hallway. Crap. If that giant got a hold of me, I didn't think she'd easily let go.

"I love you," I said, kissing her soft cheek before I scrambled out the tiny window of the adjacent bathroom, scraping a ribbon of skin off my back on a sharp part of the metal frame and landing hard on the ground outside.

Slumped against the outside wall, I held my shirt against the sting and tried to hear what was going on in my grandmother's sickroom. No sound. Security Sasquatch had probably just done a quick check on her. I shouldn't have panicked, could have just hid in the bathroom. I tried to hoist myself back in, but the window was too high. I wanted to hold my grandmother's hand longer, say a proper goodbye and rescue the cherub. It was the thing that most represented her in my memory. I wondered if I had time to go back in through the basement window, sneak by the kitchen and out to the front hall to grab it.

No. I wasn't going to steal another item from this house. I'd call the lawyers; find a way to get a visit. Have my grandmother tell them her wishes herself. Besides, it was already four o'clock. If I wasn't back by six, then Eduardo would have to take another of my shifts. I wasn't a sneaker or a stealer anymore. I needed to get back to Trove.

At Sam's insistence, I talked to his lawyers and they did a bit of digging. Philbrech & Fitch was a reputable white-shoe firm and the power of attorney and contracts my grandmother had signed were airtight. OHM now controlled and stood to inherit everything. If I pursued this, however, Sam's lawyers thought I might be able to rattle them a bit, especially if I were to file suit claiming my grandmother's mental incompetence. They sent over examples of precedent where plaintiffs in similar suits had won. I read through the paperwork trying to translate the legalese. The more I understood, the sicker I felt. I didn't want to put my grandmother through stressful and embarrassing psychological tests and competing doctor visits. I saw how weak she was. That might have killed her, and for what? A knickknack and maybe a few dollars? I thought of Esther Summerson in Dickens' *Bleak House* watching those she loved driving themselves crazy, becoming party to the endless lawsuit of Jarndyce v. Jarndyce. Everyone involved expected justice, but all they got was an expensive, soul consuming trial that eventually reduced the estate's value to zero. In Dickens, litigation was like a disease, catching and deadly. I wanted nothing of it.

"They would be willing," Sam's lawyer said, "if you were to sign a release for any material interest in your grandmother's estate, to allow unsupervised visitations."

"I'll give you the money to go after those bastards," Sam said.

If I thought she was being mistreated I would go after them in a second, but after seeing her, the only deficit in her care was company. I've taken enough from her, I thought. Now I just want to give. I just want to be able to see her.

I drove back down to San Francisco the following week and signed away my rights to inheritance for a chance to know my grandmother.

Chapter 24

There was a 7-Eleven halfway between my place and Blockbuster. After ten hours sorting and shelving movies, I'd treat myself to a large Slurpee and a hot dog. One day, I ate al fresco on the sidewalk in front of the store while the asphalt in the parking lot shimmered with heat. In my back pocket was a business card for the continuation high school; one of the teachers there was a regular renter at work.

I sat on the curb finishing off my dinner, my feet stuck out in front of me, my legs baking in my one pair of pegged acid-wash jeans. I leaned back and checked the clock behind the counter inside. It was five past five, too late to call the continuation school's office today. Tomorrow, I thought.

A teal pick-up truck, lowered to a few inches above pavement, went diagonally over the speed bump into the parking lot. Unintelligible base shook the truck's windows. The Beastie Boys flooded my ears when the driver's door opened. A pinched-faced blonde slunk from the driver's seat, yanking at her too-tight jeans.

Tori.

She didn't notice me as she walked into the store. I watched her buy cigarettes, a canister of beef jerky, and flash her fake ID for beer. She walked out of the store, stood ten feet away and lit a cigarette. I stared at her, waiting for her to notice me. She tossed the smoking match on the sidewalk and started back toward the truck.

I knew that Tori had never been a true friend, that our relationship was a convenience for her as I'd been the other girl around and the main supplier. Yet she was one of the few people who knew me. I was sitting alone, and she was getting into the truck to leave.

I called out.

She turned toward me, then squealed.

"Cinnamon!" she said. "I thought you were in juvie!" And as she hugged me, she insisted the gang had missed me, and she made a couple calls on the payphone. That night, as if I'd rubbed the wrong lamp, Tori, Alex, and Chad were all in my apartment, sitting on my Goodwill futon watching The Simpsons, smoking weed.

Chad and Tori had both dropped out of Orchard and now talked about getting jobs while they watched a lot of daytime TV. Alex had graduated and was taking a semester off before starting junior college, and also living at home.

Tori was now Chad's girlfriend—it had been his lowrider she'd been driving at the 7-Eleven—and when both of their families were home, they'd come to my place during the day and leave wet stains on the futon, dishes in the sink, and sprinkles of Chad's urine around the outside of the toilet. Chad had asked, demanded, for me to join them, and high enough I would, to get him to shut up, to make peace, but even wired on coke I didn't want to. If I came home and they were there, I'd walk around the block on the dusty sidewalk-less street to avoid being drawn in. The one I wanted, even when sober, was Alex, but at most Alex would let me sit against him on the couch and lay my head on his shoulder when he was too stoned to drive home. I thought of my non-conjurable imaginary friend, the boy, a few years older: my companion and protector. Alex was neither of these things, but sitting next to his warmth on the couch, even if he held himself stiff, kept me from sliding into more with Tori and Chad and gave me something to think about during the endless hours I scanned and stacked love stories.

Despite a party at my house every night, I led a boring life. Every day was one of two scripts. Either I'd have the day off and sleep until three, when I'd shower and eat a bowl of cereal, anticipating my friends' arrival. Or, more often, I'd drag myself into work, get a frozen yogurt at the TCBY next to Blockbuster and head back to the apartment where Tori or Chad would have already let themselves in. I'd find them eating Doritos and drinking beer, waiting for me so we could get down to the real business of the evening.

Even with Alex's contribution and Chad's occasional twenty, I still paid for the majority of our drugs and our food. Tori claimed she never had any money, that her dad was still the world's biggest cheapskate. She borrowed my clothes, and returned them smelling of cigarettes and vomit.

I got sneaky with my drawer at Blockbuster to support our collective habit and was fired for stealing. I knew there were cameras, but I did it anyway, asking myself who the hell would review all that film. Turns out, they had a whole team in Miami that did once your cash drawer didn't balance. They also had their own security apes come in while I was working, cuff me, and toss me in the back of their siren-crowned white Jimmy. It was a bluff for the benefit of scaring my co-workers, because all they did was drop me at home telling me I was lucky they'd not taken me to jail.

"I'd have to go in front of a judge for you to put me in jail," I said, rubbing my wrists and backing away from the beefy thugs in crisp white shirts.

"Don't be smart," the one riding shotgun said.

I bought the Press Democrat the next morning, looking through the columns of Help Wanted ads with a pen in my hand.

After two days of searching, I found my next job, at the Dry Creek Coffee Café off the Square in Healdsburg owned by two guys from San Francisco who had cashed out of management consulting.

"You're a Renaissance girl," Ray, the one who managed the business, said in my interview, which ended with him asking me to bake blueberry scones from a three-by-five recipe card. Remembering all of the things Socorro had taught me in my grandmother's kitchen, they came out buttery, crumbly, and perfectly browned. Then he showed me how to finish a latte with hearts or concentric circles on top.

"Only do the hearts for the people you really like," he said. "Otherwise, do the circles."

"What's a Renaissance girl?" I asked.

Ray, with his prematurely gray hair and eyes the color of cornflowers, turned to me. "You'll find out when you get to college," he winked.

Once he discovered I was emancipated, he didn't ask specifics about where I lived or why I wasn't in school. I gave him my parole officer's name as a reference; and after a week of working alongside me, he gave me as many hours as I wanted.

"I'm hiring you because I need to be home. Randall's not well. If it's too much, holler," he said when I asked him if he really wanted me to open and close solo after I'd been there such a short time.

But Ray needed me and I needed the money, so I didn't holler. After the initial rush, the mornings were quiet. After I had the fresh scones in the cases and all of the pitchers of milk full, I would nap on the couch, my ears alert for the bell if a customer came in. I learned to order coffee, flour, and sugar from Sodexo; I polished the espresso machine, took the dishtowels home to launder, opened on time no matter how wasted I'd been the night before, made circles on all my lattes, and never lied if I'd forgotten a customer's request for decaf. Although I was arguably still just a wage slave, making coffee and baking scones provided a measurable achievement and filled me with something that days at Blockbuster seemed only to deplete.

After a month, Ray gave me a dollar-an-hour raise. If I ever had to steal out of the drawer, I paid it back out of the tip jar by the end of the week when he came in to do the books.

One morning a woman in a tie-dye dress came in with her young daughter hiding behind her skirts. The mother ordered a soy latte and I made the little girl a free not-too-hot chocolate, remembering that long ago treat of Mrs. VanTassen's fudge. I thought of my mother, how she'd found a way to get us to my grandmother's without any money that rainy day. When I'd left the group home, I'd not given a forwarding number or address. Ray had told me if I was caught up with work and there were no customers I could make personal calls, so when the little girl and her tie-dye mom left, I called OHM.

"Baby!" my mom cried when she came to the phone.

She was fine, great, she told me, but my dad had left again.

"He couldn't take what the Lord asked of him," she said, our connection bad.

 180 *The Angels' Share*

A busload of tourists started filling the café, lining up for their caffeine fix.

"What did the Lord ask of him?"

A coiffed blonde rapped on the counter with the diamond in her wedding ring. "Service?" she said, raising her eyebrow at me.

"Let's not get into that now," my mom said. "I want to know when you're coming up to visit."

"I've got to go," I said, telling her I was working and where.

After that, my mother would hitch rides down and spend the afternoon drinking free hazelnut mochas supplemented by little bottles of brandy she kept in her purse. Once she borrowed the commune's car and we went to Hillsborough for dinner. The occasion for this dinner—the last time I'd see Frank before he dropped dead on the golf course—was my Uncle Victor's final visit before he went into a seclusion order. He would not be able to talk to or have contact with the outside world for the rest of his life. I'd met my mother's brother once before. He'd come to visit Julia on a weekend we were at Grandmother's together. He had just been in training to be a priest back then, but now he was the real deal, standing at my grandmother's, dressed in his robes and collar with a signet ring on his fat pinky. He acted like he didn't know how to hug when my mother threw her arms around him. This was her little brother, who had grown up living at The Pierpoint with her, the person who should have been her closest ally. She never mentioned him. And after he didn't hug her back, they spoke awkwardly if at all, cordially ignoring each other for the rest of the evening.

My grandmother, dressed for dinner with a thick collar of gold around her neck, looked over my ripped jeans and Ramones t-shirt, her face contorted like she'd smelled rotting meat.

Uncle Victor mixed everyone's cocktails before dinner, and made me a Shirley Temple, which I clutched in my sweaty palm as my grandmother retold the story of firing Socorro and Jorge. My grandmother's new maid—there seemed to be a new one every few months—called us to dinner. I'd not put my napkin in my lap before Frank started in.

"I wonder what old Jasper would think about his mighty hotel being run by a bunch of camel-jockeys."

After my grandfather Jasper had sunk the hotel and our family's fortune, an East Coast hotel chain bought the building out of bankruptcy. They advertised the famous past guests of The Pierpoint and sold the rooms through consolidators while skimping on maintenance. In the early '80s the hotel catered to conventioneers with a buffet brunch on Sundays where scrambled eggs were poured into chafing dishes out of greasy buckets. The hotel's silver was melted down and sold. Playboy owned it for a while and turned the restaurant into a cocktail lounge called Hugh Hefner at The Pierpoint, then sold it to a group of Japanese investors who planned to demolish the hotel and build an ultra-modern monument to their takeover of the West Coast. Only a dilapidated shell of its former self, it survived the 1989 earthquake and subsequent recession. When the Japanese economy burst, the investors halted their plans and the hotel had gone back on the market. I'd read in the newspaper we got at the café that a family of Indian hoteliers with five-star hotels in Bombay, Manila, and Hong Kong, and a son at Stanford, was rumored to be in negotiations to buy the property, not to tear it down, but to refurbish the original back to grandeur.

"Not too pleased, I'm sure," Victor said in reply to Frank's question. My uncle's blubbery jowls swiveled on his priest's collar to smile at me. Despite his lofty calling, I caught a whiff of my uncle's desire to please Frank, but whether it was for a peaceful last meal or a donation to his order, I wasn't sure.

"The past is past," my grandmother said, fastening the clasp of her diamond bracelet and pushing it up her arm until it fit tight. "Regrets are unbecoming."

My plate was filled with juicy fillet and grilled tomato, one of my grandmother's signature dinners and a favorite of mine. All I had to do was stuff my mouth with it and keep quiet, but instead I said, "Camel-jockeys?"

My mother reached for her glass.

"They're Indian, not Arab," I told Frank. "If you are going to be a racist, you should at least insult people properly. I believe the term is 'diaper-heads' or if you want to be more general, then 'darkies' should do the trick."

Frank Ferguson, four martinis into the evening, fixed his eyes on me from under their heavy lids. I glared back.

Uncle Victor tried to smooth it over. "Camel-jockeys, diaper-heads, those are all just words. What's important is that the family name is being restored."

"That's not what's important," I said, not taking my eyes off Frank.

Frank spoke: "Elaine, get your mouthy, ill-mannered granddaughter out of my house."

"Don't worry, I'm already gone," I said, trying to keep my voice light but knocking over my chair as I stood. As some sort of defiance, I grabbed my dinner roll and went and sat on the front steps, picking crumbs off the roll and throwing them into the motor court in hopes of attracting some birds.

"Tell us, Victor, have you had a chance to visit with Julia?" I'd heard my grandmother ask before I slammed the door behind me.

Tales of my cousin Julia—a perfect way to end this miserable outing.

Those days Julia was an Atherton debutante; I'd been expelled from high school. She'd been accepted at Stanford; I'd been fired from Blockbuster.

I picked hard at that roll until my mother stumbled out the front door.

"Linda," I heard my grandmother say. "We do not enjoy Cinnamon's unpleasantness. Have you taught her no manners? She's not welcome back."

Driving home, I railed on Frank, Elaine, and Victor.

"Manners?" I said. "However badly I behave, they're worse."

"I won't take sides," my mother said. "No matter what, I'll always love her."

My mother, adhering to the Fifth Commandment or just practicing more masochism than I, went to Frank's funeral. She continued to see my grandmother as often as she could find a ride down, though Elaine called her weight disgusting, her clothing shabby.

My mother told my father where to find me and he also became a regular at the café, taking snore-filled naps on the couch after inhaling three of my scones and an extra large drip coffee.

"Sneaking in to visit your mother," he'd say on his way north. On his way south again he'd tell me he couldn't stand the commune, would never go there again, until he did. Sometimes he'd crash at my apartment. Chad and Tori thought he was a riot and I'd come home to the three of them around the same bong. When it came to be my turn, I shook my head, embarrassed to smoke pot in front of my father, still holding onto some taboo of behaving like I wasn't a druggie in front of him. But Chad kept pushing me, and my father was settled back in his chair, his eyes glazed over seeming not to care what I did.

I took the pipe from Chad and put it to my mouth, the water sounding like it was boiling from my inhale.

Chapter 25

Sam found me working in the caves on Sunday, sorting through orders for new barrels, waiting for one o'clock when it would be time to pick up my mother's ashes. "You're related to the hotel Pierpoints, right?" He was holding a folded copy of the San Francisco Chronicle:

Julia Foxworthy Pierpoint has made San Francisco her home after graduating with honors in French from Stanford University. Granddaughter of both Jasper Pierpoint and Morgan Foxworthy, Julia was raised in Atherton, where she made her debut five short summers ago. Miss Pierpoint has been hired as the public relations assistant to Parveen Shrinivarssrian, scion of the Indian hotelier family in the midst of refurbishing the old dame of Frisco hotels. The new Pierpoint is set to open by the New Year. Can anyone say party? Mr. Shrinivarssrian and Miss Pierpoint had their concurrent graduations from Stanford in June. Word on the street is Julia and Parveen were close at The Farm. Could there be more than business going on? Once the Tattler knows, and she always does, you'll get the scoop, but until then let's raise a toast to the air of romance and mystery back at The Pierpoint.

"Know her?" Sam asked.

"A little," I said, pretending to be distracted by organizing the invoices on my desk.

Later, I fished the paper out of the recycling bin and took it back to my cottage.

There was no mention of our grandfather Jasper who had embezzled The Pierpoint into bankruptcy, Julia's mother on marriage six or seven, a father who hid behind a cloister from her or her drug-addict loser relatives. Just society gossip accompanied by a professional photo of blonde, radiant Julia. Of course the hotel had hired her; she was the perfect figurehead. Everything was surface. My head hurt. I sat up and tried to shake it off.

I looked at the clock; it was half past one. In thirty minutes I had an appointment to pick up my mother's ashes. I took the article, folded it, and stuck it on my bookshelf.

Judson Funeral Parlor had a heavy wood door, the knob set in the very center like a brass nose. I declined a cup of Sanka while I waited on a cushioned pew. A man in a dark suit handed me a box. I went to thank him and then realized that I held the whole of my mother, everything she'd been in my hands and she was nearly weightless. A jones for crank hit me like a Rocky Balboa uppercut.

Since I left Napa Meadows, I was careful around the things I knew might trigger a craving: the sound of a pop-top can, the snap of rubber, a squeeze on my bicep—the doctor took my blood pressure with a thigh cuff—but mostly I found my desires for coke, crank, and pot manageable, fleeting. Dr. Falk told me I was a situational user—more interested in the people who did the drugs than the drugs themselves, but that I still needed to be careful. Dr. Falk had also told me resolve was like a muscle and by exercising mine it would strengthen. Until then, she'd been right. But standing in this ersatz chapel, holding what was left of my mother in my hands, it was like all the calm, satisfied cells in my blood stream had been turned into hungry, agitated bits, desperate for something to make them whole again.

"We offer several upgrades," Dark Suit said, opening a glossy catalog of urns filled with cut crystal, grand script. He leaned in closer to show me and the smell of Kevin's shampoo filled my nose.

"I'm not sure what I'm doing," I said, backing away, the sharp corner of the cardboard box making a painful dent in the underside of my arm.

"It's hard on loved ones when we are left without direction," he said.

My hand shook as I wrote out a check for the cremation and then fled the air-conditioned mortuary for the hot interior of Sam's car, where I tried to get the ant farm let loose in my brain under control.

Physical pain could take away a jones. I didn't like to use it—I'd been warned by Dr. Falk that cutting, piercing, injuring skin was another addiction I could be vulnerable to—but sometimes a bite on the lip or pinching a finger in a door was enough to press my restart button, a nastier version of scaring someone to rid them of the hiccups.

In the driver's seat, I bit down until I tasted blood.

The mortician was wrong, I had direction. That was the problem. My mother had told me on at least three semi-sober occasions that she wanted her ashes to be scattered amongst the redwoods at Oh Holy Mountain. I had asked her could I take her somewhere, anywhere else, but she'd been resolute.

To someone who knew nothing about it, Oh Holy Mountain was a beautiful piece of land: on the western hills of Mendocino County, its highest hills peeking at the Pacific, showcase sunsets every night. OHM was a place where a good portion of the world wouldn't mind having their final rest. But however beautiful it was, I hated Oh Holy Mountain. And now that I cradled my mother in my arms I never wanted to take her back there.

I examined the red, weeping crescents I'd bitten into my lip in the rearview, put the box of ashes on the passenger seat and buckled my seatbelt. My mother would not want to be left in a box; my mother would want to be put on the green earth as soon as possible. Taking care of her, honoring her wishes, was one of the few ways I had left to show her respect. I knew I needed to drive to Oh Holy Mountain right away and do what she wanted: scatter her ashes near Phil's tomb, near the ocean, in the place that felt like home to her, even if it was anathema to me.

But when I turned on my left blinker to head to the highway, I was shaking again. The smell of the mortician's shampoo, the same Kevin used, lingered in my nose. I wanted to obliterate myself and my thoughts, and I knew one really easy way to do that. I knew the biker bars that sold. One was less than a mile away.

I pulled over and ground the point of the car key into my palm of my hand until I was distracted again from the craving that hung at the back of my throat. Distracted from the box of ashes, the newspaper about Julia folded on my bookshelf back home, Jorge and Socorro's car turning onto Ralston, rain penetrating the shipwreck shack, the backfire of my father's motorcycle, Eduardo's silence. I arched my neck and pushed back on the headrest, howling, my eyes squeezed shut.

To make it to OHM, I'd need a hit of something. I had an ATM card in my wallet and all the money I'd saved from my Trove paychecks, waiting in my account.

I grabbed the box of ashes and clutched it to my chest like I was fighting for possession, tears on the cardboard making a Pollack painting, letting a little of the pressure out of my head. What if I didn't go? What if I drove to the movies or Bodega Bay and left my mother in her box on the passenger seat and took her later? Later, when the idea of crossing the cattle grate into the commune didn't make me feel like undoing all the good of the last year?

I drove to the United Artists theater and watched *True Lies* with a Nebuchadnezzar-size popcorn and an extra large root beer and when I got out, my lips and hand were aching, bloody, bruised, but the jones was gone. I drove my mother home and put her on the bookshelf on top of the newspaper article, next to Thomas Hardy's *Tess*, all of them on the way to somewhere else when the time was right.

Chapter 26

The summer I was twenty, we got a new regular at the café. He'd been a year ahead of me in school and traveled in the popular, jock circle: Kevin Mitchell. I remembered him because his brother, David, got a football scholarship to USC. Not like I cared, but this was the one thing about Kevin Mitchell that everyone knew.

Kevin had been a big-deal quarterback himself. If he'd not been sibling to Orchard's football god he'd be remembered in his own right, but he didn't throw for three 12-0 seasons; never took the team farther than sectionals, and because he was standing, staring at me across the café counter pretty much every afternoon, I guessed he was not playing college football either. Unless he was at the junior college, I doubted Kevin Mitchell was in school at all.

It took him a few days before he said, "Did you go to Orchard?"

I was steaming milk, and pretended to concentrate on this while looking at my reflection in the chrome of the espresso maker. My black hair fell past my shoulders. I was maybe too pale, but my eyes were large, fringed with dark lashes. I wore a men's v-neck t-shirt bunched up in the back with a rubber band to make it fit. Even in this slightly warped mirror, I thought it possible Kevin Mitchell could think I was pretty.

"For a while," I said.

He nodded, waited a beat, then said, "Remember me?"

I looked up. There was tenseness about his shoulders that said no matter the truth, the right answer was yes.

"Sure I do." I went to say that he was the brother of David Mitchell, but I caught myself. He was probably sick of hearing it; I would have been.

"You played on the team?" I said. "Kevin, right?"

"Football, although I did play a little basketball freshman year," he answered, digging change out of his jeans pocket, ninety-five cents for the coffee and four quarters in the tip jar. He had olive green eyes, light copper hair and a mass of freckles on retreat.

"What's your name again?"

Without a thought, it came right out. "Cindy."

"You got expelled for drugs, right?"

So much for Cindy.

"That was fucked up," he said.

"Not really. I had joints in my locker; I was planning to sell them to a seventh grader."

I waited for a twitch of disgust, but it didn't come.

"They call me Cin, by the way," I finished.

He rubbed his hands on the sides of his jeans and stuck his left out to shake mine.

"Nice to meet you again, Cin," he said.

"Right," I said, feeling the evidence of who he was still in his grip.

There were other regulars, men who worked construction for the county who hung over the counter, told me they liked my smile, and tossed coins in the tip jar, but I was never sad when any of them left. With Kevin, it was different. I began to look forward to his usual four o'clock visit, an hour before closing, when the place was empty and I was dying to leave. At 3:45 I'd start a fresh pot of coffee to pour just his one cup. While it brewed, I'd lean on the counter in anticipation of seeing Kevin pull up in the green Ford truck with "Mitchell and Sons" in red italic script on the door.

He always came alone, and each day his visit lasted longer. The first week he'd gotten his coffee and left right away; for a few days after he introduced himself he'd taken his coffee to-go but sat at the tables, lingering with the paper. Now he read the sports page first, then the front section, his coffee in a cup and saucer.

"Hey, listen to this," he said one day.

With a caffeine perk going, Kevin read me the headlines.

"Local Possum Has Its Way with Widow's Garbage," he read in

newscaster basso profundo, and I laughed, my hand flying to my mouth to stifle it.

Over the next few weeks Kevin came in every day, ordered his large black drip, and tried hard to crack me up, prying my laughter loose by reading me the paper, telling me stories about Orchard and regular, silly jokes while I bussed tables and wiped down the counter to end the day. He left about five minutes before close, turning left out of the parking lot while I shut off the machines and gathered my things.

And then, one day, Kevin stuck around. He held the door open, motioned I should go first, and then as I found the right key for the deadbolt, he stood behind me. The deadbolt hit the strike plate and I jiggled the lock.

"You still party?" he whisper-asked in my ear.

I shivered. A good shiver or a bad shiver, I wasn't sure. In the weeks he'd been coming to the café, he was never mean like Chad, or distant like Alex. He tipped me, never let me bus his table, the closest thing to chivalry I'd experienced outside my childhood bookshelf. He could make me laugh. I didn't laugh much sober anymore.

"I do," I said and twisted my wrist so the bolt slid home.

"Do you guys remember Kevin Mitchell?" I asked. We sat around a box of donut holes. Chad held a fifth of Safeway-brand gin and was making a dinner of the sugary puffs and swigs from the bottle.

"The dude that played for USC?" said Tori.

"No, that was his brother."

"I remember him," said Alex.

"He's a big speeder," said Chad.

"Like traffic school?" said Tori, taking a swig from the bottle.

Chad rapped Tori with his knuckles and fell to his side, laughing, spewing gin-moistened crumbs on the carpet. "Crank, you airhead. He makes it himself, but doesn't sell it, the fuckhead. He could make beaucoup."

"He gets his coffee where I work," I said. "I invited him here to-night."

He showed, too, bringing two six-packs of Miller Lite. He and Chad talked for a while on the futon about sports and Orchard High and what his brother David was doing now. Chad asked a lot of questions and Kevin answered them rapid fire. He would, every few minutes, turn and spot me, although I'd not moved from the carpet near where they talked. I held my knees into my chest. We'd not scored any coke that night, and I didn't feel like getting stoned and eating another half gallon of ice cream. I couldn't remember the last night I'd not ingested something, but that night I drank in Kevin. This boy, this good boy, had come here to see me.

Around eleven, Kevin stood up and walked out the door without saying goodbye, leaving his beers behind.

"That dude is so shittin' lucky," Chad said, popping one open. "His parents are loaded. He lives for free on some land they own up off Dry Creek and works like never. He sat at the fifty yard line at the Rose Bowl last year."

"I think he's into you," Tori said to me.

I shrugged my shoulders thinking, we'll see, I hope so, but Kevin Mitchell didn't come back that night or come to the café for the rest of the week, which made going home to Chad and Tori snoring on my futon even less tolerable than it already was.

A week later, when I'd begun to give up hope he'd return, I saw the green Ford pull into the parking lot at his usual time. I poured him his large drip and set it out on the counter.

He wóre a Mitchell Landscaping baseball hat that hid his eyes.

"For me?" he said, motioning to the coffee.

I forced my voice to be light. "No, for the guy behind you."

Kevin put 95¢ in my palm and a paper dollar in the tip jar and went to look at the sports page, which I'd left for him like an offering at the table closest to the register. After he got his coffee in him, he came back to the counter where I cleaned, and began an imitation of Mr. Danvers. The assistant principal who'd expelled me was also the varsity football coach at Orchard who often reacted to a ref's bad call by throwing down his clipboard and stomping on it. When I rewarded

Kevin's antics with laughter, lights danced in his eyes.

When the Danvers mimicry ran out, Kevin leaned against the counter and asked with no transition, "You think about college?"

"I haven't even got my GED."

Kevin was the first person in my life who acted like this was positive, a relief.

"Don't bother. I tried the JC," he said. "Losers."

"What do you do now?" I asked.

"Hang out, work a little for my dad." He shrugged, a percentage of cocky in his movement.

"Why'd you leave the other night without saying goodbye?" I asked.

His smile disappeared.

"Oh, that. I got a little wigged."

"Why?"

"I don't do so great, you know, with people," he said. "Everyone wants to talk about David."

"Chad's annoying," I said.

"It's not just Chad," he said. "It's everyone."

"Come over again tonight?" I asked.

"I'm kinda done with people parties."

I thought of the mess that was waiting back at the apartment. I'd seen vomit in the bathroom wastebasket this morning, and I knew it would still be there when I got home. Tori coming by to borrow clothes I'd never see again; Chad drumming his fingers on the table while I called around to score for us; the pieces of demolition equipment that were massing in the parking lot of the building.

"I know what you mean," I said.

Kevin lived in a doublewide trailer on the land where Mitchell and Sons had greenhouses and stored their machinery. The trailer had white lattice covering the gap between itself and the dirt. Inside, it looked like his mom had decorated years ago but hadn't been back since. There were peach and blue throw pillows on the sofa with burn holes in them, an empty but spotless fridge, florescent lights.

I sat at the dinette table studying the contents of my near-empty purse while Kevin showered and changed. His hair was damp and stuck to the hollows of his skull. His breath smelled of mint. The setting sun filtered through the metal blinds and made parallel lines on the trailer's calico-colored carpet. Kevin offered me a Miller Lite. He popped the top and I took a sip—the coolness filling my throat.

I thought of the little group back at my place waiting for me to show up so I could buy the evening's entertainment. I liked the idea of them sitting there, eating through the last bag of chips, their surprise when I didn't show. I was with Kevin Mitchell, who was too good to hang out with them.

Kevin sat to my right at the dinette. I noticed his eyes jiggled in their sockets. It was creepy and I was trying hard to ignore it.

"Are my eyes moving?" he said.

"A little."

"I know it's gross; I can't help it when I'm nervous."

"It's okay," I said. "I understand."

Kevin darted his head forward and kissed me. He hit the table with his ribs and his bony cheek smashed mine, but the beer was in me and I knew at that moment that kiss was the best Kevin could give and more honest than a thousand kisses from Matthew or Chad. Kevin moved next to me on the carpet. On his knees he was the right height to kiss me while I sat, although I had to twist toward him from the table. We made out like this, taking breaks to chug beer.

"My knees hurt," he said as an invitation to the couch.

After a while, I pulled my sweater over my head and Kevin drew back and looked at me. His eyes had stopped vibrating.

"You're so pretty, Cin," he said. He stroked my neck where the artery ran from my chin to my collarbone and touched the ratty edge of my black cotton camisole. I was floating in beer dreamland, his fingers nice against my skin. Then he pulled my arm straight and studied it in a way that brought my attention back.

"Your skin, it's like something in a museum."

I looked at what he saw and, in the fading evening light, the interior bend in my elbow looked alabaster, perfect.

"Not even a freckle," he placed kisses back up my arm, moving the strap of my camisole so he didn't miss a spot.

Since that day against the house with Matthew, I'd fucked more times than I could remember. But never sober. A couple Miller Lites was not enough to get the job done.

"I need another beer," I said.

"I know something better," he answered.

On the coffee table he put out a rubber strap, a Ziploc of tiny syringes, and a baby-food jar, the label long washed away, filled with clear, sparkly liquid.

He drew some of the dissolved crystals into a syringe and undid the cuff of his long-sleeve shirt. He had a cluster of half-healed punctures around his elbow.

"Kevin," I said.

He looked at me. "Of course, you first."

"No," I said, the effect of the beer gone.

"But you said you liked to party."

"Not needles."

"It's faster," he said.

I had no interest in needles. The people who used them were dirty. I might be a loser, but I wasn't dirty. I clenched my wrists and elbows to my chest.

I could tell I'd hurt his feelings. But he shrugged it off and went to the kitchen cabinets and brought over a little bag of powder.

"Speed with me," he said, handing me a twenty.

I took a bump of crank on the bottom knuckle of my thumb and snorted it without the help of Andrew Jackson. Like it had burning, jagged edges, the powder scorched the inside of my nose and singed the sinus behind my left eye. I applied pressure until the pain subsided. Then I sat back with my beer and watched Kevin perform his injection. He pulled the rubber tourniquet tight with his teeth, drawing sparkle into the petite syringe. He found a healed spot, pushed the needle in, and pulled the plunger back. His blood mixed with liquid meth, then on a slow exhale, he pushed it all into his vein. I blinked and the light in the trailer got brighter, all the outlines of things were sharper, like my eyes had been made perfect, I'd been made perfect. Then Kevin was beside me, I climbed on his lap. All of the awkwardness of before gave way to understanding; being near Kevin was not enough, to experience him all of my skin had to be on all of his skin. I would have to be inside. He swung me around and we twirled in a glitter circus.

The next time I saw the clock, bright blue digits on a black background, it was three am. We'd been awake the whole time. I knew I should be sore, but I didn't feel it. Kevin was pulling the hose tight again while I found the baggie and took another bump. When the sun rose, we ran through the fields around the doublewide, naked, shrieking. We tried to climb a eucalyptus, shredding the bark as we scrambled up. I could see the red scrape marks on my legs, but I couldn't feel them.

Along the side of one of the greenhouses, a row of Meyer lemon trees grew, interspersed with tall, big-leafed plants.

"What are those?" I asked.

"Banana trees."

"Right next to the lemons?" I asked.

"They don't fruit up here," Kevin said. "Too far north."

"You should never put bananas and citrus together," I said, remembering Socorro's advice. "They'll ruin each other."

Kevin found a baseball bat and picked ripe lemons off the tree to pitch to me. Fueled by the meth, I knocked them over an ancient split-rail fence. The property on the other side was filled with gnarled vines, bent over like monks at prayer.

"What are those?" I asked, pointing.

"Vineyard," Kevin said. "Some rich guy bought the land. Gonna make wine again."

"Doesn't look alive," I said.

"Wait until spring," Kevin said. "They'll green up."

I smiled because Kevin had mentioned spring, a half year away, like we'd still be together then.

"Run the bases, Cin," Kevin said, readying his next pitch.

On his next pitch I connected, the lemon breaking apart in the air, seeds and pulp flying, and I started to run. When I turned back to look, Kevin was on the ground. I must have thrown the bat and hit him with it.

I ran to where he lay in the dust, shaking, I thought in great pain, but when I turned him over he was laughing. A flap of skin was ripped off his shoulder and his blood spilled into the dust.

"Yes, we have no bananas," he sang. "We have no bananas today!"

Somewhere in my head I knew I should be helping him back to the trailer and bandaging him up, but Kevin knew all the lyrics to the bananas song and I sang with him until we had to stop to breathe.

"I've heard there are a ton of caves that run under the vineyard, wine caves," he said, motioning toward the fence. "We should go and check them out."

I sat up, game for the adventure.

But Kevin shook his head. "'Nother time. Let's go back and clean," he said, scratching at his forearm.

"Clean what?"

For the next three hours Kevin vacuumed, scrubbed, and polished the trailer. He dusted the inside of the cabinets, unscrewed the hardware in the bathroom shower and cleaned the tile underneath with a toothbrush.

"It gets dirty under here and I'm the only one that knows how to fix it," he said, to no one in particular, but I heard it as I leaned against the doorframe watching him work. In the kitchen, I turned on the radio. Frankie Goes to Hollywood bounced from the walls, and I thought it strange the radio had been silent. At my place we always had music on while we partied. I danced a little, but my high was leaving and when I asked Kevin for more, he yelled at me to leave him alone. He was bleeding from the back of his leg and scrubbing at the linoleum. I crawled into his bed and slept.

I woke to pitch black; the clock said five am. I stumbled out to the living room and turned on the TV. It was the Tuesday morning news. I'd gotten to Kevin's Saturday night. I'd missed my entire Monday shift at the café. I called Ray and told him I'd gotten the stomach flu so bad that this was the first time I'd been able to call.

"That's unlike you, Cinnamon," he said.

He was annoyed, I could tell, but I didn't have to fake feeling sick. After forty-eight hours on meth with nothing else in my system but Miller Lites, I felt terrible.

"Do you need us to come by and check on you?" Ray asked.

I paused then answered, "That's okay, I've got a . . . a friend."

I'd never told Ray about anyone. Not Chad or Tori. But I wanted to tell him all about Kevin.

"Good, good," he said. "Get better soon. I'll try to keep things running till you get back."

I hung up and went back to the bedroom. Kevin was still asleep. His back was to me and I could count each rib that laddered down from his broad shoulders. I curled up next to him and drifted off.

When I woke again it was afternoon. I went to give Kevin a kiss and he pushed me away so hard that I tumbled out of bed onto the floor. I dressed, now feeling sore and bruised all over. My mouth was dry and I was hungry. I drank from the kitchen faucet, opened and considered the empty fridge. I was afraid to wake Kevin again; he'd shoved me hard for bothering him. If I wanted something to eat I would have to leave.

I came through my own front door to "Where the fuck are you!?!?!" scribbled on my wall in black marker; piles of Burger King wrappers and half a smashed hamburger bun on the table; a rotten banana ground into the futon; nowhere to be comfortable. I cut the molded sides off a block of cheddar and nibbled on the bit that was left. Its texture was rubber in my mouth. As the meth dropped out of my system, I felt ten times worse than any of my post-pot pity parties. I lay on the floor with my blanket and pillow, wishing I'd never been born.

I woke from a dream of my father. He was offering me a jar of vitamins, yellow ones, and I took a handful. Before I could swallow them, I woke up. I scrounged change from my car and went to the Valley Sun Grocery where I knew my dad liked to buy tinctures and supplements.

"You feeling worn down?" the man behind the counter asked.

I nodded. The world was too bleak for speech.

He measured a few capsules on his scale and slid them into a brown paper bag.

"B Complex'll getcha back on your feet."

"Do you have any yellow ones?" I managed. The man pulled at his beard then shook his head. I swallowed what I was given and went into work.

Kevin came to the café again Thursday. I said hello, sober now and mad that he'd yelled at me, shoved me away, and then not called for three days. When I didn't answer his banter like usual he left his coffee unfinished and drove off without saying goodbye. He didn't come back the next day or the one after.

I hid from Chad and Tori by going to a double feature every night that week after work. Come Saturday, I felt a lot better. I'd not had anything, not even beer, since Kevin's, and it was the cleanest I'd been since my counseling at St. Jerome's. Chad wrote some more choice phrases on my walls, but he and Tori didn't stick around if there wasn't going to be a free party, so I could sleep there unmolested, in the abandoned apartment complex.

As the week went by, I found not only did I not miss the stoner gang, the thought of them, the idea of spending an evening with them, was repugnant. Who I missed was Kevin. I must have looked up twenty times an hour every afternoon, hoping to see his truck pulling into the parking lot.

Ray asked that I drive the books out to Guerneville after close on Saturday. He came out on his porch when he heard my car pull up.

He looked exhausted, but asked how I was. I told him about my apartment being up for demolition, that I would need a raise to afford a new place.

"Randall's really sick, Cinnamon," he said. "We may have to sell the café to cover his bills. But don't worry, we'll make you part of the package or we'll find you something else."

He hugged me and I let him until Randall called for him and Ray went inside.

In my usually empty mailbox I found a final notice of eviction. I had thirty days to get out. I got into my car and started driving.

I made it halfway to OHM, pulled over in Cloverdale and called my mom from the payphone.

"My building's getting torn down," I said when she came on the line. "And I think I might lose my job." I heard her take a sip of something.

"What steps have you taken to find a new place?" she asked.

"Steps?" I said. "What do you mean by steps?"

"The things you do to find a new place to live."

"What do you do when you have to find a new place to live? I'm so tired, Mom, I know I should be fine on my own, but I'm not."

"You are almost twenty years old, Cinnamon. When I was nineteen I was a mother. Do you think I had a book of directions? Later you'll look back on what you've accomplished and be proud of your struggle," she said.

"What are you proud of?" I asked.

"What I accomplish on earth doesn't matter," my mother said.

I drove back to my apartment and saw the light on in my place when I knew I'd turned it off. Chad. I couldn't bear him any longer. Cold as it was, I slept in my car.

Chapter 27

Since moving into my cottage at Trove, I'd collected books like a bleeding heart collects stray dogs. I gathered them at flea markets, library book sales, and my best find: a box of the collected works of Dickens on the side of the road in a cardboard box. In addition to Dickens, Austen, and the Brontës, I was working on Chekhov and Cather. If I read something and liked it, I found it a spot on my floor-to-ceiling bookshelf. If not, I'd trade it in at the used bookstore for another candidate for my forever library.

I found furniture this way, too. My Queen Anne chair had been half into the ditch on Dry Creek Road, the upholstery soggy and worn. I slip-covered it in a pale yellow denim. The combination of beauty and frivolity delighted me each time I opened my front door. I sat in that chair and read from dinner until bed or entire weekend afternoons, my feet tucked under me, transported by imagination and typography to somewhere else, to a place where orphan children found protectors, opium stood in for meth, and plucky, honest heroines were rewarded.

But one Saturday afternoon, before I had a chance to get settled in my yellow chair, the phone rang.

"Cinnamon, it's Julia."

"Who?" I said, although I'd heard her fine.

"Your cousin," she said, "remember me?"

I dropped my book and set my bare feet on the floor, so shocked I considered hanging up.

"How did you get this number?" I asked. The wrong thing to say.

"Look, I'm in Healdsburg. I wondered if I could stop by."

I couldn't bear to be in the company of Julia. Even if she said nothing, her perfect presence would be judgment enough.

"When?"

"How about now?"

How about never, I thought, but I couldn't come up with an excuse so I gave Julia directions to Trove which she wrote down with what I could tell was a really sharp pencil.

I hung up and raced around, pulling what I hoped was the cottage's shabby-chic together. Beside the Queen Anne chair and half-full bookcase in the living room, I had an oval coffee table that I'd bought at the Salvation Army and painted a creamy yellow to better squire my chair, a sturdy pine table and three somewhat uncomfortable blue chairs in the kitchen nook. In my bedroom, just the mattress and a second-hand rabbit-ears TV.

I put some molding wax into my hair, which had made its comeback halfway to my shoulders, and pinned the right side back to hide my scar with two purple babydoll barrettes. I shrugged a long-sleeved lavender sweater over my faded jeans and remained barefoot.

There was the crunch of gravel outside, then footfalls, then a knock. I went to the door, my hands deep in my pockets. I really, really didn't want to open up.

She was the beautiful Julia of my grandmother's fantasy—the last five years had only honed her. Tall and slender, her long, thick hair was the color of august wheat. She wore a pale blue pantsuit with a silk shell underneath. There was a tiny silver sports car in my driveway.

Before she crossed the threshold, Julia handed me a bunch of tulips that matched my sweater.

"I'm so sorry about your mother."

"Thanks," I said, turning my back to her. I didn't want to hug her, but shaking her hand was too formal, too adult. Taking the flowers and walking away had provided decent cover for an awkward moment. I pulled a vase from the cupboard and shook the tulips into a droopy arrangement.

Julia stood just inside my open doorway with a hopeful look on her face.

"You can come in."

"These cottages," she said stepping inside, motioning at the white-washed beams in the slanted roof, the view out the picture window.

"What were they?"

"Migrant shacks."

I waited for her nose to go in the air.

"I love it," she said. "I'll bet Sunday Styles would do a story."

I doubted she was being honest, probably just another superficial comment from a superficial girl. I thought to say so, but I hesitated. Her left thumb and forefinger rubbed the fabric of her slacks hard. She'd had that same habit forever. My cousin was nervous.

"The last thing I want is to be in the newspaper," I said. Her job was getting people into the newspaper and she'd just been in it herself.

"Well, I'll be going," she said. "I wanted to tell you in person how sorry I was about your mom."

I didn't answer. My brain, so much better since I'd been at Napa Meadows, had been knocked haywire by this visit. Words and feelings stampeded through my mind and I didn't know which ones to lasso. The damage that the meth and Kevin's boot had done to my skull wasn't fully healed, or maybe even if I'd been straight all my life, Julia's unexpected visit would have still had my brain buzzing. I'd never know.

I walked behind her toward the door, already knowing that I would feel awful as her car drove out of sight. If I didn't want that achy-empty sensation after she left, I'd have to find a way to salvage this visit.

Julia was halfway to her car when I called her name.

She turned, her sunglasses already on. Although she was taller, younger, wearing pearls instead of diamonds, Julia's flawlessness sent a shiver of Elaine Pierpoint through me.

I thought about my books. What would my heroines do in this kind of situation?

"Would you like some tea?" I asked.

She stood, forehead scrunched, her keys in hand. "If it's no trouble," she said.

"None at all."

Back in the cottage, the kettle on, I sat on the counter, then raised myself up to standing to take down mugs from the cupboard's highest shelf. Julia watched me from one of the kitchen chairs.

"What brings you up here?" I asked.

"I came to see you."

"You drove an hour to see your lousy cousin who never calls or writes?"

"Yes," she said.

We were quiet again, but with less awkwardness this time.

"Have you been to see Grandmother?" she asked.

"I tried, but the security guard wouldn't let me in." That wasn't a complete lie. "I signed something so now I can go and see her. You?"

"I signed it also. They let me, but the guard stood outside the room while I was there. It was creepy. That place your mom lived at is somehow in charge."

"Yeah," I said. "They're like that."

I handed Julia a mug of Darjeeling and offered her an ice cube to cool it down. She didn't want one, but I put two in my mug.

"I'm sorry about your bad time," Julia said.

My defenses deployed. So this was what this visit was about: bestowing pity on the less fortunate.

"No big deal," I said, flicking a packet of sugar I held in one hand with the index finger of the other.

"I think a year in rehab is a big deal," she said leaning forward.

"Is this why you came here? To rub that in my face?" I asked, pretending to be fascinated with the noise I made flicking the packet.

The old Julia, the Julia from the weekends in the red toile room, would have recoiled or oozed tears. I could see her arm moving, her thumb rubbing against her thigh, but her face was serene.

"No. I came here because we are family and were, at one point, friends. I owed you my condolences and an apology for not coming sooner."

I didn't answer, but scowled.

"Look, Cinnamon, with Grandmother and us it was zero sum. To love me more, she had to love you less. But now we're grown-ups, I want us to start over."

"I'm a pretty reliable fuck-up," I said. "You might be wasting your time."

"What makes you think I'm not some mess myself?"

"Because of the way you look and the way you act and the way you live."

Julia reached out and took my wine-stained, fingernails-to-the-quick hand in her manicured one.

"Cinnamon," she said. "Listen to me."

And I did.

"I'm so terribly sorry about your hard time," she said.

The first tear that had ever spilled over the edge of my eyes in the company of Julia—I'd prided myself that she was the crybaby and I was the strong one—ran in the hollow between my nose and cheek. I wiped it aside.

"I heard you almost died," she said.

I wanted to deny this to her, to keep her at a little bit of a distance, to say the whole thing had not been such a big deal. But this was our chance, like she'd said, to start over.

"The doctors said so. I don't remember."

"What happened to the guy? The one who . . . the one you lived with?"

"The police wanted me to press charges against him, but I wouldn't. I went to his parent's house, I was hoping he'd be there, maybe even be better himself, but his mom didn't know where he was. It's like he vanished."

"What do you think happened?" Julia asked.

I had only thought about this, not believed it, but as I voiced my suspicions to Julia, I knew it was true.

"We, or he anyway, had this yellow motorcycle. We used to ride that bike up above Dry Creek Valley across ravine bridges, along narrow roads on the edges of cliffs. I think he drove up there out of his mind on crank, found the right wooded ravine, and hit the accelerator."

As I told Julia this, I could see a hiker finding the mangled bike and Kevin's bones in the woods. Like I'd already seen it on the news and was just remembering.

She said nothing, but nodded her head.

I went to the bathroom and rinsed my eyes with cold water. When I returned, Julia made light conversation about how my cottage had given her some ideas of how to brighten up her dark apartment. I was thankful for the distraction so that I could stop thinking about what might have happened to Kevin and the frightening idea that Julia was back in my life and the possibility that I had been wrong about her.

"How about your mom?" I asked.

"Married to lucky number seven and living in Vegas," she said.

"Your Dad?"

"For better or worse, the vow of silence has taken."

"What about the guy from college, the one whose family is going to reopen the hotel?"

"Parveen?" I saw her mind clicking until she determined I had to have read the article about her. How else would I have known? She smiled, I'd just proven I cared, if only a little.

"He tracked me down at school. His family already owned the property and he was curious to meet me."

"We dated a while," she added.

Julia had dated an Indian guy. I hoped there was not quite enough room for Frank Ferguson to roll over comfortably in his grave. "What happened?"

"It's a long story, maybe something better told over drinks—" she paused and blushed, probably thinking she shouldn't mention any controlled substance in my presence, but regained her air of calm. "But I suppose the most important piece is that his parents don't approve."

"Of you? Of the beautiful, talented Julia Pierpoint?"

"Of the non-Indian, white Julia Pierpoint, yes, they didn't approve, and it would break Parveen's heart to go against them. So I made it easy on the both of us and broke it off. And now," Julia paused, "we're friends, or at least I'm his employee."

Julia gathered up her things and I walked her out to her car.

"What about you," she said. "Any guy?"

I glanced reflexively at Eduardo's cottage to see if his truck was parked in the shade. It was not. "No, no guy," I said.

Chapter 28

It took two weeks, but Kevin returned to the cafe. There was a line of wine tasters ordering their end-of-day cappuccinos when he came in. He pulled a cup off the stack, poured his own drip and put money on the counter and in the tip jar. He read the newspaper as I rang up sales and foamed milk.

The crowd thinned, leaving their coffee rubble behind and I began to bus, moving back and forth between the tables and the counter. I saw there was a twenty in the jar. It couldn't have been the tourists. They dropped pennies and nickels in, if anything at all. I took the twenty out and stuffed it in the pocket of my jeans. Widening my circles with each trip, I approached his table.

"Hi," I said.

He looked up from under the Mitchell & Sons cap.

"Hey," he said.

I took the tray of dirty cups and mocha-foamed saucers to the kitchen. When I came back, his spot was empty; he'd gone and was out in front of the building, studying the For Lease sign in the window. After he read it, he continued toward his truck.

I watched him go, a stained dishrag in my hand. I felt my hope, the last bit of essence that kept me alive, evaporating. What if he never came back?

I watched him unlock his door, climb in, sit there.

"Please, please, please," I begged the empty air of the café.

He got out of the truck. I flew out the front door to meet him halfway.

"Why did you stay away?" I asked, my face buried in his sweatshirt. "Why for so long?"

"The way you looked at me when I came in that day."

"You yelled at me, Kevin. You shoved me on the floor."

"I don't remember," he said. "But if I did that then I'm horrible."

"Everything's wrong. They're tearing down my building, my mother won't help, my grandmother's disowned me, my friends aren't my friends, my dad is gone, they're closing the café, and everything is just the same big, fucking, falling-apart mess."

Kevin smoothed my hair and kept me pulled in close to him.

"Do you believe I can make things better for you?" he asked.

I nodded into his chest.

"I don't think I can," he said.

"You're the only one."

I followed him to his place. He parked my car in one of the hangar-sized garage bays and then he drove me back to my apartment. The resolve of Kevin's hand when he shifted gears made me want to sign my soul over to him.

Chad sat on my futon playing Atari. "Where the fuck are you going?" he said when Kevin passed him with a dresser drawer filled with my clothes and I followed with a duffel that held everything else I wanted from that place.

"Say bye to everyone for me," I answered, not bothering to close the door behind me.

Kevin was right about the injection hitting faster than the powder. Before he'd even fully pushed the needle into my virgin vein, my universe hit the reset button and the windshield of my mind wiped clear. We went to bed again and time passed like before, our bodies wrapped around each other, spinning in and out of consciousness, digital hours falling off the clock.

In another life Kevin would have made a great nurse. There was something reverent, sacred, about how Kevin injected me. He worked by candlelight—using a taper to liquefy the meth—and he treated my veins with perfect respect and duty. He'd throw me up before he did himself so the job would be perfect. Even the initial prick didn't hurt because I'd had a beer or two while Kevin got our date night ready on the coffee table. I loved watching the beauty of a little of my blood coming into the clear syringe, red tendrils mixing with his pure crystal and Kevin's restraint as he plunged the pink liquid back inside me. His doses screwed off the top of my head, took out my tangled neurons and combed them silky and straight. I was never tired or confused! My parents had done the very best they could! I had limitless potential!

I was in love.

Kevin worked methodically on my arms, starting from the elbow and working up and down in equal measure, alternating left and right so that the veins had time to heal up before he entered them again.

"If I'm careful, your arms will last five years," Kevin said, making another tiny puncture in perfect symmetry.

In five years, I'd be twenty-five. By that time we'd never have to abandon my arms and go to the next spot, a spot I couldn't cover—like my hands or neck—we'd be cleaned up. I'd get my diploma and convince Kevin that the junior college was not for losers. People got tired of partying and they grew up. But for now, I lived in the trailer, the warmest, cleanest home I'd ever had, with Kevin, to whom I was precious.

Although he didn't work a regular schedule for his dad, Kevin was expected to come in a few days a week, order fertilizer, walk a new job site, at least pretend he was learning the business. For this he'd sober up and in solidarity with him, I'd be clean those days, too. My favorite part about Kevin being sober was he got hungry and I loved to feed him. He'd eat my beef tenderloin, bowls of roasted potatoes, chocolate cake, making up for the days when he wouldn't eat a thing. We'd rent movies and watch them from the pastel couch. Those sober days were for me the good life, but for Kevin it was just a passing state, something necessary to keep up the ruse of being a Mitchell boy. When he got back from hauling pool filters or spreading mulch, he would, sometimes even before he kissed me hello, head to the kitchen cabinet for his paraphernalia. And if he pushed the button, I would annihilate myself, too.

In the landscaping business of the early 1990s, Kevin had access to every noxious chemical he needed to make the cleanest crank north of Modesto. He told his father he was working on a new kind of fertilizer concentrate and kept the beakers and tubes in one of the garage bays spotless. He made enough for us and would sell a little to his friend at the hospital who got us our supplies. His dad gave him a salary that covered most everything, but if we needed more he could make one or two calls and have rolls of twenties by the end of the afternoon. The meth dealers he knew sold the crap they got from Mexico and used what Kevin made.

Anything I asked for, Kevin got. Christmas came and he brought me a tree, my first real tree that smelled of pine and grazed the ceiling of the trailer. He let me fill a bag with ornaments at Macy's and we strung lights together, drinking cocoa and listening to the radio on a stormy Christmas Eve.

Rain pounded on the trailer's roof when we were done, but as we sat admiring our work, I could not see a leak or feel a draft. "Let's sleep out here tonight," I said.

In the morning I opened boxes of lingerie, a light green cashmere sweater, a bottle of Paris perfume. And I put it all on at once: the nightie, the cardigan, the scent, and danced to the Waltz of the Sugarplum Fairies that flowed from the radio.

All this made Kevin happy.

That afternoon, though, he left me at the trailer with a rental of *It's a Wonderful Life* and went to visit his parents without asking me to come. The previous night and through the morning I had been satisfied. But, although I tried to tell myself not to be greedy, I wanted what money couldn't buy: to meet Kevin's parents, to be a real girlfriend.

"We'll go to dinner there sometime," he'd said when he came back that night, a new red scarf around his neck, but three, six, nine months later it had yet to happen, and when his dad stopped by to give Kevin a schedule or check the seedlings, they talked outside and I waited in the trailer, silent, watching like a junkie Grace Kelly in *High Noon*.

"If I brought you home," Kevin said one afternoon when I'd been pestering him, "it would make my mother cry."

Kevin had convinced his parents he needed some time off before college or taking over the business. He said his mom called it "getting his ya-yas out" and his dad said he'd wished he'd had a few more years of freedom before he'd gotten married and taken over Mitchell and Sons. Kevin's brother, David, had graduated from USC, gone to law school, gotten married, and produced adorable twin girls for them to grandparent. This let Kevin off the hook in terms of growing up. So far, as long as Kevin showed up for the little work they requested and dropped by with flowers for his mom on holidays, Kevin's parents didn't ask any questions.

David was the only one in the family I'd ever met. After another Sunday dinner I'd not been invited to, and Kevin had to attend because David was in town, his brother followed him back out to the land.

"Let me in, Kev," David said, nice at first then pounding at the trailer door while Kevin and I sat on the couch, the TV on mute, pretending not to be there.

"You're going to break it," Kevin shouted, finally opening the door.

David was taller and wider than Kevin; he seemed a giant in the low-ceilinged doublewide.

"What the hell is wrong with you?" he asked. His eyes landed on me. "Who's this?"

"This is Cindy," Kevin swallowed. "She and I hang out."

"Hi," I said from the couch, holding the pillow to my front like I was naked.

David checked the trailer, looking in the bathroom, the bedroom, but everything was, of course, spotless. He didn't think to look in the kitchen cabinets. Who would keep drugs in a kitchen? Kevin followed him out the door as he walked the property looking for something, anything that would explain his little brother's glassy eyes and skinny frame. David searched the greenhouses and found nothing but the seedlings. He looked in the garage and saw the lab.

"What's this?" he asked Kevin. I trailed behind them, listening.

"I'm concentrating fertilizer for the seedlings. Ask Dad. Fuck. Just 'cause I'm not perfect like you doesn't mean something's wrong with me."

David lingered in the garage, and while he'd seen a ton of coke in his days at USC, he was now a family man living in Newport Beach and had no idea what comprised a meth lab or how easy it would be for his brother to construct one.

"Something is up with you, Kev. I'm telling Mom and Dad. They like to pretend they don't know, they may not do shit, but there is definitely something wrong out here."

He climbed back into his car without acknowledging me and backed out the driveway.

"He's gonna tell your dad."

"Don't care," Kevin said.

A month later his father bought Kevin a bright yellow motorcycle for his twenty-third birthday; we rode the roads above the Dry Creek Valley to celebrate, high as drones.

For almost two years, I felt lucky that I'd pierced Kevin's indifference toward people and become the one he wanted to be with. Healdsburg Coffee Café had closed, Ray and Randall had moved back to the city and I'd lost touch with them. The old apartment was torn down and I'd again not left forwarding information with anyone. Other than calls to the OHM payphone where my mother would whisper her problems on one call and then deny them the next, I interacted with no one from my pre-Kevin days. I stayed in the trailer, on the couch, watching shows I'd never seen but were in the lexicon of everyone else my age. For two years my companions were Gilligan, Laverne, Sam, and Diane. I could make an entire day of going into Santa Rosa for a frozen yogurt, a movie, and a refill of birth control pills.

But after I'd caught up on the 70s and 80s via syndication, I could no longer deny that the isolated tweaker life that satisfied Kevin wasn't enough for me. Although I never wanted to see Chad or Tori again, I thought that some of Kevin's friends, especially if they went to the JC or had jobs, might be what we needed. For my birthday, he asked what I wanted.

"A party with other people," I said.

Kevin called up his friend, the one who worked at the hospital, who came by with his girlfriend. They snorted, we shot up and then played Liar's Dice. We had a quarter-sheet cake from Safeway with Happy Birthday on it. I forgot to wish on the candles, leaving the cake intact on the table, because none of us was interested in eating. On her second bump of meth, the girlfriend took a knife and began to cut the cake into tiny squares.

"One hundred pieces?" she asked me, so amped she couldn't sit. "Do you think I can do it?"

When Kevin and I started in on our third dose, his friends, who were potheads at heart, smoked out and went to get groceries. In what seemed like a minute, they were back and she was cooking sausage and omelets on the two-burner. The cooking meat had a stench I couldn't identify and I tiptoed up to the pan. But I didn't see sausage, I saw little gray mice, shriveled up, frying away. I screeched and skittered to the back of the trailer where Kevin had started cleaning. I burst through the bathroom door, to tell him his friends were cooking mice on the stove. Before I was halfway through the doorframe, he'd risen from his hunch over the sink, his hands raw and bleeding from the bleach, and walloped me back out into the hall.

I hit the wall headfirst and slid down. My legs shook, from the impact or the speed, I wasn't sure.

"Fuck, I thought that was an earthquake," said the boy, who'd come running back when the trailer shuddered.

"You okay?" asked his girlfriend.

"You were cooking mice," I said, as if that would explain everything.

"What are you talking about?" the girl said, bringing the pan to show me.

In it were two normal sausages. I'd been hallucinating.

"Want some?" she asked.

When Kevin sobered up, he asked how I'd gotten the black eye and the egg-shaped knot on my head. I told him I tripped and hit the counter and he got ice and held it gently to my face.

"Did you have a good birthday? Did you like your party?" he asked stroking my hair.

I wanted to tell him that he'd given me the bruise and once the drugs came out my birthday hadn't been fun, but I knew from times before when I'd told him about the awful things he'd done to me when he was high, he'd lie on our bed and cry, beg forgiveness, and make promises he didn't keep. I told him I loved my party.

A week later, my face had healed enough for us to go out. We were sitting in a booth at Denny's when Kevin said, "We could get a little house in Santa Rosa; we could go back to school."

I'd mentioned ideas like this a dozen times and Kevin had brushed them aside, annoyed.

"We have a little house," I said carefully.

"We have a trailer. I want you to have a real house."

"If we had that kind of house, you couldn't have your lab," I said.

"It's time to give that up. I've taken advantage of my parents for too long."

When we were first together, he could go a couple of days between highs, but now, even if he was going to meet his dad, he would snort or shoot a little meth in the morning and be back on it the minute he came through the door.

"You don't seem excited," Kevin said.

"I am," I said. "But we've talked about being sober a lot."

Kevin pulled me over to his side of the booth and sat me on his lap. He would have never been able to do that when we first met. I was pot-chubby then, but now I was skinnier than I'd ever been. He pushed a piece of my black hair behind my ear.

"To you, Cinnamon Monday, I solemnly swear: I'm going to make everything up to you."

The sober phase that started that day was the longest one we ever had, but it was less than two weeks before I woke up in the middle of the night, found a syringe on the coffee table and Kevin disassembling the oven.

Chapter 29

After that first visit, Julia called every few days to check in. We talked mostly about our grandmother. They were moving her to a nursing home and we could go visit her together once she was settled. But the personal was slipping into our conversations.

"I don't know why," I told her about Eduardo's coldness.

"Sometimes, we are more than friends," she said about Parveen.

We'd generally talk in the evenings and the nights that she didn't call I began to miss having someone to puzzle through the day with. I started to sometimes call her first.

One evening I'd been working in the caves and came home so hungry that I started eating some chicken salad straight out of the carton. I'd eaten more than half when the phone rang.

"Chronicle, D6," Julia said without a greeting.

I went to my counter and shook loose the food section from the day's unopened newspaper.

"Bottom left," Julia said.

In the City Finds section there was a review of a taqueria in the Mission that served the City's best carnitas and a to-die-for banana-caramel dessert. *Los Tres Amigos* run by Jorge Meza and his wife, Socorro.

"We found her! Let's go right now. Open till ten!"

"Maybe another day," I said, that bit of mayonnaised chicken glop churning in my stomach.

"You're kidding, right? I've never been able to stop thinking about Socorro and I know you haven't either. Give me one good reason why you don't want to go."

I could think of one really good reason, but I was afraid to tell Julia. I agreed to leave in fifteen minutes and pick her up on the way.

On Valencia Street, my Breck girl cousin drew attention. I, with my black wisps of hair and stained shirt and jeans, blended right in. I'd been to the Mission a lot, back when I was in high school. I'd probably bartered drugs right in front of Socorro and Jorge's restaurant and not known it. Los Tres Amigos, quiet now in the post-dinner lull, proclaimed its name in red letters with gold trim on the one spotless window. From that window—I held Julia's wrist so I could look before going in—you could see the kitchen, a long bar for a quick burrito dinner and a few wooden tables for two or four in the way back. Socorro was cleaning the grill and her profile was recognizable, but barely. She was three times the weight she'd been when she worked for my grandmother. Her hair was no longer braided and wrapped in a bun, but instead was short, curly, and highlighted with silver. But the angle of her chin, how she stirred while she cooked, made her unmistakable.

"Come on," Julia said, pulling at me to go inside.

"Miss Cinnamon, Miss Julia?" she exclaimed when she recognized us, yelling for Jorge and rushing out from behind the counter to hug us both.

"Pulgita! Julita!" she said over and over.

Jorge came out of the back room carrying a case of napkins, which he dropped on the floor when he saw us. Before we could protest, Socorro set a huge plate of rice, beans, and her carnitas, with warm pressed tortillas in front of us at the long bar. My nausea from the chicken salad, steady on the drive down, took an upswing; I could only move the good food around on my plate. Julia was digging in, so I managed one bite.

She asked us what we did and where we lived. She gasped when Julia told her she was helping re-open The Pierpoint.

I told her I worked at a winery, but left out all else.

"I'm sorry your grandma is sick," she said, wiping the already clean counter after we told her the story. On a little stand hung a bunch of bananas. Several feet away was a red bowl filled with lemons and limes. On the menu board that ran the length of the kitchen I saw "Bananas con Dulce De Leche." Socorro lifted our glasses of water and wiped again.

"But I cannot forgive, although I pray to God everyday. She treated us bad. After twenty years with her, Jorge and I were living out of our car for a month until he found a job as a dishwasher here. We saved every penny until we could buy the place, and every month that went by that I couldn't send money home to my family, I thought of your grandmother up on the hill with her fur coats and her jewels and this has made my heart hard."

"It was wrong, Socorro; I'm sorry I didn't help you more," Julia said.

"You were little girls," Socorro clucked. "What could you do?"

The one bite of carnitas mixed with the gloppy chicken had begun to fight for possession of my stomach.

"We were fourteen and fifteen, we could have done something," Julia said.

Jorge set up the napkin holders near us and started refilling.

"I'm sorry you had to see that day," Socorro said to us.

With her apology, I ran for the bathroom, but didn't find it and vomited instead in the alley out back. I held to the building's corner and retched onto the already stinking asphalt.

I looked up to see the three of them staring at me.

Julia ran inside to get me a glass of water.

"Our food makes you sick?" asked Jorge.

"No, I make myself sick," I said.

Socorro took her handkerchief from the pocket of her apron and cleaned my face. I thought about that first time when I'd peed on the floor and she'd been called to wipe it up.

"It was me, Socorro, it was me. I stole that diamond. I stole it and let her fire you instead of telling the truth."

Socorro and Jorge looked at me like I was speaking in tongues. Then Jorge shook his head and let out a long, low "No."

Julia arrived with the glass of water.

Socorro folded the handkerchief back into her apron pocket, raised her hand, and slapped me hard. The healing cuts on my lips burst open. I tasted blood. She raised her hand again but Jorge grabbed it and said, "Socorro, no te puedes."

"You're the same as your grandmother," Socorro said to me. "Get out."

"What's going on?" Julia asked, frozen in the doorway.

"Julia didn't know," I said.

"Know what?" Julia looked panicked.

"Out," Socorro said, raising her hand again. I grabbed Julia and made for the door.

When we were back in the car, Julia handed me tissue after tissue as I cleaned my face and hair. She got ice from the corner store, put me in the passenger seat, and began to drive. Then I confessed again.

"I can't believe you didn't tell me."

"I know," I said, resigned. I could see a red, hand-shaped welt was rising on my right cheek in the rearview mirror.

"You're inconsiderate." Julia's tone was sharp. My skin pricked with fear at her tone, but I knew telling the truth was the right thing to do even if no one liked me after.

"Wasn't every minute I was dishonest inconsiderate?" I said.

"You'll say anything to justify your behavior," Julia said. "How could you have done such a revolting thing? And then lied about it? And then told her without even giving me a warning? This was my first chance to see her too, you know."

She drove, trying to cross Market Street in traffic. I wasn't sure I could take being trapped in the car with a hostile Julia for the time it would take to get back to her place in the Marina.

"Why don't I just drop you and you can take a taxi. Then you won't have to ride home with your inconsiderate cousin."

"No, I won't," Julia fumed. "Right now, I don't have enough family to have the luxury of shutting you out."

"Eventually you'll find out enough about me to be permanently disgusted," I said. "Then you'll leave."

Julia pulled over into a red zone and killed the engine.

"I'm not leaving you," she said, turning to me. "I'm not. But can you make loving you a little less costly?"

We glared at each other until I looked away. Julia maneuvered back into traffic. I held the ice to my face in a sea of red lights as the car started the incline of Franklin Street. We crawled past the back side of Davies' Symphony Hall, and the War Memorial Opera House, where as girls we'd climbed the steps in matching velvet coats, each holding one of Elaine's hands, to our seats for the Nutcracker.

"Do you remember that year that Grandmother took me and you didn't come?" Julia said, not sounding angry anymore.

"I remember," I said.

"Well, she didn't tell me you weren't coming until the curtain went up. And then I cried. She took me to the bathroom to get me to stop and we missed Clara's dream, where the tree gets big. Remember? Grandmother told me that blubbering made me ugly. But that just made me blubber more. She was furious. We left before intermission. She never asked me to go again. I was miserable without you there, and I think she was, too."

Chapter 30

There were times our third year together I'd find Kevin standing in the door of the trailer watching a spider spin its October web, or he'd read me the paper and do imitations like he used to back at the café that would still make me laugh, but mostly the drugs made us quieter, less curious. I stopped bothering him to meet his parents or nagging him to be more social. Instead, sitting beside him in the garage lab, I'd watch, with fascination, diamond-like crystals precipitate from the murky brew of red phosphorous, Drano and lye.

That I couldn't tell twilight from dawn was no longer an inconvenience. I never needed to be anywhere, so what did it matter? In the darkness or the light, Kevin would tell me he loved me and I'd answer back, moving my thinning body against his. I think there is a chance we might have died that way: skeletons in love. Then came Tony.

Tony was a speed freak. He'd gone to Orchard, too, in David Mitchell's class, but had moved to Vallejo, been in juvie, then Soledad, and was now out and back in Santa Rosa. Like an English gentleman calling on his new neighbors, he drove up the rutted road to the trailer in his beater Honda, one front light busted out.

Kevin and Tony, once their mutual disgust for Orchard and David's overachieving were established, frightened me with how well they got along because I thought Tony was different from us. He had been shooting up longer and had needle marks that covered his neck, the indents between his fingers, the side of his calves. His gaze never rested and thoughts caterwauled out of his mouth. Tony was out of viable veins and would trapdoor by picking off a scab, injecting at that site, and patting the scab back down again so it could re-adhere.

Tony called me Kevin's old lady. He got two air rifles, one for Kevin and one for himself, and with man-boy excitement, they'd go shoot cans and bottles, then animals.

"It's just crows and jays," Kevin said to me when I begged him to stop, telling him about the bird that swirled in the dust near the trailer, its wing broken by a pellet, for half an hour before it gave up. "They're shit for brains anyway."

"It's Tony who's shit for brains," I said.

"Pot and kettle, old lady," Kevin answered.

On a raw January day, I didn't shoot up because I was sick, trembling with fever.

"You'll be fine," Kevin said, putting me on the couch, covering me with a blanket.

I wanted him to take me to the doctor, but I knew if I asked now, he'd refuse. He and Tony wanted to go ride the yellow motorcycle in the storm.

"Sleep it off," Kevin told me, biting his nails, his eyes wiggling.

"Come on!" Tony yelled from ten feet away. He was jumping, shaking the trailer as much as the wind, impatient for the ride.

They took off into the storm and rain began to pelt the roof. I thought to get up and look for a thermometer, but I had trouble sitting, my breath ragged, fast. When the whine of the motorcycle came close to the trailer, I made my way outside, holding onto the backs of chairs and the door with shaky hands. My calls to Kevin were swallowed by the wind. Tony turned the bike so mud and grit sprayed on me, and they drove off. A surge of adrenaline had me whirling like a dervish trying to get the filth out of my hair and clothes. I made it to the shower, but couldn't get the water warm enough.

Sitting at the bottom of the shower stall, I was sure Tony wanted to kill me. I could picture it. He'd suffocate me with a pillow on the floor behind the bed. Tony would be happy to get rid of me. I was the only thing between him and a lifetime supply of crank, gratis, while his heart raced his kidneys to the reaper's finish line.

I went and got into my car, but it wouldn't start. I'd not left the property on my own in a long time. I crawled into the cab of Kevin's

truck, revved the engine, and drove to the main road. I put my chin against the steering wheel to try and stop my teeth from chattering.

I wondered where to go. The truck's headlights illuminated a windbreak of cypress trees across the road that swayed in the storm. Oleander bushes grew on either side, shielding the vineyards from the exhaust of the roadway. In the headlights, between the bushes and the column of trees, I saw a boy and a girl, my imaginary friends. Although I couldn't make them out, I noticed they'd aged with me, were no longer little. My view of them was obstructed by the wind blowing the oleander bushes back and forth. I blinked. They were still there. I got out of the car.

I had to push against the gale, the icy rain stinging my face. The truck was running behind me, its low beams on. I pulled aside the waving branch of oleander and found nothing. In the time it had taken me to cross to the other side, they'd vanished.

"I'm here, I'm here," I called to the boy and the girl as loud as my aching throat allowed. "Don't leave without me," but no one answered back.

When he sobered up, Kevin bartered speed for antibiotics from his friend at the hospital. I stayed in bed for a week and Kevin cared for me, feeding me soup, giving Tony enough meth to get lost for a while. But once I got better, Tony came back. I lost Kevin's attention and began to dream of suffocation again.

Kevin worked less and less reliably for his father. He'd agree to run a job and not get up early enough to pick up the workers. He'd agree to meet his dad at a new client's and then not show up.

"Isn't he going to fire you?" I asked when he hit the snooze button yet again.

"He'll never do anything," Kevin said. The few times his dad stopped by the trailer after Kevin dropped all pretense of being a good son, he'd toot his horn to let Kevin know he was coming, never pounding on the door like Kevin's brother had done or using his spare key to get in and find out what was going on. We didn't bother cleaning up the drugs anymore; had he come inside just once, he would have seen everything. But, if Kevin didn't come out when his dad blew the horn, Mr. Mitchell simply drove away.

One night I wanted a coloring book. I drove Kevin's truck to Albertson's and chose the Flintstones, with plans to do each picture in detail. In the express line, I held the coloring book and a box of Crayola crayons while my hands twitched and my feet tapped. The thought of the built-in sharpener filled me with glee. I chewed at the side of my mouth, waiting for my turn at the register. Someone two check stands over caught my eye.

"Cinnamon?"

It was Mrs. Ranzetta. I thought to dash from my spot in line, but she was already at my side.

"Sweetheart. It's been forever!" She hugged me. "Jorie's down at Santa Barbara. What are you up to?" she asked, then added, "You look thin."

"I'm taking care of my nephew," I said, holding out the crayons as if it would prove my lie true.

"I thought you were an only child," she said, followed by, "Are you all right?"

My mind whizzed by any reasonable answer.

"You know, I need to get back to him . . . he's adopted . . . I've got to go . . . he's all alone . . . sick . . . I've had too much coffee."

I dropped the coloring book into a magazine rack and left without saying goodbye.

Back at the trailer, Kevin was already in his scrubbing ritual. Still thinking of Mrs. Ranzetta, I went through cardboard boxes in a closet and pulled out a copy of our '86/'87 yearbook. I was a freshman and Kevin was a sophomore. I opened the book, pages falling out of the spine, and searched for myself. There were no candids of me—I skipped too much school and didn't join clubs, but there were plenty of Kevin and even more of Marjorie, who'd been homecoming princess for our class.

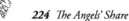

I found our '87/'88 yearbook. Then, Kevin's smile had been easy and wide. Now, he had a front tooth going black and two more on the bottom were already gone.

I looked at the photo of me, my last year: sophomore. I wasn't smiling, but I had a roundness to my cheeks. The collar of my army jacket was flipped up. My hair had been growing out of its punk cut, thick and glossy. Now it hung limp around my face. If I ran my hand across my scalp, entire clumps would come loose.

I stared into the mirror. My face was discolored, savage. My lips stood out swollen and dark, my brow was furrowed and my eyes bloodshot.

A hermit and a madwoman, I thought.

And then with a high school yearbook in my hand and Mrs. Ranzetta fresh in my head, I had a vision of how Kevin and I would get cleaned up. We'd have to start by going to his parents. Mrs. Ranzetta would help, too, I was certain. They'd show us how to manage. How to make a list of what mattered. Find doctors who knew what to do. His mother might cry when she saw me, but if she'd look in my eyes, she'd see I loved her son and I wanted to be good. I ran to catch Kevin and tell him. Tell him, again and again and again, it wasn't too late for us.

"Kevin," I sprinted toward the kitchen, my mind plotting a start to our better life. We'd give Tony a pound of crank, the yellow motorcycle, and the air rifles, and he'd go away and find another host to bloodsuck. Maybe we'd turn him in.

"Kevin," I called as I got close, "I know what to do."

His first blow hit my face. I slammed into the refrigerator, felt something near my temple crack, and then hit the floor. He stood over me and landed a kick in my side. I grabbed the shag carpet for traction to get away, but the next kick to my hip hit just as hard.

"Don't. Bother. Me. While. I'm. Working!" he raged in the rhythm of his kicking, my ribs, my hip, my face. He grabbed me by the hair and threw me into the wall. Pain supernovaed the right side of my head where he'd ripped away scalp. I scrambled under the dinette where it was tougher to get at me and he kicked the metal pole that held up the table instead of me, which hurt him enough to break his focus, curse me, and then get back to the task of scrubbing the already spotless oven.

I crept like a serpent toward the door with hope that if I stayed low, he wouldn't come after me again. Blood from my mouth and scalp smeared across the linoleum. I made it down the aluminum grate stairs, into the driveway, and passed out.

Chapter 31

Saturday morning after the vineyard's first big storm of winter, a loud knock woke me up. I'd fallen asleep re-reading *Jane Eyre*. I walked to the door, still in my robe, my hair sticking every direction, my index finger marking my place in the book. Eduardo Delgado, neatly dressed, stood on my front porch.

"Good morning," he said. "May I take you to breakfast?"

My hand went to my hair, trying to smooth the tangles. When had I last brushed my teeth? Was my face even clean? After months of being available to talk, grab lunch, hang out when I was presentable, it was now when I was disoriented and disheveled that Eduardo decided it was time.

"No thanks," I said shutting the door leaving him outside.

I stood, my warm cheek against the cold door, waiting for him to go. He didn't budge.

"I can't stop thinking about pancakes," he said through the door. "I thought you might come along."

I was starving. I wanted to say yes. I was curious to see what it felt like to sit across from him at breakfast, what we'd talk about, what silence between us at so close a distance would be like, but it had been so satisfying to shut the door on him, to refuse him for once, and there was no way I was re-opening it.

He waited another minute and then I heard the thud of his boots on my step and the crunch of gravel as he walked back toward his place. I turned my back against the door and slid to the floor. As Eduardo's distance from me increased, my elation about having the last word turned to the disappointment of knowing that I'd barricaded myself too well. If I kept this up, even the most intrepid might be defeated. I heard him start his truck and roll past my cottage, stopping long enough to roll down the window and call out, "When your nuclear winter sets in, Miss Monday, I hope you know where to go."

Weird thing to say, I thought.

And then I remembered the boy, the boy who'd played in the creek with me. Once I started in with the Naughtons, I'd forgotten him. I'd not been there the following year when apple harvest had come in. Had he waited for me? Had he kept our game alive while I dealt drugs to kids littler than me? Had he tended our sanctuary while Matthew's mouth, smelling of microwaved beef ravioli, gnawed at my chest? And had that boy's father, after twenty years of following the crops, found a foreman's job at a Dry Creek winery? I opened the door and ran out in the road, yelling his name. But I was too late, his truck was gone.

I left a note on his door.

"Are you the boy?" it said. "Are you the boy I knew at the creek?"

Chapter 32

Eduardo didn't return to his cottage that day, and the next morning he wasn't in the caves. I tried to keep busy, but looked up every time there was a sound.

Pedro came in about ten and told me Eduardo was up at the farmhouse going over the details for Sam's upcoming trip: the vineyards and the contacts Eduardo had with winemakers in Spain and France.

"Pedro, before you got the job here, where did you work?"

"Inglenook," he said, pulling on his galoshes to walk the muddy vineyard.

"Before Inglenook?"

The digital timer on my desk went off telling me I needed to go tend to the tanks. I ignored it.

Pedro looked at me. "You want me to punch down?" he asked.

"I'll do it," I said. "I just want to know where you worked before Inglenook."

Pedro wrinkled his forehead like I'd asked him something deeply personal. The timer beeped again. I ignored it.

"Many places," he answered. "My family, we followed the crops. Now please, Cinnamon, go punch down before the cap hardens."

Sam was doing a favor for a vintner buddy of his who had harvested his three acres of Malbec, but had gotten into a dispute with the winery he'd hired to do the work and was now having us ferment the grapes for him. It had arrived in refrigerated trucks and I had pumped it through the crusher-destemmer a second time and then into some older redwood tanks we weren't using where finally the whole mess of it—the skins, the pulp, and an errant stem or two—was heating up to a nice 84 degrees.

Big enough to dip a Volkswagen beetle in nose first, the tanks were filled with two-thirds juice, one-third pulp. Juice mixed with the skins to turn the Malbec a bright inky purple. The escaped drips looked like electric violet Kool-Aid.

The problem, not just with Malbec, was that the juice was heavier than the pulp and so the pulp would float at the top, dry out, and make a solid cake, sometimes a yard thick if the tank was full. And if you didn't watch out, the cake would harden and you wouldn't have enough of the juice in contact with the skins to impart pigment and tannins to the wine. Some newer wineries had hydraulic presses pushing cake back into the juice at programmed intervals. But here at Trove we still pushed the skins down by hand.

The timer reminded me of the intervals, and that's what had gone off when I was giving Pedro the third degree. I shoved back my chair, ready to go push the cake down, but my phone rang. It was the oak cooperative from Beaune calling. I'd been waiting for an update on our shipment of new oak barrels that was two weeks late. It was closing time in France and if I didn't talk to them right now it would have to wait the weekend. I needed to get the info quickly, and go push down.

But the call wasn't simple. They couldn't find the shipping invoice and they put me on hold. Another minute went by and the timer beeped again. Then another, then a third. Beaune was a testy cooperative. It was best, I'd discovered, to move at their pace—let them smoke their cigarette, talk to each other, do whatever—eventually they picked up the line with the information you needed. If they went through the hassle of coming back to the phone to find you'd hung up on them, it might be days before they were willing to call you back. Another minute elapsed and the timer beeped again.

Eduardo came through the cellar doors. I caught his attention by waving the egg timer. I covered the heavy black mouthpiece of my rotary phone when he was close enough and said, "It's Beaune. I'm on hold. Can you punch down?"

Eduardo gave me half a nod and continued toward the old tank room. I sat back in my chair and waited for Philippe to finish le pause cigarette or whatever was taking so long and find me the tracking number on the freight.

To punch down one of the redwood tanks, you hooked yourself to a harness on a ceiling pulley, climbed the ladder on the side of the tank to a twelve-inch square platform, and plunged a paddle, not unlike something you'd use when canoeing, into the mass of pulp and skins.

I'd not thought to remind Eduardo about the harness. Often I was lazy and didn't put it on, which was stupid. But he was such an Eagle Scout that I figured I didn't have to risk a French hang-up by running down the hall to remind him one of the basics of fermentation safety.

Several more minutes went by before Philippe returned, assured me the oak had shipped in July on freight, and gave me a tracking number. I put down the receiver and was ready to call the shipper for an arrival date when I realized Eduardo wasn't back.

I'd been on the phone ten minutes at most and he'd probably punched down the caps and was off for lunch, although it was on the early side for that, and he'd just gotten in. Besides, I'd been waiting all morning to talk to him. I walked down the cave's long hallway and opened the ceiling-height sliding doors that were shut to keep the heat and stink of yeast-eating sugar and burping alcohol to a minimum. The ventilation units hummed.

"Hello," I said.

I heard a weak call from the second tank.

"Eduardo," the shout died in my throat as I flew up the ladder.

If the cap was too hard to break with the paddle by yourself, then protocol was you were supposed to get a second person with a second paddle and harness to take turns finding the cap's weak spot. Much like my laziness with the harness, I would instead step on the cap, tapping with the paddle to find the thinnest section to work on. The combination of no harness and walking on the cap was double jeopardy and Eduardo, in a hurry to get my job done, must have taken the risk. Like ice on a pond, the cap could seem strong at the edges and then swallow you up closer toward the center. Eduardo was treading grape juice, holding onto pieces of broken cap, in too deep to grab the edge of the tank and pull himself out. Like quicksand, the more he'd struggle, the farther he'd fall into the hot pulp. Even if he could hold on, he couldn't be far away from losing consciousness from the carbon dioxide.

I reached out to him with a second paddle, but whenever he grabbed on, I started to lose my balance. Shit, I thought, Sam's up at the farmhouse and Pedro's twenty acres away by now. There was only me, and if I fell into the tank, too, we'd both drown.

"How about if I throw you the harness?" I said.

"What's the ballast?" his voice was weak, failing.

"Me?"

"You don't weigh enough," he gasped.

I tried again with the paddle, no luck. I wanted to run, find someone else, someone more reliable in charge of saving Eduardo. But, I knew how quickly the carbon dioxide could kill him. If I went for Sam or Pedro, Eduardo would be dead before I got back. My brain, still unreliable when stressed, started scrambling. Think, Cinnamon, think! I tried again to reach him with the paddle and failed, and my mind opened to the deathly hollow that I might not be able to save Eduardo. *Oh please*, I begged, *not this.*

Ten percent of an idea came into my head and I ran toward it, toward my bottom desk drawer where I had dumped a pile of one-pound fishing weights Sam had bought to keep tarps over the grapes in case of hail. We never used them, but I hadn't bothered to move them out of the cave. I loaded my jean and fleece pockets up with the little lead bells and sprinted the extra weight back down the hall, winded before I'd gone halfway, my lungs on fire from the exertion, but this was my chance to do right, to make one thing right and I pushed through the pain. I flew up the ladder, threw Eduardo the harness, tied the other end of the rope around my waist, and waited until he'd snapped in.

I turned to jump. It was about twelve feet to the floor.

"No," Eduardo's voice was calm, solid, now that he was attached to me. "You'll give yourself the Heimlich. Go down the ladder, slowly."

I did what he said and by grabbing the rungs below me and pulling myself down the ladder I was able to hoist him a few feet out of the juice, a few inches for every rung. Once he left the liquid weight behind it got easier, but when my feet were back on the cement floor it was still not enough to get him over the rim. I knelt and he came higher; I could see his face and shoulders. I went lower, laying myself back on the cement, hoisting him out of the tank and suspending him in the air above me. We stared at each other under the lights of the cellar, gobs of hot Malbec from Eduardo's clothes splattering me with purple, the rope between us taut, my hand on the knot that tied us. We traded places now, me kneeling, then standing, then starting up the ladder again while Eduardo inched down to the floor. The rope pulled against our ribcages, straining from the weight of the wine in Eduardo's clothes and the lead in mine. Once he touched ground, Eduardo unsnapped the harness and collapsed against the warm wood staves of the tank. I untied the rope and climbed down the ladder, sitting next to him while we caught our breath. Mine came back first and I began to take out the lead bells from their hiding places in my clothing, lining them up on the cold cement floor between his right leg and my left. I peeled off my fleece, leaving only the thin long-sleeved t-shirt underneath. Normally, that would not be enough to keep me warm in the caves, but right now I was radiating steam from the panic and exertion.

"Thanks," he said once he could talk again.

"You're welcome," I said, setting the last of the weights out. I'd added twenty pounds to myself. Pretty nifty little trick, I thought, for someone who flunked algebra, biology, and PE.

"I'm an idiot around you," he said.

"I don't always wear the harness either," I said.

"Not just that. Knocking over the table. Taking so long to tell you who I was. Now this."

"All those things matter less than how unfriendly you've been since the day I started here. And all that time you knew me."

Eduardo moved his hand toward the floor, picked up one of the lead weights and closed his fingers around it.

"I didn't have the courage to tell you, Cinnamon. Every day since we started working together and every night since you moved in near me, I've wanted to. But I thought: what if you didn't remember? Or worse: what if you didn't care? I've dreamed about you for so long. Having you close was enough. I didn't want to mess it up."

I put my head in my hand and rubbed my forehead, smearing purple everywhere.

"What happened to you?" he asked.

"I was on hold, with Beaune," I said.

"No, back then, back when we were kids. When I came the next year, you weren't there. Our stuff was, but you never showed up."

"I had to leave that behind," I said, ashamed to tell him what a failure his partner in survival had become.

He'd never given me the chance to look at him so closely, so long. Now, I saw the resemblance to the boy, the square forehead, outlined with a sweep of black hair. His eyes were an inky brown, almost indistinguishable from his pupils. His cheekbones were raised and delicate. Sitting close together on the cold concrete, our backs to the vat that almost killed us both; my teeth began chattering. Eduardo got up, and offered me his hand.

"It's gone," I said when he'd pulled me to standing.

"What's gone?" he said.

"Our creek," I said, my soaked t-shirt cold on my skin. "They built houses on the fields there. You can't get in."

"You're wrong," he said. "You just have to know the way."

Eduardo pulled me close and kissed my neck where soft cotton met my collarbone, then hovered above the spot. It was everything to stand still. I thought I might evaporate if he kissed me again. As if he knew, Eduardo eased back, picked my fleece up from the floor and helped me into it. I pulled the collar up around the spot, then stepped into him, tucking myself into his body, letting him protect the place where his lips had touched, where my neck curved into my shoulder.

That was the first kiss, I realized, I'd ever gotten sober.

We stood together, leaning into each other, not talking for a while. After five minutes or maybe fifty, I felt a draft and looked up. I'd left the sliding doors open. Facing us, Sam stood in the doorway.

"Mr. Gladstone," I said, pulling away from Eduardo. "I was on the

234 *The Angels' Share*

phone and the timer went off and then he went to punch down—"

"You stupid kids. Stupid! You're supposed to wear a harness," Sam interrupted, as angry as I'd ever seen him.

"It was my fault," Eduardo said. "I didn't follow the rules."

"Go home and change," Sam ordered Eduardo.

Eduardo looked at me and I nodded. Still dripping Malbec, he squelched down the hall, leaving Sam and me alone.

"You remember I'm leaving this afternoon?" Sam said, too agitated to even look at me.

"Yes," I said.

"How long has that," he motioned toward where he'd seen Eduardo and me, "been going on?"

Where should I start?

"Wait," Sam said waving his hands in front of his face. "It's none of my business. Just be more careful, goddamit. The both of you." He turned and walked down the hall and let the door of the cave slam shut behind him.

Chapter 33

We entered the creek from Eduardo's side. It had once been an apple orchard, complete with boarded-over cottages in a row. Unimproved versions of the ones we now lived in.

"You lived here?" I asked.

"That one," he said, pointing to the one on the end, "three harvests in a row."

He showed me the break in the fence and we climbed through into the forest beyond.

I gasped when I saw the gully we'd chosen as a larder, the earthen bench we'd carved into the bank. After all this time they had been preserved just as they were. Several inches of water ran down the center of the creek bed from that first rainstorm. This would probably be the last time we could come here until the rainy season was over. Eduardo put his plaid work-shirt down over the damp moss on our carved bench and we sat, listening to the birds chirp the same as they had thirteen years before.

"Tell me where you've been since the last time I saw you. Why you never came back," Eduardo said after a while.

"I played apocalypse as a kid," I said. "And Sam found me with more meth than blood in my veins, my jaw kicked in by a steel-toe boot. Isn't that enough to fill you in on what happened in between?"

"I want to know everything about you," Eduardo said.

"Some things I don't remember," I said resting my chin on his shoulder. "And some things I'd rather not tell you."

"I'm sorry," Eduardo said.

"For asking what happened?"

"For not preventing what happened."

"How could you?"

"I'm not saying I could have. But I did promise to take care of you, and I did mean it, and I'm sorry that I couldn't."

"Answer my questions, then," I said. "How'd you get to Davis?"

"Got lucky. My dad found steady work so we could stay in one place."

"Inglenook?"

"Yes. I spent my last three years of high school in Napa and got a guidance counselor who believed in me."

"Tell me about Mondavi Girl."

"Mondavi Girl?"

"The blonde. With the Jetta."

"Alison? She lived on my hall freshman year. Gringo goddess I wanted in some sort of sicko reverse-conquistador way."

"And she wants you in the regular conquistador way. She spent the night."

"When I got the winemaker job, a lot of people from Davis got friendlier. Alison was one of them. She threw herself at me that day, and after all those years of waiting, I decided what the hell. Not the best night of my life."

Quiet again.

"I want to make you dinner," he said. "Right now."

It was getting dark, the bit of light that filtered through the trees slipping away. We hiked back up the bank of the creek, me following Eduardo.

"Doesn't it bother you that Sam redid my place, but expects you to live in yours as is?" I asked.

"He offered to fix mine up, but I said no," Eduardo said, extending his hand to pull me up the last, steep bit. "I didn't want to live in my parents' house once I came back from college, so I just moved in. For now, it suits me fine."

Chapter 34

Eduardo dropped me back at my place to shower off the chill of the creek while he picked up dinner makings at the store.

He was back before I'd got my hair dry and was already chopping onions and garlic for spaghetti sauce when I came out. I washed and tore lettuce for salad at the table. The cordless rang. I wiped my hands on a dishtowel, reached the counter with one extended arm, and answered it.

"Miss Monday?" asked Sheriff Tully.

I looked at the clock. Eight twenty-five on a Friday night.

"Speaking."

At the tone of my voice, Eduardo stopped chopping.

"I'm finalizing my report. Cause of death was organ failure due to ingested amatoxin. Probably a suicide. Before I file it, I wanted to check in, make sure you didn't have anything else to add."

I told him I didn't.

"We've got two options: I can go back up to the commune for another look, see if there is something that the responding deputy or coroner missed, or we can close the case."

"It's my choice?"

"No, but I'm of two minds and you're the only interested party."

That would have been my chance to say my father foraged wild mushrooms. He knew the edible from the poisonous by heart. My mother didn't and also she hated tromping through the woods. She'd never gather mushrooms on her own and if he'd given them to her to eat, it was no mistake.

I opened my mouth to tell the Sheriff why maybe they shouldn't close the case without talking to my father, but again I saw my parents together in the field, my father drawing something in the air with his finger, my mother laughing. I was the only interested party, the Sheriff had said so himself, and that was how I wanted to remember them.

"You don't need to go back to OHM," I said.

"Miss Monday," he said after the last formalities, "I offer my condolences."

I thanked him and had the chance to hang up, to disentangle myself from the law hopefully forever, but instead I asked, "Why do you trust me when you've never seen me cry?"

The detective paused. "Miss Monday, there are approximately thirty communes left in Mendocino County and the population is aging. When I need to contact the family, the children of the deceased, there are a wide range of responses. Some break down, some don't. I figure the ones that don't have done some of their mourning already."

After I hung up, I went back to chopping the carrots and cucumbers for the salad. Eduardo watched me from the kitchen. After a few minutes had gone by, and I'd not said anything, he set the table.

We ate a while in silence. I told him his sauce was the best I'd ever had. Then I told him what the detective had said and what I hadn't.

Eduardo filled his glass with more Zinfandel and offered some to me. I shook my head.

"I wish I could be someone else, start over. Someone who grew up in a normal house with a normal name."

"What makes someone normal?" Eduardo asked, puzzled.

"I wanted to be Cindy."

"There's not a cell in you whose name is Cindy," said Eduardo. "You are the anti-Cindy. Nothing conventional about you. And you're more beautiful because of it."

He was as serious as I'd ever seen him.

"What did you know? You were nine," I said.

"I knew enough. Survival is no joke."

"I had tangled hair, ratty clothes," I said.

"Your hair flowed down your back and shoulders like Rapunzel. I don't remember your clothes. I remember your hands. I watched them when you talked, I thought they might turn into birds and fly away."

I had no retort to that.

He took my palms in his, opened them, and traced along the lines.

"Do you doubt me, Cinnamon?"

"Entirely," I said.

"You have no faith in my memory?" he said.

"Not a bit," I whispered.

"You smelled like honey and earth and something that I cannot name, and if I could capture that and put it in my wine, it would sell a million bottles. You smell like a girl and since no other girl smells like you, they're all wrong to me. I knew who you were at Sam's party the minute I saw you. That's why I knocked over the table, ran away. You'll never, ever be Cindy, Dios Mio. After knowing you, Cinnamon, I could never love a Cindy."

"You won't love me."

"Why not?" Eduardo asked.

I unbuttoned the cuffs of my shirt and rolled them up, revealing the full effect of knotted veins and the double path of scars. He held my arm in his hand and examined the red tracks from my wrist to the hollow of my elbow.

"You saw a little of this that day at my desk. It disgusts you."

"I did see it and I was surprised, but if you saw disgust on my face it was with my own cowardice, not with you."

"Do you still do it?" he asked, sounding less shocked than I'd thought.

"No," I said. "I've been sober since Sam found me in the vineyard."

"Then what does it matter?"

"It matters because I'm an ex-junkie who works with booze. Because my father might have murdered my mother. My grandfather bankrupted his own family. I'm trash and you won't want me."

"I want you," he said. "I want all your pieces. You're not trash."

He cupped the back of my head with his hand and kissed me on the mouth once. He was quiet, his eyes intense. I stared back, aware now that his silence in the caves had not been disinterest. It had been restraint.

"Enough," he said, standing. "Dishes, then dessert."

While we took our plates to the sink, I anticipated all the ways this night might go wrong. That Eduardo would make a comment or a gesture that would remind me of Matthew or Chad. Or he'd open a pop-top can. Or he'd try and kiss my arms in a cutesy attempt to make my scars all better and follow that same path toward my jugular as Kevin had. I wanted to warn him, explain the minefield he was walking into, how many traps he faced in the wideness between us. He washed; I dried. In my tiny kitchen our sides touched while we emptied the basin of dirty dishes. Working together, we found a rhythm of him soaping the inside of a glass or a plate, rinsing, and me drying the water drops, putting it away, and swiveling back to take the next piece from his hand.

After we finished, Eduardo turned on my rabbit-eared TV, and we lay on my bed watching the eleven pm Creature Feature on KTVU, my head buried in the crook of his arm, taking turns reaching into a bag of Mint Milanos.

Of course, I thought more about him than the movie. He seemed focused on the screen, his hand tucking mine into his chest. At commercial, he turned to me and stroked my temple. He looked at me with such seriousness it was hard not to laugh. His hand tucked hair behind my ear. My fingers flew to the side of my head.

"I've got a scar there," I said, covering it.

"I know," he said. "Does it hurt?"

"No," I said. "Sort of."

"I'll leave it alone," he said.

I nodded and then, because I felt bad, because I wanted him to know that even if I had scars he couldn't touch, that I wasn't impossible, I pushed up on my elbows and kissed him. He turned off the TV, set my head back on the pillow, and stared at my face again. The nightlight from the bathroom reflected in his eyes.

"Why are you looking at me like that?" I asked, unable to bear the intensity of his gaze.

"Because I can't believe you're here, after all these years that you are real and not imaginary."

"You thought I might not be real?"

"My mother thought I'd made you up. In her mind, white girls don't play with brown boys. But I knew you were real, I knew you'd come back. And then you did."

Eduardo touched my mouth with his thumb. He put gentle pressure on the lower lip. Touch, kiss, touch, kiss. Not a darty peck like Kevin's or a slobbery maul like Matthew. Light, but increasing power on each return.

"You're not breathing," he said, pulling up.

And I took a breath.

He kissed me again, the two of us in sync like divers sharing a respirator far below the surface.

Eduardo shifted his weight and I felt his erection against my thigh.

I realized I was in unmapped territory: a man, a bed; no beer, no crank. Drunk, high, or stoned, things happened on their own. I'd never had to remove a piece of my own clothing; it was pulled up, pushed aside. The idea of my participation, my active consent, was terrifying.

"You're not breathing again," he said. Then his hand was on my cheek, his eyes near my eyes. He took my hand, laced it with his, like he'd found me, was pulling me to . . . safety. "Are you okay?"

"I'm okay," I said. "But I need to stop for now."

Eduardo nodded, his hand covering my navel, holding the side of me so in sleep I could only turn closer to him, not fall or turn away.

In the morning, Eduardo said, "I want you to come to Sunday dinner at my house."

"Tomorrow's Sunday."

"Exactly."

"What about your mom?"

"What about my mom?" he said.

"She doesn't like me."

"Probably not."

"Why not?" I had been hoping he'd say I was being ridiculous.

"I'm the only son. I could be dating La Virgen and I think she'd have some reservations. Plus white girls don't play with brown boys, remember."

"Last time I looked, the Virgin Mary was pretty fair skinned."

Eduardo laughed. "You will never be the daughter-in-law that she pictured. No one will be, of course, but you blow the visual at the get-go."

"Who said I wanted to be a daughter-in-law?"

"No one," said Eduardo, sitting up. His boxers were dark blue with green stripes and I liked them very much.

"So now, I'm not only white, but I'm too modern."

"I'd safely say you are post-modern," said Eduardo as he pulled on his t-shirt.

"I'm not Catholic."

"That'll be another problem."

"Then why are you bothering? And why are you getting dressed? Are you bored of me already?"

"No, I'm late meeting the New York distributor. Remember?"

I ignored the rational response and kept going.

"Why do you want to introduce me to your mother? Things are just starting. I need more than thirty-six hours of good before we complicate things."

Eduardo sat on the bed, lacing his work boots while I watched him, the brown blanket wrapped around my knees.

"Look, I don't hide things from my family," he said. "My dad knows. He's known since I knocked over that table. My mom is tougher. But she loves me. In her heart, she wants me to be happy. And from now on, when I'm there on Sundays and you are not, I will feel like a liar. And I am not a liar. Come with me, Cinnamon. Come with me on Sunday."

Chapter 35

When Eduardo went to meet the distributor, I thought about calling Julia, seeing if she'd meet me, but I decided I was too lost in the trance of the previous night and I'd be terrible company. I drove to Healdsburg and wandered the square, determined to find an outfit that would help win over Eduardo's parents. I believed that if I had the right clothes and said the right words, they'd accept me. I'd never seen Alma in pants, so first I had to find a dress. It had to be a dress.

Eduardo, the movie, replayed in my head all day. Even with the distraction of town, I couldn't stop picturing him in the caves, talking to the distributor: his dark hair back in a ponytail, his plaid work shirt with just one button undone.

I went into a boutique on Healdsburg Square where I always admired what was in the windows. Everything was so expensive and nothing made me look like a dark-skinned virgin. I carried a few things around the store, let a saleslady start me a room where I tried to shake the images of Eduardo out of my mind long enough to pull two paychecks' worth of long-sleeved burgundy silk over my head.

"Stunning," the saleslady pronounced, peeking in the room while I stood facing the mirror, trembling from the memory of the pressure of Eduardo's thumb on my lip.

The person in the mirror would need new shoes. The person in the mirror would need beige-colored undergarments. The person in the mirror would need make-up and a haircut.

"It's not me."

"Oh, it's you," she said. "Isn't it?" she asked another shopper.

"Pretty," the woman said, meaning it.

I hung all the new, expensive things back on their hangers and left the store with promises to come back after I'd thought about it.

On the way back to the car I lingered outside the Oakville Grocery and stared at their selection of mushrooms: tiny white enoki, wrinkly shitake, golf-umbrella portabellas, milk caps the color of Orange Crush soda, selling for twenty-five dollars a pound. I thought of my mother. I had a vision of her gulping down that plate of poisonous mushrooms, swallowing without chewing. I drove to Goodwill and found a dark green velveteen dress, which fit but was unlined and scratchy with sleeves that ended in a Dracula-like point on the back of my hand. When I pulled it over my head in the dressing room, the edge of it draped fluid across my navel and tumbled down my hip. I imagined Eduardo running his hand along that same path and had to sit down on the plastic bench in the dressing room. My God, all we had done was kiss; how was I going to be able to function if we took this any further?

The sun burned orange and low when I returned home. Eduardo's truck was still gone. This distributor handled high-end restaurants on the East Coast, places where an artisanal wine could develop a following. With Sam gone it was Eduardo's job to make sure Trove would stick in the distributor's mind. I guessed Eduardo had taken him to dinner.

I went up to Sam's to water his plants. I ended up reading a chapter on Malolactic Fermentation out of a new *Concepts in Wine Chemistry*. Malolactic was happening to the red Zinfandel in our barrels right now. The tart, sharp malic acid flavors of the newly harvested grapes were being mellowed into the rounder, lusher lactic acids we wanted to be Trove's trademark. Given this second fermentation, the wine became easier to drink, more approachable right out of the bottle.

As I hurried back down the path to my cottage that cold December night, I saw the lights were on at Eduardo's. I knew I should go home and wait for him to come to me, but I couldn't. I took all three of his steps in one leap and knocked on his door, breathless. He opened.

His radio was tuned to a hockey game. He'd been folding laundry.

I stood in the doorway not knowing what to say.

He took my hand in his, pulled me inside and shut the door behind us.

Chapter 36

Sunday, Eduardo and I walked up to the ranch house for dinner. Alma opened the door all smiles, and I thought, okay, this won't be as bad as I'd feared, but after she hugged her son, she only patted me on my shoulder like she was trying to shoo an insect.

I gave her the bouquet of white ranunculus I'd bought at the expensive florist.

"From the field?" Alma asked wrinkling her nose.

"No, no, from a store," I said and she made a face like that might be worse. I asked if I could put them in a vase for her.

She nodded and I followed her into the kitchen. Carnitas simmered away on her tidy stove, nothing boiling over, the good smells transporting me back to Socorro's kitchen on the nights when Frank and my grandmother were eating elsewhere, the safety of Socorro's arms where I'd run after a scraped knee. Maybe I could never make right what I'd done to Socorro, but if I could get Alma to accept me, then these Sunday night dinners could become *my* Sunday night dinners, a cornerstone in a regular life with Eduardo and his family.

Alma pointed to a cabinet to her right and said, "That one," metering out her English like each word she had to speak of that foreign tongue in her house was an insult.

I thought she'd get one for me, but she'd turned her back so I guessed she wanted me to pick one on my own. I took out a large blown glass vase I thought would hold the flowers well.

Her spatula clattered to the counter and she took the vase from my hands.

"Wrong," she said, putting it back.

She gave me a cheap glass vase that was too small for the length of the stems. The blooms separated and the arrangement that had looked so elegant in the bouquet now looked leggy and cheap.

"Shall I put them on the table?" I asked.

"No," she said, dismissing them and me while she turned back to the stove, taking flautas out of the hot oil. I stood for a moment, watching her work, her hair pulled into the same, flawless bun she wore every day. I wanted to offer my help, but my eyes were smarting from her rudeness and the scratchy Goodwill dress was irritating my wrists and collarbone.

I should go home, I thought. Tell them I'm not well. Try another night.

Eduardo came into the kitchen, saw my face, put his arm around my shoulder, and pulled me into a corner of the living room beside their flocked Christmas tree.

"Hellacious," I said.

"No, purgatorial. If Mama wanted hellacious, you'd know."

"I don't think I can manage a whole night of this," I said. "It's the first time doing drugs has sounded better than the alternative since rehab."

Eduardo went serious. "Don't even joke," he said. "My uncle is coming. When he gets here, she'll stop with the insulting part of the evening and move on to the ignoring part."

"This is a mistake," I said.

Eduardo steadied me with a hand on either shoulder.

"She's a good person, you just need to be patient, pay your dues and she will accept you. She will, I promise."

Dues? I thought. Why should I have to pay my dues? I'd not done anything to Alma.

Eduardo's Uncle Chuy arrived with a dozen roses for Alma in a red velvet box.

"The most beautiful flowers I've ever seen," she said distinctly.

Chuy didn't hug me, but he pumped my hand with enthusiasm and slapped Eduardo on the back after he met me. Pedro and Chuy sat on the couch and talked fútbol. Alma hummed while she brought food to the table. Eduardo was right; once Chuy arrived, Alma ignored me.

Eduardo held my hand under the table while Alma babied her brother with food.

Alma's food was as good as Socorro's, maybe even better. She made her own tortillas, Socorro's had been store bought as my grandmother didn't like hearing the grinding of the mealing stone in her house. Alma's tortillas were the best I'd ever had and I took more every time the basket came around trying every dish inside them.

"This is delicious," I said in halting Spanish. My compliment started a round of accolades to the chef. Alma nodded at them, at me, not meeting my eyes, not smiling, but the next time my glass was empty she refilled it with Coke from the two-liter bottle on the table. I hadn't really wanted anymore, but I thanked her anyhow.

"De nada," she said, and I thought maybe I heard just a trace of sincerity in her voice.

After dinner we sat in the living room and drank Drambuie from cordial glasses while Pedro, Alma, and Chuy talked in Spanish I could not keep up with. Eduardo offered to do the dishes and I joined him. We sudsed up one basin of the sink and the steam from it fogged the windows. I opened one a crack to let the steam out and washed while Eduardo dried.

As I worked, the points of my velvet sleeves got wet, so I folded them up. We filled the rubber dish drainer by the side of the sink and then Eduardo laid the pots and bowls around the tile counters on unfolded dishtowels. "Feliz Navidad" came on the am station. Singing along to something as hokey as "Feliz Navidad" didn't seem like something the quiet, brooding Eduardo would do, but he belted out the words and I joined him on the chorus. It got hotter in the room, my dress got itchier, but I felt good. The evening was almost over, I'd survived, and Eduardo and I were giddy from the song, our closeness and the stepping around each other as we worked in the kitchen became a little dance. He leaned over and kissed me on the cheek. A pile of dessert dishes came crashing to the counter. Alma had brought them in and let them drop, because she saw the kiss, I guessed. We stopped singing.

"Drafty," she said, reaching past me to close the window I'd opened. Something grabbed her line of sight and, like a heat-seeking missile, she zeroed in on my arms. *My arms!* Trying to make myself comfortable, I'd forgotten how important it was to keep my arms covered on tonight of all nights. The wet sleeves were now rolled back to my elbows, exposing the knotty scars, which pulsed red from the dishwater. Soap bubbles attached themselves like magnifying glasses showing off every bit of skin I'd wanted to hide. I tried to pull the fabric down but she grabbed both my wrists, her clench like a vise.

"What is this?"

The radio went to commercial.

"What's wrong with you?" she demanded in English, suddenly more fluent.

I stepped back, yanked my wrists from her, locked my hands to my sides.

"What's wrong with your arms?" she shouted. Conversation in the living room ceased.

"Tiene heridas, Mamí," Eduardo said.

"Why?" Alma asked, her mouth straight, one eyebrow raised. "What did you do?"

I wanted to bolt, away from her accusing eyes that stripped me back down to who I was at my core, which when I forgot how to pretend, like now, was not much of a core at all.

I tried to think of something I could say to sting her, make her back off, but I wasn't at dinner with Frank Ferguson any longer. If I wanted Eduardo, I had to stay calm, make this work. Face Alma, I thought, and tell the truth.

"I was a drug addict. For many years I injected methamphetamine into my veins using a needle. At first I was careful, but in the end I was not. I injected so many times that some of my veins collapsed. The rest developed scar tissue."

"Alma," Pedro was in the doorway, his tone a reprimand. I'd never heard him sound that bothered. I could see Uncle Chuy sitting on the couch rubbing his hands together, staring into space.

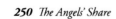

"No drugs in my house," Alma said to me, fierce. "Out."

"I don't do drugs," I pleaded, glancing at Eduardo.

"Mamí," Eduardo said, a warning in his voice.

"Look at her arms, mijo," she shouted at her son. "Quien nace burro muere rebuznando."

"What did she call me?" I demanded from Eduardo, Pedro, my voice rising. Neither one answered me; Chuy was still hiding in the living room. Cowards, all of them. Eduardo was afraid of his mother and had let her bully me since the minute I'd got here. Pay my dues. Bullshit. I'd already paid my dues in life and with Alma. She thought she was so superior, so much better than me. Well fuck her. Fuck her little despotic Sunday dinner. If she got to say exactly what she thought, then why couldn't I?

"Whatever you think about me, Alma, you're wrong. You're worse than wrong; you're a rude closed-minded bitch."

It was like I'd pulled a pin from a hand grenade. Everyone froze. A monster-truck-athon commercial in Spanish was the only sound in the room: *Sábado, Sábado, Sábado.*

I threw the towel down and ran from the Delgados' house, away from that disastrous dinner, one that had been as bad as any at Frank's table. She deserved it, she deserved worse, I kept chanting as I stumbled home, my breath making smoke in the chill night air. When I got to my porch, I turned and waited, expecting Eduardo to come running after me, then hoping he'd come, then as the night grew darker and colder around me I realized Eduardo was not coming after me at all.

Inside, I paced my cottage, fuming at Alma's predetermination from day one that I was not worth her good opinion. Pissed that Eduardo had talked me into coming to dinner, hadn't defended me and had let me run off alone. Angry even at Pedro for not sticking up for me, doing what was right, letting me fail so badly.

I waited for Eduardo, but he didn't come, and he didn't come and he didn't come.

After midnight, a knock.

"Come in," I said, my voice controlled, but when he came through the door, a scowl on his face, I lost it. I rushed for his chest, and when he did not close his arms around me, I punched him in the shoulder as hard as I could, then the face, catching him right above the eye.

"You lied!" I shouted. "You said it would be okay!"

Instead of shielding himself from the blows, he grabbed both my hands and held them to my sides while I struggled to get loose.

"You called names," he said, holding me still. "You can't ever, ever call my mother a bitch, do you understand?" His voice cold, final.

I let out a sharp, high screech and yanked my arms from his hands. Instead of hitting more, I whirled around, running to the other corner of the room, pushing my back up against the wall, between the bookshelf and the corner as far away from him as I could get.

"And it's okay for her to call me whatever she did?"

"No, it's not."

"Then give her the lecture, not me."

"Where do you think I've been?" he asked me, his voice cracking.

Where I'd hit him above his eye was now bleeding, dripping down his cheek. I wanted to get a cloth, stem the damage I'd caused. But I wasn't sure what he'd do if I came close.

"Didn't you see how hard I tried?" I said, feeling I'd grown smaller or the room bigger, either way the distance between us increasing by the second.

"Whatever I saw," Eduardo answered, "I didn't like it."

Eduardo wiped at his face and looked at his bloody hand. He looked at me and shook his head. The bottom dropped out of my stomach, the room, my world. I was stupid and out of control. I hated myself.

This time, Eduardo walked out on me.

After he left, I sat on my bed, wrapped in the brown blanket, rocking. First I considered telling Sam, begging him to cut his trip short and have him come home and fire the entire Delgado family. If I pushed hard enough, if I gave an ultimatum, maybe he'd do it. Bile pulsed in the back of my throat and with it came a stealthy little craving, not hard and fast like I'd gotten at the mortuary, but trickling, sweet-talking, wrapping itself around this mess and offering its services as a solution. You don't want to call Sam, it whispered. That's all too complicated. I can fix it all and quick, too, it said. The Hanky Panky out on Stony Point, the Blue Room on Roseland only twenty minutes away. Buy yourself a day or two, a little pain-free vacation from all this reality. Then you can figure all this out.

"No, no, no!" I shouted at my walls.

I began to pick at my arms, still rocking, the blanket left on my bed. I couldn't make it through this night without something. I just couldn't. The car keys, so close, hanging just inside the kitchen door of the farmhouse. Just a little walk and a little drive and then I could obliterate myself on top of everything else.

I went out the door, in a hurry to self-destruct when a rake of thorns swept across my forehead. The rose vine that climbed up the side of my porch had come loose and I'd run into one of the thick branches with such velocity that thorns came off in the skin of my forehead and cheek. I sat on my steps sobbing as I pulled the barbs from my skin, the pain bringing me back, making me remember I had other choices. Eduardo wasn't speaking to me and Sam was gone, but I had Julia, didn't I? I went back inside, put a washcloth to my forehead and dialed Julia's number.

Chapter 37

After I told her everything, Julia offered to come and pick me up, but I couldn't wait the hour it would take for her to get there; I needed to get away, get distance between me and the places where I could find cheap meth. But the time alone in the car wasn't good either. I kept replaying the scene and getting angrier with Alma's conclusion jumping, Eduardo's limp defense of me. Most frustrating of all, I saw how I was also responsible for what had happened, or at least for the way it ended.

When I got to Julia's apartment, I told her I couldn't stand thinking about what had happened anymore, and I'd do anything to stop feeling the way I did. She gave me one of her sleeping pills.

"Prescription won't be strong enough," I said. "Remember, I'm an addict."

But ten minutes later, when I tried to get up from her couch, I almost fell over. Julia guided me to her bed as I listed to the side.

"What are you laughing at?" I asked Julia as she tucked me in.

"Your forehead," she said. "It looks like you got attacked by a fork."

The sedation played my brain like a harp. "I found him, then I lost him again," I said.

"Don't worry," Julia said. "Just sleep."

In the morning I watched her get ready for work in a haze, my head almost completely under the blankets.

"I want you to come down to the hotel for lunch," Julia said.

"I'm lousy company," I said, inching myself even farther into the covers.

"Don't be ridiculous," she said, grabbing her purse and car keys. "I'm taking you to lunch at the hotel. Twelve-thirty. We'll be the first people served by the kitchen—the staff needs practice. Pretend you're fine, get dressed. Stop feeling sorry for yourself, Cinnamon. If you want to mope, do it after lunch."

I'd only been to the hotel once, when I was maybe nine or ten, around the time Playboy had sold it to the Japanese. Uncle Victor thought we should see it and drove Julia and me up to the city. I had expected to see pretty ladies dressed like bunnies multiplying in the lobby, but The Pierpoint lobby was deserted except an unshaven man snoring on the bench near the revolving door. On the wall behind the front desk, a rust-colored water stain started at the ceiling and worked down the wall like an artery. Victor rang the bell until someone in jeans and a workshirt came.

"What kind of place are you running?" Victor asked.

I could just see over the top of the grimy marble counter. "The hotel is closed, sir," the man said. "I'm here shutting down the phones."

The counter had once been cream or maybe white. I wet my finger and rubbed the part nearest to me. A little gold streak shone through the grime twinkling at me even under the fluorescents.

"This is an embarrassment," my uncle said.

The man behind the counter shrugged. My uncle tugged my cousin and me out of the lobby without the promised hot chocolate.

On the way back to Hillsborough, Victor had sobbed so hard we swerved into other lanes, the drivers honking long and hard, giving us the finger as they passed by.

"Do you want to get off the freeway Uncle Victor?" I asked. Julia was scared to near petrification between us.

Victor muttered on about the hotel, our family. Still crying, still causing other drivers to navigate around his erratic driving. I gripped the door handle and held onto Julia until we turned up the driveway at Grandmothers.

After that, I never had any desire to see the shabby innards of the Pierpoint Hotel again.

Following Julia's instructions, I pulled into the workers' parking lot—the grand front entrance was still shrouded in scaffolding and black mesh. A security guard checked my name off a printed list and I ascended from the basement in the freight elevator.

The doors opened into a dark little hall. I followed the light then stopped short. The main lobby opened like a cathedral. The bellhops' chrome trolleys stood in a mirrored row facing the street. Wooden columns as thick as redwood trees flanked the bank of revolving doors to the street. Everything shone like new under the gilded chandeliers that had replaced green of fluorescents. I walked over to the front desk, the place I'd stood with my uncle years before and touched the slab of cool white marble, the golden strands running through it, sparkling full strength in the improved light.

In a few weeks this lobby would be busy with staff and guests—bells and chatter filling the space—but for right now the place had a sacred sense, like my sanctuary down at the creek or the wine caves when I was working there late at night, and I took in a deep breath, filling my lungs to capacity, letting it out slowly so as not to disturb the spell The Pierpoint was casting on me.

At twelve-thirty exactly, Julia came from her office, carrying a big box with a red bow.

"What is it?" I asked.

"Your Christmas present," Julia said. "You're getting it early."

The host poured our water with a flourish as if the restaurant were filled with visiting dignitaries, although other than Julia and me it was empty.

"We're having a party here on December thirtieth, first a press event and then just family and friends, before the grand opening on New Year's Eve. I put an invitation to you in the mail. I hope you can come, Eduardo or no."

"He called me this morning," Julia continued. "Went to some trouble to find me at the hotel."

"Why?"

"He said you'd had an argument and then not shown up for work.

He was worried. I told him you were with me."

"Did he want to talk to me?" I asked.

Julia didn't answer. "Open your present, Cinnamon," she said, pushing it across the floor to my side of the table. "It will make you feel better."

I undid the ribbon on the glossy box, which was taller than it was wide and filled with white tissue paper. I peeled away the layers, lifting out what Julia had placed inside.

The bronze cherub.

"A copy?" I said.

"No," she said, "the original."

A yellow tag hung from the bow. Butterfield & Company Auctioneers, it said.

"How?" I asked.

"Well," Julia began, "once when I was arguing with the OHM lawyer he said it was the highest appraised item in her estate. I called everywhere in the city that appraises bronzes, told them I was interested in buying such a thing, and one told me that he had given an estimate on something similar that was up for at auction this month at Butterfield's. All Grandmother's things, Cinnamon, they were up there on the block, no reserve. Remember that beautiful clock she had in the morning room? Went for almost nothing."

I set the cherub on the table and inspected the tag again.

"Oh, Julia," I said. "Where did you get that kind of money?"

"I took a little velvet bag I had down to Union Square and sold what was inside."

"That's too much," I said.

"Shut up," she said, grinning.

I held the cherub in my arms and gazed at it, remembering the times my grandmother had taken her jewelry and redeemed it to give my mother and me another chance. All the mornings in the rose garden, all the times she'd shown me her direction by pointing the cherub. That I now held something she and I both loved. I cupped my hands on the heavy base. Julia had given me the perfect imperfect altar to my grandmother, to my mother, to everything they'd wanted to give me and couldn't.

"This is the best present I ever got," I said.

"It's the best present I ever gave," Julia said, holding up her water glass.

I placed the cherub on the table, its arrow pointing toward my cousin and returned her toast.

"I want to give you a present, too," I said, setting the glass down, leaning toward her. "I want you to know that I'm sorry."

"For what?"

"For all of the mean things I did and the horrible things I said at the Fortress of Frank."

Julia laughed. "That's such a perfect name for that place. I rechristen it!" she clinked my glass again with her fingernail. "And for such a great name, I forgive you, Cinnamon Monday, for any and all things. Here's to the end of the Fortress of Frank."

The waiter brought us champagne and a basket of warm rolls.

"I think you have to give the same present to Eduardo," Julia said breaking off a little piece of bread. "I think, if you can, you should tell him you're sorry."

I drove back up to Trove that night and placed the cherub on my yellow coffee table. I thought about getting it a tiny set of casters so I could spin my fortune each morning, have it point me in the direction of the day. *Use it better than I have, Cinnamon.*

I remembered a Lazy Susan I had picked up at the flea market for condiments but then never used. I put the cherub on it. Telling myself I was joking, I spun it around. The cherub spun in an ellipse once, twice, and ended with the arrow pointing away from Eduardo's house, but toward my bed and the clock on my nightstand that read 12:02.

I brushed my teeth and put on my long-sleeved nightshirt . . . 12:11. I spun the cherub again, thinking I'd give her another chance to point me toward Eduardo's. This time the bow pointed toward the driveway, the road. I thought about the mail. I hadn't checked Sam's all week. He'd made me promise to empty it once a day when I agreed to water the plants.

I put on boots and a coat over my nightshirt and shivered down the long driveway to the mailbox. Sam's box was bursting, and even my box had a small stack of mail inside. Back in the cottage, I dropped Sam's in a grocery bag to sort the next day and went through my own little pile: two credit card solicitations, Julia's engraved invitation to the opening party at The Pierpoint, and a slip saying I had a certified letter waiting at the Healdsburg Post Office. I recognized the return address: Philbrech & Fitch, LLC. I had a letter from Oh Holy Mountain's lawyers waiting for me, and I guessed it wasn't a holiday card.

Chapter 38

Sam was back early on December twenty-third. I'd seen the black Town Car pull up to the farmhouse, but I'd not gone up to say hello. There was no need; he was at my door within fifteen minutes. He bear hugged me, pulling me tight to him. Instead of resisting, I hugged him back.

"I missed you, Darlin'. How's the fort?" Sam said, setting me down.

I told him we'd barreled the Malbec; I showed him the cherub and the invitation to the opening party at The Pierpoint.

"You're taking Eduardo, then?" Sam asked.

"I'd like to," I said. "But I'm not sure he'll come."

"He'd be a fool to say no," he said.

"When you were gone, Eduardo and I, we had an argument." And I told Sam the whole story, who Eduardo was, how long I'd known him, how much I liked him, what a disaster the dinner was, how angry he'd been, how the previous day in the caves, our first day working with each other after the fight, Eduardo had reverted back to his silent self, acting like I didn't exist.

Sam sat on one of my kitchen chairs and thought.

"I've got to get you more comfortable chairs," he said first. Then, "That day I saw you in his arms, the day I left," Sam said. "I've not had feelings that powerful for a long time. I thought maybe this old man was jealous, but on the trip it hit me. It wasn't jealousy; I was afraid. If something happened between you and Eduardo and then went sour you might leave me. I'm seventy-two years old, Cinnamon, and I'm not one of those people who does well alone."

I sat down across the table from him.

"I don't want to leave, Mr. Gladstone. Even if Eduardo can't forgive me, and it's not fate for us to be together, I won't leave. You're a part of my life now; no one's ever been kinder to me."

"Fate," Sam repeated, then clapped his hands together and stood up.

"What?" I said.

"Dinner, my house, eight pm," he said. "You have to be there. It's an order from your boss."

At eight, I went up to the farmhouse to find Eduardo already there. A fire burned low and hurricane lamps illuminated the table, a trio of wineglasses at every place. Sam motioned for me to sit across from Eduardo, while he sat at the head, making us clustered around one end of the long table.

Discussion over dinner went back and forth between vineyard owner and winemaker, discussing who Sam had seen in Spain and France. I'd gone back to the expensive boutique that afternoon and bought that silk burgundy dress with long sleeves that buttoned snug to my wrist. I blanched every time I thought about how much it cost. But the burgundy was good with my coloring, it didn't itch, and I would wear it for Christmas dinner with Sam and also to the Pierpoint party.

"Doesn't she look so pretty in the candlelight?" Sam asked, watching Eduardo to make sure he looked at me. I colored red.

"She does, Mr. Gladstone," Eduardo answered.

"It's Sam, dammit," he said. "Neither one of you ever calls me Mr. Gladstone again without you getting a week's worth of pay docked. I'm not someone you've just met. I care about you, I see you every day. I'm Sam!"

"Okay, Sam," we said like scolded children.

After dinner Sam brought out a bottle of Madeira he'd purchased on his trip. He stood and poured each of us a tiny glass out of the black bottle.

"First," Sam said, "I talked to the distributor you charmed, Eduardo. He's hand-selling Trove Zinfandel everywhere. Just wait until they taste our '95."

We all toasted, Eduardo hitting my glass but not meeting my eyes.

"Second, to my two newest employees. I'm lucky to have you both." Eduardo looked at me this time and with even pressure, we touched glasses.

"And to honor you and the fate that's brought you back together after all these years, I'd like to tell you a story of how I came to own this vineyard, or how I came to be in the position to own it. Why I think you kids knowing each other when you were little is not a coincidence, not something to be taken lightly."

Sam's chair scraped the floor as he got up from the table. He paced in front of the fireplace as he spoke.

"In 1963, my high school sweetheart, Cynthia, who I'd married after Korea, had cleaned out our bank account and run off with my brother. She was wrong to do it, but I was damaged goods after the war, and she'd taken longer than most would to give up on me. I lived in a weekly hotel in the Tenderloin, working as a floor sweeper at the Buick dealership on Van Ness.

"Buicks flew off the floor in those days and salesmen made a nice living for themselves. I tried to work my way up, but for a year I'd been sweeping the floor while the nephews and sons of the owners were promoted to salesmen in weeks. I'd gotten to spending all my time and paycheck at the bars between work and my roach trap on Eddy Street. I thought about robbing the safe, stealing a car, buying a gun, and hurting my brother. But I was a coward, thankfully, so instead of stealing a car, I borrowed one. On my lunch break, I took a brand-new convertible, silver with a baby-blue interior, and drove it down to Fisherman's Wharf. I walked to the end of a pier and thought about spending my last three dollars getting drunk at a wharf bar, leaving the keys with the bartender, and tossing myself in the Bay. The foghorn sounded and I turned around, shielding my eyes against the sun. At the top of Russian Hill, something glistened like a jewel, winking at me. The bar and the Bay weren't going anywhere, so I ran the car up there and found the source of the sparkle: the sun hitting a metal garbage shoot coming out of the back of a Victorian mansion they were about to demolish. The old place wasn't in that bad of shape and looked regal from the street. But down it was to come, to be replaced by one of those concrete towers you see there now.

"Now, Cynthia, the one who'd left me for my brother, and I had a cat, Humphrey. I'd never been much of a cat lover, but Humphrey would crawl up in my lap and purr. And it was about the only affection I could stand after the war. She took him when she left and I thought about getting another, but the hotel didn't allow pets. So when I saw a cat that looked a lot like Humphrey walk out from under the bushes in front of this old Victorian, look at me square, and walk around the side to the backyard, I followed him. He sat at the tradesmen's entrance when I came around the side, and as I approached, he twisted his body through the open door and disappeared inside.

"The tradesmen's entrance led into the cellar, where, in this old house, the coal chute and furnace had been. I called out into the dark warren of rooms, but the workmen were all at lunch; the place was empty. I heard a little noise and thought it was the cat. He was behind some baseboards, digging and scratching. The floor was packed dirt and the beamed walls weren't plastered. I knelt down and saw the cat was bothering with the corner of a metal box. I pulled it out, and took the box, about the size of something that would hold a pair of children's shoes, back to the light at the door. It had a little, rusty padlock. I found a stone in the yard and beat the lock off.

"The first thing I did when I saw what was inside was to drop it. Then I scrambled to pick up the contents: a stack of hundred-dollar bills in a yellowed paper sleeve, a sapphire ring as big as a robin's egg, and a lady's choker with three good-sized diamonds and a bunch of smaller ones that sparkled as bright as that garbage chute in the sun.

When I dropped the box, I must have spooked the cat into a thicket of blackberry thorns that had overgrown the back fence of that once fancy house. I called to him, but he didn't come.

"Lunch hour was about over, so I hustled from the house to a park across the street and sat on a bench in full view of the Victorian, the box on my lap.

"In a few minutes, the workers returned. A crane with a wrecking ball was creeping up the steep side of Russian Hill. I sat on that bench and thought as hard as I ever had in a Korean foxhole.

"I'd been gone too long at that point. One of the managers liked

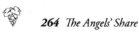

me, but he was off that day, and I didn't have too long before someone at the dealership called the cops. I had two days left on my hotel room for the week and all my belongings were there, but I couldn't walk through the Tenderloin with this box. I'd been held up once before for a bag of groceries, and there was nowhere to leave my treasure if I did want to go back to the hotel.

"One of the workers directed the crane up the last section of the hill. I carefully slid the money and jewels into my pants pocket and left the box under the bench. I stood, holding the keys to the borrowed car, and walked across the street to a workman who leaned against the crane smoking a cigarette.

"I asked him a few questions about demolishing the old place, and told him it was a shame. He explained to me that the residents had died and their heirs had sold out to a developer. That was exactly what I wanted to hear.

"I crossed the street to the car, put the keys in the glove compartment, walked three more blocks down to Polk Street and a payphone, where I called the dealership, quit, and told them where to find the car. Then I hailed a cab for the airport."

"You're making this up," I said, interrupting him.

"Nope," said Sam. "I bought a ticket to Hong Kong with the cash, had some new suits made, and went jewelry shopping. No one had a sapphire as big as mine, but I saw a good comp for the necklace, and then I went to Bangkok and sold everything, took the money and put it into tax-free munis back in the states. I bought a boat, a big one, and planned to spend the rest of my life sailing around the world."

With Sam's weathered skin and wiry frame I could picture him on a boat's deck, looking at the horizon. He'd never told me anything about the boat, or his life before buying Trove, but it made sense. "Where's the boat now?" I asked.

"I thought I loved the ocean and its freedoms. But after a number of years I came to hate it. There was nothing but flat water stretching in every direction, like some sort of desert and I had dreams on that boat worse than anything in Korea. In them, I was looking for someone, a woman, I used to think it was Cynthia, but when I found her, I grabbed her by the shoulder and turned her over; she was rotted, her face eaten away. I was too late. Too late for her, which I thought meant it was too late for me.

"I'd sailed around the Mediterranean and made friends with a man who owned vineyards in the Cote d'Or. I went to visit him there. Dry land. My bad dreams stopped in Burgundy and I decided that I would come back to California, buy a vineyard, make wine.

"Then Pedro and I found you when we were walking the vineyard," Sam turned to me. "Just like in my nightmare, but you weren't dead, and when you survived, it was the second miracle of my life."

Eduardo let out a huge exhale.

"Fate has been good to me," Sam said. "If I'd ignored that shiny trash chute, I'd be fish food at the bottom of the Bay. If I'd stubbornly stuck to what I thought I wanted I'd still be driving that boat around, waking up in a sweat. What I'm trying to say is don't ignore what fate has given to you."

Sam drained his Madeira and set the glass back on the table.

"Now, this jetlagged old man is going to bed," he said. "Will the two of you clean up, please?"

He shut his bedroom door behind him. Eduardo and I looked long at each other in the candlelight.

"I'm sorry I let things go so wrong the other night, Cinnamon," Eduardo said. "It was my fault and I hope you will give me and my family another chance."

I wanted to accept his apology, to give him one of my own. But much like I imagined Eduardo struggled to tell me who he was for all those months and couldn't, it seemed impossible to form the words or speak them. I nodded a little, but mostly looked at my lap where the burgundy sleeves fastened at my wrists.

When it was clear I wasn't going to say anything, Eduardo crossed to my side of the table. He kissed me gently on the top of the head.

"Merry Christmas," he said.

Chapter 39

I spent Christmas Eve in Sam's guest room at my suggestion, and woke up early to make us both pancakes as Alma had the day off. He'd gotten me a red cashmere scarf and a dozen fragile glass ornaments from a Christmas market in Madrid. I gave him a book on the history of the Italian Swiss Colony. Over pancakes, sniffling from something he'd caught on the plane, he asked if Eduardo and I had made up.

"Not quite," I said.

"Alma has a temper. I know it, she knows it, and her son knows it," Sam said. "But I do believe her to be a good woman. People read Steinbeck and think *The Grapes of Wrath* ended with the New Deal, but that's only for gringos. The migrants lived *The Grapes of Wrath* before, during and after the dust bowl. Something Alma doesn't tell anyone, is when they worked in the fields, she lost babies. Miscarried them or right after they were born, all to things that any decent doctor could have helped. Six of them that Pedro has told me about, maybe more. Eduardo is the only one who survived. Any woman who could live the migrant life, to face so much hardship and come out of it with the dignity of Alma Delgado is a tough lady, a survivor. Much like yourself."

Alma lost six babies? I swallowed.

"Give it time, Cinnamon," Sam said, easing into his brown leather chair, my present in his hands. "She was unfair. Be patient, try to forgive her for what she said, and forgive yourself, too."

Eduardo went to church with his parents on Christmas Eve and spent Christmas Day at their house, but at night his truck was outside his cottage and the lights were on. I put on a jacket and shoes a dozen times to go over there, to thank him for his apology and offer one myself, but I couldn't make it past my porch. The cherub sat in the center of my table, its arrow pointing at my bed. I was tempted to spin it, to see if it might change its direction, but instead I took its initial advice and went to sleep.

The morning of December twenty-sixth, the first business day since I'd gotten the slip, I was at the post office when it opened. The letter from OHM's law firm, printed on thick, creamy linen paper, informed me that since my mother's estate had now been settled, her equity investment would revert, equally, to the other shareholders in OHM, LLC, on January 1, 1996. Ms. Monday, her executors, or kin had until December 31, 1995, one week away, to clean out her home or else personal property would be removed and also redistributed.

My mother's box of ashes still sat on my bookshelf. However tempting it was to leave her tangle of stuff up there for OHM to deal with, this was the opportunity to be true to my mother's last request and scatter her ashes. And maybe someone up there would tell me something about my dad they didn't want to tell a detective. I felt ready to go, but there was no way I wanted to head there alone. I could count on three people: Sam, Julia, and Eduardo. Sam's sniffles had turned into a cold that had him in bed. The Pierpoint was opening in three days. If I called Julia she would drop everything and come, I knew that, but I couldn't do that to her. I crossed the gravel drive and knocked on Eduardo's door.

"I got this," I said when he answered, holding out the letter, "and I need your help."

As Eduardo slowed his truck to cross the Oh Holy Mountain cattle grate, I closed my eyes and breathed in the new leather, the car's vinyl and upholstery, a smell I didn't associate with OHM or the broken-down cars that had gotten me there before. We parked in front of the Holy House. I took the box of my mother's ashes and Eduardo's hand and led him down the path.

The redwood grove in between the Holy House and my mother's

dome was shrouded in a bone-chilling mist. I stepped off the path, my boots sinking into the moss and the leaves, the trees dripping Northern California's liquid sky. Still walking, I opened the flap on the box, and looked at the pile of chalk-white. My mother said OHM was where she wanted her ashes scattered, but she'd never said specifically where. And I was uncomfortable with the idea of some ashes in one spot and some in another. It seemed like she should stay all together, not be parceled out in little lonely bits. Eduardo, who'd walked with me off the path reached out and grabbed my shoulder, saving me from walking into a low branch wet with dew and sap. His touch left me with goose bumps. I wanted to take his hand again, but I'd asked him to come as a favor, as a friend, I couldn't expect that things would be the same between us.

We came around the corner to the clearing where my parents had been sitting in the swing that one magical day. I remembered how butterflies had filled the meadow making the whole scene seem unreal. The swing was still there on that winter morning.

"Wait here," I said to Eduardo.

Near the base of the giant pine that held the swing, there was a hydrangea bush as tall as I was, its blue globes of flowers fading. I knelt down and parted the leaves near the ground, dug away a little dirt and placed the box of mother's ashes in the crown of earth where the roots became stalks. There, the cardboard blended in, looked protected. I let the leaves fall back into place, dusted off my knees and joined Eduardo back on the path.

He'd seen what I'd done and took my hand again when I was close enough. Silently, we walked through that last grove of trees to my mother's place.

I couldn't get the door to budge and my hands shook worse on each try. Eduardo threw his hip into the water-warped door and it creaked open to reveal the familiar inside of the tiny hut: kitchenette with a table for two, orange shag carpeted floor with a few cushions strewn about, a near-empty bookshelf, and the ladder to the sleeping loft. It felt colder inside than out and, even with the chill, smelled of underarms and dirty laundry.

"We should have brought some boxes," Eduardo said.

"I'm not taking much," I said.

The kitchenette was bare except a few plates, forks, mugs, and an aluminum pan still caked with whatever had cooked in it last. I scraped at the pan with a knife. Gray lumps in gray sauce. My mother's last meal.

On the bookshelf there were some of my dad's old Down Beat magazines, a framed miniature version of the portrait of Phil in the Holy House, and the Gideon Bible my mother had gotten outside the supermarket back when we lived in the shipwreck shack. Leaned away from it, in the corner of the bookshelf, was a green leather-bound copy of *Jane Eyre*. The one I'd stolen so many years before from my grandmother's library. The one my parents had told me they gave away.

I touched the book like it might be a mirage.

"To Elaine" was written on the flyleaf. A slip of paper fell out. It was in my father's hand and dated June twentieth, over six months ago, not long after I'd seen them happy, together, in the swing. It was addressed to me and sealed, but didn't have a stamp.

Dear Daughter,

I was having some pain so I went to the doctor and he said I had advanced stage colon cancer and needed to have my colon out and crap into a bag for the rest of my life. He thought it might have also spread to my lungs and my brain, but I refused the x-ray.

I've collected a bag full of Death Cap mushrooms and have asked your mother to cook me something with them. I want to have a nice last meal, but she's refusing. She's still hung up on all that Bible shit. She says she can't live without me. That if I off myself I'll go to hell.

If she wants to be with me in the afterlife she'll have to find a way to send herself to hell, too. I'll eat the mushrooms raw if I have to and die on a

wander from here to the coast, but I'd rather she cook me a meal and I go to sleep in her arms. She says she won't, but we'll see.

Sincerely,
Stephen F. Monday

P.S. I was smoking too much weed when you were born and I've come to realize that naming your child for your own entertainment is wrong. I apologize. If you still want to change your name, please know I'd be supportive. I've never said sorry enough, but I'm starting now. SFM.

Chapter 40

"Can you take these lemons up to Alma's place?" Sam asked me, still sick enough to stay in bed, a few days after Christmas. "She said she'd make me some of those lemon bars I like now that the Meyers are ripe."

"Alma's?"

"You can't avoid her forever."

Like a child dragging her feet to her room, I took the bag of lemons and trod up the hill to the Delgados'.

I was relieved to see Pedro sitting on the front steps.

"Ah, Cinnamon," he said, making room for me. "Alma is inside taking a nap," he said as if to explain his low voice. "Dolor de la cabeza."

"Sam asked me to bring some lemons for the bars she was . . ." I trailed off and Pedro nodded his head yes.

I sat next to him on the steps to his house and we looked out at the bare brown vines.

"When do the leaves come back?"

"Not till March. Before then it is all root work. All winter you think nothing is happening, but those plants are working all the time."

Eduardo sprinted up the hill. He must have seen me heading toward his mother's place and wanted to avert World War III. He bent over when he reached Pedro and me sitting together on the step, breathing hard. His work boots and overalls were covered with mud.

When he caught his breath, Pedro offered him a drink of water. I continued to sit on the stairs as they moved inside.

"Come on," Eduardo said, beckoning.

"I don't think so. Your mother is trying to get over her headache," I said.

"She's sleeping. Join us."

I followed them in and watched Pedro shake the lemons out of the sack into the fruit bowl.

Eduardo filled three sunflower-decaled drinking glasses with water from the tap and we stood around the yellow-tiled bar in the kitchen drinking silently. When they were done, Pedro and Eduardo went back out to the porch to talk. I took the three glasses and carefully rinsed them in the sink, quietly tipping them upside down to drip the water out onto the drain board. I dried my hands on a dishtowel, folded it, and then noticed the lemons were next to the bananas. I picked up each lemon, removing them from the bananas that would mold them. Before I was finished, I heard someone come into the kitchen behind me.

I turned, expecting Eduardo wanting me to walk with him down to the caves, but it was Alma, watching me. Maybe because of her headache or maybe the nap, her hair was down, glossy and beautiful, the silver threads like the filigree through the black. I thought she'd accuse me of breaking in, yell at me to get out, but she didn't. Her eyes were fixed on the counter where I'd separated the fruit. She looked far away, like she might still be half dreaming or remembering something someone had told her long ago.

"I want to apologize for the things I said at dinner," I told her. "I've never said sorry enough, but I'm starting now."

Chapter 41

I'd put the green leather-bound copy of *Jane Eyre* on my middle book-shelf where my mother's ashes used to be. I took the cherub off its casters and pointed him in the direction of the vineyard.

It was nearly time to leave for the party at the Pierpoint and I buttoned up the sleeves of my burgundy silk dress. I looked in the mirror and realized I looked different. My face no longer had any hollows or lingering bruises, under the silk sleeves my arms had some muscle, my balance was steady, my thoughts clear.

Eduardo came over in his one tie, a bolero, and stood beside me getting it even while I put on lipstick in the bathroom mirror. It was raining again. He'd driven his truck right up to my steps so that I wouldn't have to get my new shoes muddy.

Pretend to be who you want to be, and reality will follow.

The rain and holiday traffic made us late crossing the Golden Gate Bridge. By the time we arrived, the hotel's parking garage was full, so Eduardo dropped me in front of the hotel, said he'd find a spot and come back. I had been picturing walking in on his arm, and I was disappointed, but not disappointed enough to stand outside in the downpour until he came back. The bit of dry space under the stately awning was crowded with TV cameras, tourists, and San Franciscans all trying to get a sneak peek at the new and improved Pierpoint. I showed the doorman one of the passes that came in my invitation and he let me inside.

A jaunty ragtime tune bounced from the Steinway. The room was a golden dazzle of polished wood, honeyed lights, and Christmas swag. Julia and a tall, handsome man I guessed must be Parveen were talking with the reporters who had been admitted for an interview and a tour.

One hour, they'd been told, then friends and family only.

Julia was leading the group through the renovation of the historic fixtures and furnishings of The Pierpoint. Parveen was following, his hand hovering near the small of her back. I stood in line to get myself sparkling water with lime from the bar. Julia saw me there, turned the last bit of the tour over to Parveen and came to me.

"I thought Eduardo was coming?" she asked, her forehead showing her concern.

"He's just parking the car. The hotel's garage was full."

Julia checked her watch. "I'm afraid he won't get in once security closes the doors for the party. Let me go out and tell the doorman to let him in."

I watched her go and saw Parveen leading the reporters en masse also to the front entrance, leaving behind a group of maybe thirty people: half San Francisco hipsters, half traditionally dressed members of Parveen's family. I walked up the grand staircase so I could take in the whole sight, the tree, the people and all the restored grandeur of my family's legacy below in one vista.

Julia passed the foyer's columns, went out the revolving door, and was lost in a sea of heads. I stayed on the mezzanine, watching, waiting for my cousin and Eduardo to come back.

The piano player finished the ragtime tune and started Beethoven, the *Moonlight Sonata*. My attention was fixed on the doorway: I caught a glimpse of Julia, still outside, hold out her hand to a dark-haired man in a bolero tie.

Again, I lost sight of them. I started down the curving staircase, wanting the waiting to be over, wanting to be with them both as soon as possible more than anything else. Halfway down, I saw Julia again coming through the revolving door, Eduardo at her side. The sight of them stopped me short.

I wanted two. A girl and a boy just my age. But I could never get them to appear.

Eduardo and Julia crossed the threshold of the new Pierpoint. There they stood, solid and real, searching for me, amidst columns that looked like trees.

Acknowledgements

I am indebted to those who helped me write a better novel by flagging trouble spots and suggesting fixes: Laralyn Melvin, Caitlin Zittkowski, Meg Waite Clayton, Liz Amini-Holmes, Ronda Breier, Christily Silvernale, Mark Holmes, Libby Hlavka, Laura Leichum, James Logan and Amy Santullo. Thanks also to Meg Brunner, Librarian at the Alcohol and Drug Abuse Institute at the University of Washington and Andrew Levi, winemaker at Skipstone Ranch, for helping me get the technical details closer to fine. To my agent Andy Ross who pulled the novel out of the multitude he receives, and to Winter Goose for publishing it. Kristina Rust for her artistic eye, and Wendy Cervera and Ilsa Brink for their web skills. Also to Mary Bisbee-Beek, my publicist, equal parts cheerleader and corner coach. And for providing me a room of one's own, The Santullo family for the use of their beautiful Inverness farmhouse where I wrote the first draft of The Angels' Share. Also, thank you to my husband and daughter who provide a wonderful place for this writer to call home. I'm lucky that in my life no imaginary friends are necessary.

About the Author

Born in San Francisco, Rayme Waters spent much of her youth in Northern California as well as a few years in Sweden. Previously nominated for a Pushcart Prize and a Dzanc Best of the Web Award for her short story "The Watertower".

Follow Rayme:
raymewaters.com
Facebook: facebook.com/Rayme-Waters
Twitter: @RaymeWaters

CPSIA information can be obtained at www.ICGtesting.com
Printed in the USA
BVOW081237060912

299663BV00005B/27/P

The End